ANYTHING BUT MINOR

A Sports Romance Comedy type book, but really not a comedy...or maybe it is.
Who the hell knows? Not me.

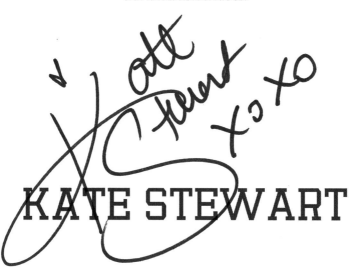

KATE STEWART

ANYTHING BUT MINOR
Copyright © 2016 Kate Stewart

ISBN-13: 978-1535247535
ISBN-10: 1535247533

All rights reserved. No part of this publication may be reproduced, distributed, or transmitted in any form or by any means, or stored in a database or retrieval system, without the prior written permission of author.

This is a work of fiction. All characters, organizations, and events portrayed in this novel are either products of the author's imagination or are used fictitiously. Any resemblance to actual events, locales, or persons, living or dead, is entirely coincidental.

Editing
Edee M. Fallon, Mad Spark Editing
www.madsparkediting.com

Cover Design
Amy Q

Formatting and interior design
Jersey Girl & Co.

DEDICATION

For Patty Tennyson, Charleston, and my hero, John Hughes...but mostly for Patty Tennyson.

Thank you for being the amazing friend you are. I love you.

Prologue
Alice

"Ladies and gentlemen, we're just about ten minutes outside of Charleston. Current conditions are sunny and seventy-three degrees. We hope you've enjoyed your flight. Please keep your seatbelts fastened as we prepare for landing. We know you have a choice in air travel, and we appreciate you flying with us."

Seconds later, a more muffled Darth Vader order was barked at a faster speed.

"Flight attendants, prepare for landing."

Freedom.

That was the only thought that crossed my mind after my mother's unexpected, tearful, and mortifying goodbye at the Ohio airport.

"Remember your virtue. It's the most sacred thing a woman

has," she said as she eyed the man behind me with distaste.

"Mom, don't start this," I said as she looked me over with threatening tears. I'd never had the heart to tell her. At twenty-four, I hadn't been a virgin for years. She'd raised me to wait for marriage. I'd let Brian Callahan lift my skirt instead. A move I regretted, but I'd been far too curious.

"You keep yourself safe," she urged again as she looked around us for any sign of disorder. My mother, though nurturing at times, had the bedside manner of Carrie's mother from that terrifying Stephen King movie. Though I was never beaten for menstruating or locked in a closet to pray, she'd sheltered me to the point of almost making me wear a chastity belt to my senior prom. It had been a miracle she'd even let me go. Though I'd never been much for breaking the rules, due to her constant harping and paranoia, I was convinced I would burn in hell for taking a hit off a joint at a senior party, which I snuck out to attend.

And when I lost my virginity, I was even more convinced my soul had no safe haven to depart to. It was only months later that I realized if I didn't remove myself from her iron grasp, I too would start to reach that level of crazy.

She wasn't so much religious as she was paranoid. She feared everything and everyone and was always sure she could find a motive in someone else's kindness. She remained unmarried after my runaway father divorced her when I was five. I knew I was all she had, but I had to get away. I'd only remained well-rounded due to my movie mothers: M'Lynn, Clairee, Truvy, and Ouiser from the movie *Steel Magnolias*...and, well, *Uncle Buck*.

College was a five-year blur. I rarely ventured from my dorm room at Cornell. It took all of those five years of school and even a few more years of flight time to slip into my newer, less terrified self. College had only salvaged me until summer hit, and I'd ended up right back in hell: Dayton, Ohio.

If I wanted any semblance of a normal life, I had to move far away from her, where I wouldn't feel like I had to report my every move.

No, *this* freedom would be completely different, and the cloudless, neon blue sky through the rectangle window to my right told me so. I pulled up the forecast on my iPhone as soon as the crew announced it was safe and saw that sunny skies would be a constant for the next week. True spring was in full swing in the south and a far cry from the bipolar weather from which I came.

I'd just left the dreary, bleak slosh of my former life behind and quickly discarded the thick sweater I'd boarded the plane with. Charleston had mild to non-existent winters, beautiful sandy beaches, and was now my home.

That alone was enough to sell me on the move.

That and the fact that I would be one of a few manning the entire flight simulation program at the newly built Boeing plant.

They say all good things come to those who wait, and as I deplaned and began walking toward the exit, all I could think about was that I'd waited long enough. I'd been dying in a gray hell, longing for a taste of everything for as long as I could remember, and I would take a bite out of it all. I'd spent too many years of my life living vicariously through movies.

That day and every day that followed would be the best days of my life.

I saw my new Prius make its way down the circular lot at the airport entrance. I flagged the driver down, and as soon as he spotted me, he smiled and got out of the car to help me with my bags. He was an older man, mid-fifties with salt and pepper hair and kind blue eyes. He didn't look like he'd missed a meal...his entire life. Carl was sweating like he'd just run a race as I reveled in the crisp spring air. I made a mental note to toss my sweater in the trash at home, as soon as I located...home.

"Ms. Blake?"

"That's me. You must be Carl," I said as he shook my hand with a smile.

"Call me Alice. Thank you for going out of your way to help me today."

"No problem at all. I was happy to do it. So here she is," he said as he pointed out a few features of my Toyota while he tucked my large suitcase safely in the trunk before handing me the keys.

"You can drive me back to the lot, and I'll answer any questions you may have."

"No need. I've researched it enough," I said as I took the wheel and began syncing my iPhone.

"Just a few more papers to sign and it's all yours," he said with a slight southern lilt in his voice. I loved the accents associated with the south. So far, every single person I'd contacted in regards to my move had been nothing short of friendly and personable.

After buckling my belt and taking a look around the cabin, I asked for the address to the car lot and ordered Siri to start directing me.

"There's really no need. I'm happy to give you directions," Carl offered. I turned on the AC, despite being completely comfortable, and I saw his instant, but silent thank you.

"I'll be relying on her quite a bit, so I need to make sure we get off to a good start," I said, slightly uneasy.

He simply nodded. "You said you were working at the new Boeing plant, correct?"

"Yes, I start tomorrow."

"Well, it's less than a quarter mile from where we're sitting. We'll be driving by."

"I know. I've researched that, too," I said as I flushed slightly. Google was my vice.

"New city, new job, this is an exciting time for you."

"It certainly is," I said as I listened to Siri guide us out of the airport. I spotted the plant, the place where I would be spending the majority of my time, making sure well-trained pilots lifted and landed safely. But I was far more fascinated by the palm trees playing peekaboo through the sunroof.

"I've never seen a palm tree," I whispered in awe.

"Welcome to the Palmetto State."

ANYTHING BUT MINOR

By the time I had made it to my new fully furnished condo, I was running behind to meet the realtor.

"I'm so sorry," I rushed out, barely able to take in my lush surroundings as I met a casually dressed woman at the door, my overstuffed suitcase and carry-on in tow.

"No worries. I had to walk my Skeeter, anyway, so I swung by when you texted." I was sure "Skeeter" was a pet name but got no further explanation. She turned the key and gave me an animated face with big eyes. "Well, take a look around."

I braced myself. Renting from afar was scary business, but so far the drive into the complex had been absolutely beautiful. I'd even spotted a free roaming alligator on the pond bank on the drive in. I was tempted to stop and take a picture. I held my breath and then let it out in a huge and happy gust as I took in my new digs.

"Oh wow," I chimed as I walked into the spacious kitchen with marble floors and new appliances. Adjacent and across the bar top was an even larger living room complete with dark wood floors and a stone fireplace. I was convinced it wasn't just a home but a haven.

"The pictures really didn't do it justice," she said as she watched me closely. "I had the maintenance man put your boxes in the living room. They arrived today. I didn't want you to have to drag all that stuff up yourself."

I barely heard her as I looked at the beautiful furnishings. Things I'd never dreamt of in a place of my own, things without doilies under them. My mother loved doilies, crosses, and lace. I shivered at the memory of my old bedroom.

"It's"—I damned near teared up—"perfect."

"Ahhh, hon, you're going to love it here! It's a lot quieter than the other complexes in the area. What is it that you said you do?"

"I'm a flight instructor."

"Wow," she said, clearly impressed as I took a look at the leather couch and big screen TV. "Well, here you are." She walked over and dropped the keys into my waiting hand. "Your copy of the rental agreement is on the counter. You said you've never been to Charleston?"

"No, ma'am. I've done a bit of research on the web." I turned to her, my chest bursting with excitement. "Thank you."

"I think I'll call you in a week. Just to see how you're doing."

I looked at her with a curious glance.

She gave me a knowing smile. "Oh, honey, you don't know where you are...yet."

When she shut the door, I clamped my hands over my mouth to cover my squeal, but I knew she'd heard it. Ten minutes later, I was dressed in an oversized white tee, pink panties, black Ray-Bans, and knee-high socks, sliding across my new hardwoods to Bob Seger. And it *was* the best day of my life.

You know that part in the movie *Top Gun* when Kelly McGillis walks around, sex clad in aviators and an oversized bomber jacket while the gorgeous buffet of pilots sit a little straighter in their chairs and do their best to intimidate their new instructor? In that movie, Kelly took zero crap as she fired at will, demonstrating her expertise and rightfully gaining the upper hand. I'd imagined something similar for my first day as an instructor.

This was *not* that.

First, the white-walled classroom was freezing, and I was positive my nipples were perked up in an embarrassing display through my tight, thin, pink sweater. My pilots were all in their late thirties to early fifties and looked nothing like a young Tom Cruise or Val Kilmer, aside from *one* man who seemed completely uninterested in a damn word I was about to say. I was disappointed not to see one woman in the class of around fifteen pilots, but it was expected. It saddened me to no end that the majority of those in the air were still men. The percentage still 97% men in the industry.

Well, I was in the other 3%, and I was sure that these men felt that same contempt for me as they did sexy McGillis because they all looked bored or pissed to be there. I studied them for several moments as they rudely kept busy on their cell phones.

"It's not the same plane as you are used to, gentlemen," I said with certainty and in lieu of a greeting. "More advanced, glass flight deck, larger wingspan, and it's faster than anything you have *ever* flown. And you *don't* know how to operate it."

That got the attention of the only good looking pilot in the room. At least I knew I had read *his* thoughts.

"I've been in the air, gentlemen, and often. If you want to compare swords with me, simply open up your packet and take a look at my flight log. I don't need your respect, but I do need your attention."

One by one, cell phones were set down, and all eyes landed on my nipples.

Well, it was progress.

2
Alice

I looked over the cell phone pics I'd taken over the last few weeks. Cotton candy sunsets, a dead jellyfish, the infamous and ancient Angel Oak Tree, Market Street traffic, a horse with an eye patch. Charleston, in a word, was...*amazing*! The realtor had been right. The city itself was a best-kept secret. A secret that was apparently spreading due to the significant amount of wandering tourists, myself included. I'd spent hours roaming the city on a self-tour.

I'd never really been the type to get lonely. I'll just go ahead and put it out there.

I'm an alien.

Well, that's not *exactly* true, but when I was young, my obsession with aircraft kept me out of any form of a circle of friends. It was easy to play pilot when you were six with the Sunday school kids. When you're eleven, and you prefer to put together airplane models instead of shopping at the mall, that you weren't even allowed to frequent, it can start to become an issue. I had a handful of friends in high school, and even *they* gave me some odd looks from time to time.

Okay, maybe I was a bit *too* informational, less conversational.

In the last week, and in my new city, I felt more at home than ever in my own company. The pace was far slower than what I was used to. I'd spent five unnecessary minutes in the checkout at the store because of the person in front of me chatting with a cashier. It seemed no one *outside* of a car was in a hurry.

After rush hour, the city settled into a contented purr of crickets, wind, and calming water. Yesterday, and after endless meetings my first week, I drove straight to the beach a few miles from my new palace. I sat in the light beige sand and watched people pass by as I inhaled the sea air and watched the sky turn pink.

Pink.

The clouds were lit so beautifully, I felt myself tear up. I had a new addiction, and it was the city itself. Half of my addiction to flying was due to the fact I was a sucker for scenery and my new city fed my addiction in spades.

Armed with my new Prius, I drove around the peninsula of downtown Charleston and familiarized myself with the layout. It was an ocular orgasm, something on every single corner: cobblestone streets, expansive southern mansions, postcard harbor views. I couldn't get enough. I took three tours, one walking, one by bike, and one by horse-drawn carriage. It had only been a week, and I was in love. I stopped for lunch at a local spot called Barbara Jean's and ate the largest chicken fried steak in the history of the world. It was steak fried like chicken, topped with a creamy gravy that "tastes so damn good," according to the waitress, "would make you smack your mama." I finished my late lunch and walked for hours, completely in a daze, instantly in love with my southern piece of paradise. Trees covered in flowing Spanish moss swayed as I worked my tired feet down the streets, admiring the consistently lit lanterns that dated as far back as the 1600s.

I wanted to be a part of it all.

Running out of ideas but with endless possibilities, I decided my next move was now up to my new planet, and just as the thought crossed my mind, I ran right smack into a vendor passing out flyers.

I quickly scanned the pictures on the pamphlet and dead center was my planet's answer.

Go to Anchor Park!

Nervous was a feeling I was no longer used to. I'd pitched too many games, faced too many opponents to feel the old yet familiar shitty feeling that had started to eat at me this morning. I needed something to take the edge off and pounding into Melo-dee last night hadn't done a damn thing to help the slight shake in my hand or the new sheen of sweat that covered me as the words kept circling my head like the fucking vultures they were.

Last chance.

"We've got this," Andy said with confidence as my uncertain eyes met his. "Fuckin' A," he said emphatically as he clapped my back with his glove before he made his way out of the locker room. I gripped my cap sitting on my locker shelf and put it on then kicked my locker closed.

Only one thing would get me picked up this year: *performance*. I had the best stats of any pitcher in the minors. I'd solidly pitched my way into earning the invite to the big show. An invite I'd worked for my whole life.

Do or die at this point.

"Get 'em, Rafe," Waters, the right fielder, barked out as he passed me. I took a deep breath. If I didn't get tapped on the shoulder this year to play in the majors, it wouldn't be because I didn't play with every fucking bit of talent I had.

That would never be the reason. And just before tunnel vision kicked in and I took the field, I whispered in ritual, "You love this."

I've never been much of a fan of baseball. In fact, I'd never been a fan of any sport. So, sans foam finger, I headed to Anchor Park with every intention of knowing everything about it by the time I left. Surveying the stadium, I noticed a majority of the people around me sported team shirts, so I purchased a bright red baseball cap with a green team logo as a souvenir. I felt the sense of community as the players took the field. I took my seat directly behind home plate. Scanning the bright green field and immaculate stadium, I was impressed, and then I looked down to Google the Swampgators on my iPhone.

I prayed to two Gods in my life. The one I believed kept my soul safe but frustrated me with answered prayers in cryptic life lessons and another who fed me a world of information at the palm of my hand.

As I researched, I realized I was at the very first home game, and the Swampgators had an incredible season last year. Even more impressive was all minor leaguers were an affiliate of a major league team, meaning they were all signed with them. I spent a few minutes brushing up on the basic rules of the game while the Swampgators warmed up on the field. I really had missed *everything* athletic in life and was working overtime to make up for it. The announcers asked us to rise for the anthem, and I quickly put my phone away as I held my hand over my heart and finally looked up.

Jesus, Lord, God help my sin-filled mind and cleanse me, Amen.

I had no idea what I expected when I truly got a look at the players, but I was pretty sure God was making up for my lack of Val Kilmers in my first instruction class. Everywhere I looked, the male form was accentuated in perfect clothes. A sea of solid man-butt swam before me as I stuttered out the words to the country's most famous song. All of the players were lined up, eyes focused forward as I ogled them shamelessly while they paid tribute to their country. Tan, tattooed bulging arms, thick thighs, and muscular backs all saluted me as I remembered something else I'd never had much liberty to explore: *men*.

As soon as the short fireworks display ended, and the smoke cleared, I remained glued to my seat as I watched the Swampgators take the field.

"Go get 'em, Bullet!" A woman shouted next to me, obviously seasoned in the sport. She nudged me with her meaty elbow and pointed. "This is his year. I can feel it."

The woman was dressed in an old team t-shirt and a hat of her own littered with stick pins. Her skin could only be described as leathered from years of sun, but she had kind, pale blue eyes and gave me a small smile as I addressed her.

"Who's year?" I asked as she kept her sights on the man who had just reached the pitcher's mound.

"Rafe, that's who. He deserves it."

"I'm not following," I said, looking over at her. I could feel her excitement as she motioned to the mound. A faithful and dedicated fan sat next to me, and I was excited about the possibility of asking a few questions.

"First game?" she asked as if it was a cardinal sin. Her leathered skin wrinkled around pursed lips in distaste.

"I just moved here," I replied as my only defense.

"Forgiven," she said as she kept her eye on the field. "Rafe Hembrey, he's the pitcher. Should've been picked up by the big club last year, but for some reason, they haven't called yet. They're absolutely crazy for it if you ask me. He's better than half the big league starters. They won't pass on him this year. I just know it."

"Well, then," I said as I cupped my hands around my mouth. "Get 'em, Bullet!" I gave my attention to the object of my company's affection and froze when I saw him look in our direction. I stared back with my jaw slightly slack while I took him in. He was impressively taller than most of the other players. Then again, he was on a mound of dirt. Out of nowhere, a ball sped toward me, and I flinched. His pet name was no longer a mystery.

"Jesus, he's faster than last year!" the lady to my right exclaimed as I realized he hadn't been looking our way at all but was entirely focused on the catcher crouched a few feet in front of us.

"Sttriiike," the umpire called out with authority.

"My name's Beth, but my friends call me Dutch."

"I'm Alice, nice to meet you..." I left it open-ended because I wasn't sure what she wanted me to call her.

I studied Rafe's form as he again wound up and extended his arm and leg in perfect rhythm.

"Strriiike," the umpire called out again as Dutch clenched her fists and did a fist bump *with herself*.

"Last year he pitched a no-hitter."

I quickly Googled the term. "Impressive."

I was thoroughly captivated, and I had to give most of the credit to the man on the mound. Even as a newcomer, I knew he was having an excellent game. I was just as vocal as Dutch as we chanted and raised hell. Well, I mostly echoed her, but I was having a blast doing it. I looked around me to see the others in the stadium just as engrossed. I felt like I was sitting in a family of strangers. An obvious family man stood next to Dutch and me with his blonde toddler on his shoulders. She shook a noisy tin can of what I assumed were beans with the Swampgator's logo and the name of a sponsor below it. I studied it carefully.

Andy's Brew House because local is better.

Engrossed in my first game ever, I realized hours had passed, and I hadn't moved from my seat.

"Striiiikke," the umpire yelled for what seemed like the hundredth time. I and those around me were solidly impressed as the Bullet threw pitch after perfect pitch.

The game ended in a Swampgators victory, and I turned to Dutch to thank her for the company.

"He really is impressive. I can see why you're a fan. Thank you for the company."

"Honey, he's *the* best. And when he finally gets the call, I can say I told you so." She looked at me in question. "So you in?"

"Am I in?"

"Well, I don't see no one else behind ya," Dutch said with obvious sarcasm.

"What does *in* entail?"

"Every home game, rain or shine, for the season."

I stared, stunned, but my mouth moved before I could think it through. "I'll do it!"

"Good, because you're actual seat was one down. You're sitting in my dead husband's chair. I have these two for the entire season. I'll meet you outside twenty minutes before game time. If you aren't here, I go in alone."

"Oh...I'm terribly sorry...Okay," I said as I stood quickly and looked back at the chair in apology. Dutch gave me my very own fist bump before she yelled one more time, "Good job, Bullet. This is your season!"

"Thanks, Dutch!" he called back to her as I froze where I stood. This time, I was sure his eyes were on me because he was far closer. Dark hair was tucked under a ball cap and underneath the brim of that cap...was perfection. His eyes penetrated mine as I stood motionless. I damned near sat back down just to drink him in. It was a brief moment, maybe a few seconds, but it was enough to catch it all. The dark curl of sweaty hair beneath his cap, his strong nose and chin, ridiculously full lips, and dark eyes all burned into my memory as he disappeared from the field.

"See you tomorrow," Dutch barked and pushed me out of my stupor.

"Tomorrow?"

"It's a three-game series," she said as she pushed past me after shoving a game schedule into my hand.

"See you then," I said as I followed the crowd's direction. "Oh, wait...Dutch!"

"Yeah, Alice?" Her voice had a hopeful lift to it as if she was waiting for an invitation of some sort.

"I want to pay for my seat. If you can tell me how much I'll owe you—"

"Just show up," she said before she gave me a nod and got lost in the crowd.

Knowing I had a full day of work and plans to attend another game the following day, I decided local *was better*, and on an adrenaline high of my first baseball game, I found myself parked at a cocktail table next to the entrance of Andy's Brew House. Even with legal freedom and the ability to do so, I'd never been much of a drinker. I hated to lose control over any of my senses, but I'd decided that my celebration of the *best day ever* deserved to be toasted with at least one local beer.

The bartenders, clearly understaffed, tossed out draft glasses left and right at the counter full of happy Swampgator fans. The bar was small and had a homey feel to it. It was littered with baseball memorabilia, and there was a TV screen on every wall streamlining nothing but highlights of the game itself. "Centerfield" blared over the patron noise as one of the bartenders approached me. She was a stunner with long black hair and a petite figure. Her Swampgators V-neck tee did little to cover her bulging cleavage, and her long tan legs were fully bared aside from her nearly non-existent black shorts. I felt like a mutt sitting there with sweat-matted, blonde hair tucked underneath my cap and a simple, white halter top and shorts.

"I can tell you're probably new to this place, but if you want a beer *this* century, next time you come to the bar, and know what you want to order first, okay? What'll you have?"

"Uh," I said as I watched her face twist with worry with each passing second I hesitated. "Anything on draft," I answered as I let her off the hook. Minutes later, she delivered my beer and a fresh bowl of peanuts. I realized I hadn't done a thing about my appetite for the latter half of the day and started to shell and shove them in my mouth. My mouth bursting at the seams and dry from the salt, I gripped my cold beer and took a healthy swig.

The result was instant. I turned my head and blew everything in my mouth out in disgust just as the bar crowd roared to life in greeting...of the two men who had just walked in and stood next to me.

"What. The. Fuck!"

I turned to see the source of the voice covered in half eaten peanuts and spewed beer. I looked up as the man Dutch had called Bullet towered over me, and his hazel eyes burned a hole straight through me. Mouth gaping, I quickly started to apologize as I stared at a set of lips made for a movie star. If Angelina Jolie had a lip twin, it would definitely be this pair.

My eyes drifted down to his ruined shirt, which clung to his expansive chest and nicely cut tan arms, and then back to his lips which now twitched with amusement. "Andy, I don't think she likes your stout."

Another set of eyes pierced me that belonged to the man standing behind him. The man was just as handsome with reddish blond hair and blue eyes that watched me carefully before they narrowed. "That's blasphemy," he replied to Rafe with a hint of humor.

"I told you the last batch was shit," Rafe said as he perused me, his conversation still with the man he called Andy.

Not only had I covered Rafe in disgusting peanut residue, but I'd also just insulted the bar owner and apparent brew master.

"Oh jeez, I'm so sorry. It's not that I don't like the beer. I *hate* it," I pushed out quickly as I stood, grabbed a few napkins out of the dispenser, and began to dab and swipe at Rafe's ruined shirt. Andy burst out laughing as I stuttered on. My eyes widened. "No, God, what I meant to say was I hate beer in *general*, and, oh crud, your shirt is totally ruined."

"Maybe I should take yours," he whispered as he bent down and stilled my hands.

I looked up at him. He was ridiculously tall at least 6'4" and had my height by almost a foot. "I don't think it would fit." More laughter from his friend as I continued. "I'm certain it won't fit. Oh...you meant that sexually," I said aloud as Andy's faced turned crimson with his hard chuckle.

"You're a doll," Andy said as he motioned to the bartender. She quickly walked over to him. He whispered in her ear then looked to me. "I'll have something else delivered. You'll like this. I promise."

"Th-thanks," I said, taking my hands away from Rafe, who still held them as he stared down at me with the same amusement.

"Sorry again."

"It happens," he said as he wiped his face with the only clean part of his shirt.

"Forrest Gump," I said with a laugh of my own.

"Sorry?"

"Uh, just that part where...never mind. Sorry...again."

Rafe gave me another curious look before he and Andy made their way to the bar. I slumped into my seat and waited for my new drink. Congratulations and back pats were passed around as the guys took a seat and fresh beers were delivered to them along with a soaked bar towel and a fresh Swampgators t-shirt for Rafe. I held my breath as he ripped off the soiled shirt and saw his tan skin, and the barely visible etch of tattoos on his ribs below his arm and muscular back. I let out a sigh of approval as I pushed the bowl of peanuts away.

I drank down the delicious pineapple concoction set in front of me and tried to breathe through my embarrassment. I could do a lot of things well, but flirting had never been one of them. I'd never really had a chance to practice the art. Once my humiliation passed, I sat alone, a silent observer of what looked like a ritual at the bar.

I'd been doing it my whole life...watching crowds that belonged together congregate before my eyes and feeling like I didn't belong. I'd left the bitterness behind with my schoolgirl age. It was a whole new world for me. As an adult, I realized I had a choice to mingle and try to find my own people or blend, and due to my bitter beer and peanut explosion, I decided that night to blend.

Dutch *never* had company. In the years I'd been playing at Anchor Park, I'd never seen a single person sit next to her. I was used to the noise she made, but when I saw a pint-sized woman with a loud mouth echo next to her, I almost blew my first pitch. That had never happened...until tonight.

I glanced over my shoulder to see she was still there. She looked comfortable but alone. I studied her for a spell. Her blonde hair was a mess under that red hat. Underneath were large doe eyes and suckable, plump lips. I'd watched her chest heave when she'd panicked and saw a perfect quarter sized set of nipples strain against her tank.

I'd spent the first twenty minutes at the bar trying to ignore the image of those nipples and failed.

"You pitch like that this season, there's no stopping you," Andy said as he sipped his beer and looked in the same direction I was with a smirk. "She's out of your league."

"And you think that because?"

"She has manners. She said crud, not *shit*. She's reserved and doesn't have her legs spread. Not your type."

"Just because you have a hard-on for your help doesn't make you a saint," I said with my own smirk as Andy's face hardened. He glanced over at the bartender, Kristina. Relief covered his features as he realized she hadn't heard then he gave me his death glare.

"So you changing your mind or what? You still have good years left."

"Nope, this is it, so you better make it good," he quipped. "As soon as you get the call, I'm out."

"You're just going to brew beer and run this bar for the rest of your life."

"I've played my seasons. It's time," he said with conviction.

"You'll miss it," I stated with the same certainty.

"Maybe...Fuck, I know I will." He shook his head in aggravation. "My mind's made up. Let it go. The focus is on you this season. They're going to call."

"Let's just put it out there," I said, aggravated. "This is my last—"

Andy cut me off with a look of understanding and his signature "Fuckin' A."

I clinked glasses with him and turned back to look at the blonde who made me more curious by the minute.

"Fuck it, I'm going in," I said as I finished my beer and set it on the bar.

"Too late and it's a good thing," Andy said with authority as I looked over my shoulder and caught her walk out the door. "This season, no distractions."

3
Alice

After a week of preflight instructions came the fun part. Locked in the cabin of the simulator, one by one I repetitively guided each pilot through the basic steps of the dashboard, detail by detail. Exhausted by the first few hours, I almost didn't recognize the mouthwatering hint of cologne and deep blue eyes of the newest pilot who took the seat next to me.

"I read your flight log. Pretty impressive," he said as his eyes roamed over the controls with familiar confidence before landing on me.

I smiled in welcome. "Thanks."

"Trey," he said, extending his hand to me.

"Call me Alice," I said, giving him a brief but firm shake.

"Al-ice," he said with appreciation as he gave me a broad smile.

"The first thing you need to know," I said as I pointed out protocol, "is—"

"I've done my homework," he said as I lifted a brow. "How

about I give it a try, and you let me know how I'm doing?"

I looked at him skeptically. "That's not really the suggestion of—"

"Just give me a shot here," he whispered while a different kind of suggestion played off his tongue. I finally took the time to appreciate him as we stood and switched seats.

"This is an eighteen million dollar plane, Captain," I warned.

"I take care of my valuables," he whispered, now in complete control. I studied his profile as he initiated flight with every step perfectly. His dark blond hair was combed back neatly. He wore a white dress shirt, dark khaki chinos, and tan boots. His flight skills were impressive, his appearance remarkable. I'd always imagined the man of my dreams as another pilot simply because we would have a solid foundation on our one thing in common: the love of flying.

As Trey picked up speed and sent us both into the computer generated clear skies, I briefly wondered if it was a beginning.

I ran through the spring drizzle toward Anchor Park, a far cry from yesterday's perfect weather, to meet Dutch at the gates. She was covered head to toe in yellow plastic and rubber, her weathered face the only thing protruding from her get up. She looked like a rubber duck, a disgruntled rubber duck.

"They'll probably tarp the field but here..." She extended a bright red poncho that matched my hat.

"Thanks," I said as I wrapped myself in the plastic just as the rain picked up.

We made our way to the nearly empty stadium as the teams warmed up. My eyes drifted over the players and landed directly on Rafe, who seemed to be looking our way. Dutch gave him a short wave, and he nodded, his attention directed at me. I felt my cheeks flush slightly as I kept my head down, still a little embarrassed about the previous night.

Within two innings of a downpour, the weather shut the game down as it flooded the stadium, and Dutch and I with it. We said quick goodbyes with a promise to meet the following day, twenty minutes to game time, as I scurried out to the street. The water was already over a foot deep and climbing as I plowed through the street in front of Anchor Park directly across to the parking lot. The rain was cold and unforgiving as it covered both my feet and I attempted to flee. As I approached my Prius, I stood back in shock just as the tires started to be consumed by water.

"OH MY GOD!"

Just as fast as I realized my new car was in danger, a large F350 pulled up next to me and a window let down. "They don't call this the low country for no reason, doll. Get in." I looked in the cab of the truck to see Andy looking over my shoulder with concern. "The tides coming in. You aren't getting out of here in that tin can. You might as well weather the storm and see if she survives."

"I'm not leaving my brand new car to drown!" I said, exasperated.

"You have about ten minutes until you both do," he said with a smile. I realized then the water was close to knee high. I'd parked in front of the riverbank, and it was pouring onto the grass next to it.

"Thanks, I'll just move it."

"It's too late to get it to the upper deck. The streets are done. We need to go." I looked past the gravel behind me and saw the streets were running with at least two feet of water.

"But—"

Before I could get my argument out, the back door of Andy's cab opened and a shirtless Rafe came toward me with purpose. I was just about to address him when he scooped me into his arms. My body reacted before I had a chance to think it through. I saw his eyes widen as he dropped me to the flooded ground beneath us.

We both began choking, and Andy roared with laughter as both Rafe and I fought for air. I pushed off the ground, spitting water out of my mouth as Rafe placed a hand on his knee and glared at me while he massaged his throat with the other.

"What the fuck, woman!"

"You don't go barging toward a woman who doesn't know you and scoop her up, moron!"

"Well, you don't throat punch a man for trying to keep your stubborn ass from drowning!"

All words left me as the unrelenting water poured over the both of us and we stared each other down. I was completely thrown as I studied his perfect body.

Arms, abs, abs, more abs, abs, abs, abs.

Rafe cursed and made his way to the back of the truck and jumped in. I watched helplessly as the water rose over the tires of my Prius.

"Come have a few beers with us. When the rain slows, we'll come back," Andy summoned as Rafe pulled out a fresh t-shirt from a duffle bag in the back of the cab and put it on. I stood there weighing my options and relented when I realized there really was only one.

I pulled myself into the massive blue truck and put on my seatbelt.

Andy looked at Rafe in the rearview and chuckled as Rafe tried to silently clear his throat and then turned his attention to me.

"So...?"

"Alice," I said as I pulled his passenger mirror down and pushed the plastic wrap off of my head along with my hat. I fisted my hair in a ponytail and pulled it through the elastic on my wrist.

"Alice," Andy said as if his friend fuming in the back seat made no difference to him at all. "Ignore Rafe. He was already half-cocked because the game was canceled." He grinned back at Rafe before he took off. His truck plowed easily through the rising water. "So how do you know Dutch?" I caught Rafe's curious glance and pushed the mirror back up.

"I just met her last night," I said as the two shared a confused look in the rearview.

"She let you sit in Herb's chair," Andy said in slight shock.

"Yes, she told me her husband died, and I could have his seat."

"That woman has occupied those two chairs since the stadium opened and never sat with anyone, let alone gave away his seat," Andy remarked.

Still soaked and terrified for my Toyota, I shrugged. "She let me."

"Huh..." This seemed like a mystery to both men in my company. A brief silence followed before Andy spoke up. "So what do you do?"

"I'm a flight instructor at Boeing."

Andy winked at Rafe again in the rearview as I rolled my eyes. "So you're a pilot?"

"Yes, I studied aeronautics and got my masters at Cornell. I just moved here last week."

"Cornell," Andy said again with a smug smirk. "Hear that, Rafe?"

"Impressive," he said in an uninterested tone.

I snapped my head back and faced him head on. "I use my brains instead of my brawn to make a living. How do you see that working out for you?"

Rafe smiled then, and not just any smile, one that said he'd seen me naked. "Brawn's working out just fine for me."

I rolled my eyes and faced forward.

I had to fuck her.

It's all I thought about on the way to the bar. The woman was tiny but had just the right amount of everything from what I'd gathered at the bar last night, including the sexiest brown eyes I'd ever seen. But it was the fire in them that I wanted to feed off of.

Andy made small talk as I studied her profile. She was covered in plastic and still appealed more to me than half the ass I'd bedded in the last few months.

"So you go in and teach a bunch of pilots to fly every day?" Andy asked with interest.

"Yeah, pretty much. There's a newly built plane, so I'm getting them ready to pilot it."

"Like Kelly McGillis in Top Gun," he said with a wink.

She turned to him and gave him a full smile. "And you're like Sam Malone from Cheers."

As if on cue, they fist bumped, and she...giggled.

"So, are you single?" Andy said as he looked her over.

Wait. A. Fucking. Minute.

I glared at Andy in the rearview, and he gave me a deviant smile.

"I am," she said with a nod. "I've been flying for the last two years since I graduated. I haven't had much time for anything else."

"Well, welcome to Charleston," Andy said with a hint of pure southern bullshit. I had no idea what angle he was playing, but I knew he wasn't interested in Alice. He'd been in love with Kristina for two damned years.

"Does it always flood this badly?" she asked warily.

"When the tide comes in, and it rains this hard, yes. This town becomes soup, but it's mostly downtown."

"I missed that in my research," she said as if she was disappointed.

"King tides came this year. They only come around every hundred years or so. Gotta keep up with the rain and tides if you go anywhere downtown," Andy said as we pulled up to his bar. "Come on, pilot Alice, I'll buy you a beer."

"No thanks," she said with another giggle as the two completely ignored me. "And no special treatment. *You* are the ball star."

"Then I'll buy you a drink for throat punching Rafe," he said as he gave me a quick wink before he slammed his door, but not before I heard Alice say, "Well, in that case."

"What's your fucking angle," I hissed to Andy as Alice excused herself to use the restroom an hour later. I cracked open a peanut and tossed the pods back in my mouth as Kristina delivered fresh beers to us.

I gave her a thank you and a wink. Andy cut his eyes my way.

"No angle. I told you she's out of your league, and if you'd listened to one word she's said in the last three beers, you'd realize it."

"I heard her," I said as I sucked down the froth off the top of my mug.

"Then you heard her say she's new to baseball."

"Yep."

"You didn't hear shit. You were too busy staring at her nipples."

"So were you."

"I have a dick. I noticed," he shot back, unoffended. "I'm your best friend, and I'm telling you there's no way she'll be into you, so forget it."

"I don't want her to be *into* me. I want to be *in* her."

"Well, good luck with that."

"What makes you so damned sure I couldn't get her?"

"You aren't ready for *real*, and your career is about to take off."

"What the hell does that have to do with fucking her?"

Andy narrowed his eyes at me. "You're not that stupid. And you're not that big of a prick."

I saw Alice as she approached our table with a smile and nodded at Andy. The truth was, I didn't know why I was suddenly so intent on having her in my bed. I pushed the hair off my forehead and looked at her, *really* looked at her. The woman was stunning with a heart-shaped face and lips. Her large brown eyes screamed innocence. Without a stitch of makeup on, she was simply beautiful.

"Sorry about earlier. I was just goofing around," I heard myself say.

"It's fine," she said before she took a sip of her drink, and my eyes stayed glued to her lips.

Andy cleared his throat as I watched the liquid ease down her throat.

I had to fuck her.

I looked past Rafe and out the window, losing hope for my Prius. The rain hadn't stopped since we got to the bar.

"It'll be okay," Andy said reassuringly.

"Thanks," I said, unbelieving of his words with each minute that passed.

"I'm going to run back to my office for a bit. You two good? Gloves off, Alice?" Andy looked to me then to Rafe. "I'd watch my wandering hand if I were you...Bullet."

"Funny," Rafe spouted back, his eyes on mine. I felt the hairs on my neck rise in awareness. His eyes were almond shaped and beautiful, but the look in them reeked of a smug man. I may not have been a well-practiced flirt, but after years around pilots, I was well versed in cocky, horse crap detection. Rafe had cockiness in abundance.

"Ladies' man, huh?" I said, unimpressed.

"Maybe," Rafe said with pride as he tipped his beer, oblivious, taking it as a compliment.

"Every available woman in Charleston has the t-shirt," Andy said with a hard pat on the back that made Rafe's jaw twitch.

"Would. You. Fuck. Off," Rafe said with menace as Andy honored his request and retreated down a hall behind the bar.

"Soooo," I said as I stared at my drink.

"You aren't drinking much," Rafe noted as he observed the level of my drink.

"I don't like to lose control of my senses."

"Uh huh, well, it can be a good thing once in a while." He grinned broadly as my breath hitched.

"Yeah," I agreed as my horse crap meter ticked up a notch. He leaned in a little farther as he started to try to work me. "I mean, sometimes a woman just needs to let go."

Rafe was flirting, and I was ready to run for the hills.

I wanted to explore men, and the body beneath the t-shirt in front of me matched with the face of an ad model would be a good start. But lowering my panties for a one night stand with a pitcher playboy I'd have to look at every home game for the next several months did not appeal to me in the slightest. Covered in goose bumps and the heat that built from his whisper, I looked up to meet his smoldering eyes.

"Lesbehonest, I mean that literally. I'm a lesbian."

I took a large pull of my drink through my straw to keep from bursting into laughter from the look on his face. It was one of utter confusion and slight disappointment. I was sure the conversation couldn't go anywhere from there, and I was right. Thirty minutes later, I was dropped off with a silent goodbye wave from Rafe and a "see you at the next game" by Andy to my safe and sound Prius.

It was the best day of my life.

~~Almond Milk~~
~~Granola~~
~~Turkey cutlets~~
~~Asparagus~~

"Please stop him!" I heard as a little boy raced past me down the grocery aisle. I turned to see Kristina from Andy's bar running full speed to catch the giggling child. She pulled a can from the vegetable shelf as she ran after him. "Dear God, don't make me use this." She laughed and took aim at his head in jest as I gripped the little boy by the arm and stopped him just before he cornered the aisle. He looked up at me in shock.

"Thank you," she said, out of breath, as she caught up with us. "He's five years old and thinks that *everything* is a race." She looked down at her son and then back to me. "Hey, I didn't even realize it was you. Thank you."

"Alice," I said as the boy fought against his mother.

"Cut it out or no Minecraft!" The child stilled instantly. "I'm Kristina, and this...oh God, I don't know what this is."

"I'm Dillon, Mommy!" The dark haired replica of her reminded as he pointed proudly to his chest.

"Yes, yes you are," she replied with an exhausted sigh. "Thanks again for stopping him. This," she said, holding a can of green beans, "is the only thing I've managed to get since we got here. Oh God, I left my purse in my cart!" She handed me back Dillon's arm then raced away.

I looked down at him as he smiled up at me with devious eyes, wheels spinning in his mind. "I eat children," I said in warning.

He looked up at me, his smile slightly disappeared as he tried to gauge if I was serious or not.

Kristina rounded the corner again, relief on her face and purse in hand. "Pizza and green beans it is," she said as she reached into the freezer and grabbed a Baron's cheese pizza.

"Well, at least you're getting a vegetable in." I tapped the can of green beans with my finger.

"Mother of the year," she said with a groan. "It's like the Lord is testing me." She leaned in a little farther. "The sex wasn't even worth it. But he is."

Dillon started to pull his mother away as he eyed me, and I gave him the crazy witch-who-eats-children eye. I smiled at Kristina with an added, "Nice to meet you both."

"See you at the bar?"

I agreed with a smile. The woman was beautiful, stunning really. I pondered what it was like being so attractive. And then for a fleeting moment, I wondered if Rafe had ever hit on her.

"Warm up, Hembrey," Rod, my pitching coach, barked as I lay back on the grass of the field and looked up at the blue sky. I wasn't into it today. I wasn't pitching, anyway. I wanted to be on the waves. I had spent the entire winter perfecting my pitch. I'd spent countless hours alone or with Andy doing what I did best. I remained on the grass as my trainer, Mitch, pushed my hamstrings to the grass and twisted my form the opposite way.

"Get your head in, Rafe," Mitch warned as he hovered above me and pressed my legs.

"Grow some tits and I'll think about it," I snapped back.

"Jon got a call this morning," he said in a whisper. "And I know it was about you."

I stilled my legs, and he shook his head adamantly, silently telling me to keep our conversation on the down-low as he resumed movement.

Jon Rustenhaven was the manager of the Swampgators and was both my greatest ally and enemy. He had zero tolerance for bullshit, which was a good thing when you managed a team full of competitive athletes at different ages full of fire and ambition. Tempers often flared, and egos got bruised. It was part of it all. And though I hadn't given him much reason to, Jon watched me closely. I'd had an outburst on occasion but had long ago learned to handle my temper. Andy had helped.

"What did Jon say?"

"I don't know. He closed the door, but I heard your name. He knows it. We all know it. This is it."

"I'm not banking on shit," I said, pushing away from him before standing to grab my stretch bands.

"Just thought I'd let you know," Mitch said. "Conduct yourself and you've got it."

"I blew up *once*," I said as I turned away in disgust. "When are people going to forget about it?"

"And no one blames you, but it was your father," Mitch said as he gave me the truth. "No one will ever forget about it."

I had a few days before the next baseball game but had surprised myself by following the series that the Swampgators played against Columbia the past weekend that had resulted in a Gator's victory. Rafe had only pitched one game but had dominated, and I found myself silently cheering him on.

In dire need of company and with the following day off, I found myself at Andy's talking to Kristina. I'd spent my days in a cold, white classroom that was far less than alluring than my romanticized version. Though rewarding in a sense, it was less exciting than I'd imagined. I missed the air. I missed flying, but I refused to admit taking the job was the wrong choice. In fact, I was in flat out denial. I convinced myself I had to give it time.

"Asshole," I heard Kristina grunt as she eyed the bar slip left by a man who'd just ran her around for the better part of half an hour. He stuffed his face and openly ogled her, as well as made inappropriate sexual comments. She lifted her fingers into a crunched V, the tips pointed in his direction.

"Crappy tip?"

Still giving the man the strange gesture, she addressed me. "They should make it a requirement after high school that *every* human wait tables. It would teach manners and humility."

My curiosity got the best of me as she kept her fingers up until the man was safely out of the door.

"What are you doing?"

"I just cursed him with uncontrollable anal itching," she said with seriousness. I burst into laughter as she tilted her head and eyed me with a small amount of humor on her perfectly painted lips. "It works."

"Okay," I said, pushing my drink toward her in a polite request. "I'm a good tipper."

"If Andy didn't beg me to stay," she said as she gripped my glass and set it on the bar well, "I'd be doing something else by now."

"Like what?" I asked as she gripped the bottles. I noted the ingredients of my drink and typed them into my phone. Boredom may make an alcoholic of me yet.

"Like...hell, I don't know...something where I can be home with my son at night."

"Well, if it makes you feel any better, I'm not a huge fan of my job right now, either."

"In that case," she said with a wink, "this one is on me." I shook my head to protest as I looked her over. Kristina really was a stunning woman, and if she knew it, she showed it poorly.

"Shopping for something new?" I felt the tingle start in my spine as Rafe whispered in my ear. The rumble of his deep voice completely counteracted the small numbness I felt from the alcohol. "She's completely straight."

I huffed as I turned in his direction. This time, I was able to control my breath, but the effect was the same. Dark, thick green lined the outside of his irises, and I could see the caramel clouds of brown that filled the rest of them. He was too close, and our lips almost touched. Those lips were a beacon, full, inviting, and the undeniably sexy smirk he wore made them far too tempting.

"I'm not shopping and unlike you, I don't think *every* woman is interested in me."

"You assume too much," Rafe said as he nodded at Kristina, who set down a fresh beer in front of him with a smile. He thanked her then turned his attention back to me. "We got off on the wrong foot. There's no reason to get defensive. I love lesbians."

I heard a loud bark of a laugh come out of Kristina, who looked at me with bulging eyes. I nodded in confirmation but could tell she knew better.

"That's wonderful, Rafe, really." Thinking on my toes, I hid my smile. "Hey, you're a local celebrity of sorts." I saw his eyes narrow as I continued. "They're having a gay pride party at the park in North Charleston this weekend. You can be my date and endorse your love of lesbians."

"I have a game," he said as an excuse.

"It's before your game."

"I have plans."

"Now you do," I quipped back.

"Fine," he said as he looked me over with scrutiny. "I'll go, but you have to do something with me if you think you're wo-*man* enough."

He was dressed in dark cargo shorts, a V-neck, white tee, and his ball cap was backward. No matter how hard I tried, I couldn't stop staring at the curve of his bicep as he lifted his beer. My eyes wandered back to the beautiful, hard lines of his jaw and the ring of indents on the side of his mouth that accompanied his smug smile. They were intoxicating. I was starting to regret my declared sexuality.

"Fine."

"Meet me here at 8 A.M. tomorrow and bring a bathing suit, or...whatever you type of women wear."

"Now you're stereotyping," I snapped.

"Jesus, Rafe," Kristina said as she eyed our exchange with humor. "With that statement, you'd make lesbians everywhere proud."

"I'll just grab my dyke wear and see you here," I said as I left

Kristina the tip I promised and made my way out the door.

"What the hell did I say?"

Kristina laughed and held her stomach as she answered. "I think by trying to be accommodating, you offended her."

"I don't even know why I asked her," I said, pounding my beer as a headache kicked in.

"If I had to guess," Kristina whispered as she leaned over the bar, "I would say you like her."

"She's gay."

Kristina burst out in laughter again as she slid a freshly poured beer down the bar. "I think she may be gay for *you*, Rafe."

"Bullshit," I said as I paused and looked up at Kristina, who nodded once in the direction that Alice left. "Are you telling me she's *playing* lesbian?"

"I'm just saying"—she bent over the bar and gave me an eyeful of cleavage, which I appreciated for half a second—"exactly, Rafe." She motioned to her chest. "I must have done that a few times and her eyes never hit pay dirt once. She's bluffing."

"To keep me away," I said, stunned.

"Yes, big head." Kristina walked down the bar as I sat there fuming. The woman had managed to piss me off twice since I met her and had made a fool of me.

Oh yes, there would be fucking.

I'd decided on a night of southern favorites—*Fried Green Tomatoes* and *Steel Magnolias*—but would start it off with *Forrest Gump* while I doused myself with spray on tan. I felt it necessary due to the pathetic, pale tint of my skin. Standing in my living room while it dried, I repeated the words to the movie as I moved my arms back and forth in a windmill. Naked and feeling foolish for going to such efforts to look better in my newly purchased bikini, I mentally beat myself up for trying.

Rafe.

Just the mental image of him staring me down did things to my insides. Even if he acted like a monkey man who liked to build big fires to impress his peers, he was nothing short of gorgeous. He didn't seem my type at all. Rafe didn't think through the words that came out of his mouth or his actions, either, but I had to admit, it was a flaw of mine as well.

I'd accused him of stereotyping, but in the back of my mind, I'd done the same to him.

The man was the definition of arrogant and an athlete to boot. I could probably measure his depth and intelligence by the amount of space he allowed between his penis and the toilet water. God, and the sad line he used about letting go wouldn't even make it into the cheesiest of '80s flicks I watched on repeat.

And it seemed like he'd been getting away with it for a long time. I decided not to over analyze as I tried to relax while prepping for what I was sure was going to be a disastrous date...with a man...

who thought I was a lesbian.

I was dripping with sticky goo and was just about to shower it off to make it look more natural when I caught movement in the corner of my eye.

I felt the jolt of terror race through me as I pressed my legs together to keep from peeing and ruining what I was sure was an expensive rug.

A huge cockroach raced across my wall, and as I began to scream, I swear it started to scream with me as it scurried away. I grabbed the can of tanning spray and raced toward it while I yelled at the intruder at the top of my lungs, unloading the can on my cream colored wall. The bastard refused to stop or even acknowledge my ammunition as I used half of the can. Nothing in my well-educated brain reminded me that if it was safe to spray on human skin, it would be more than safe for a cockroach that could survive a nuclear war. As it made its way to safety, I realized I had just tanned a cockroach.

Nervous laughter burst out of me as I scanned my walls and went straight for a broom in my hall closet. I made a beeline back to the living room and began to beat the ever loving crap out of every surface of the space. Hours later, with newly striped tan walls, my borrowed couch was torn apart, the room in utter disarray. I realized I was blackened by the tanning spray that I was supposed to have rinsed off and still fully naked. I crouched in my living room, still on the hunt, and felt utterly insane. I must have looked like Leo DiCaprio did when he lost his mind in that movie *The Beach*.

A knock on the door startled me as I looked at the clock. It was 3:00 A.M. I quickly pulled on my Yoda onesie and raced to the door as I zipped it.

"Hi," a woman said on the other side of the frame. She looked tired, and I felt her pain. I had only hours until I met Rafe as a black lesbian.

"Can I help you?"

"I live downstairs. I think the question is *can* I help *you*?" She grinned in a sleep-filled smile as I realized the noise I must've made during my epic battle.

"Oh God, I'm so sorry. I had this gigantic..." I didn't want to say roach because who in the heck wants to admit they have a disgusting bug in their house? Just as I was about to deny it, I saw one slightly larger bug than the one inside my condo crawl up the wall on the siding behind her and then suddenly take flight.

"Oh my GOD!" I pulled her into the house and shut the door as I looked through the peephole.

"Hey now, what in the world is wrong with you?"

I turned to her with wide eyes. "There's a gigantic roach outside, and it's FLYING!"

She burst into laughter as she pushed me gently from the doorway and opened it. "I take it you aren't from around here?"

"No." I pushed out a breath. "Please, God, I've already dealt with the thought of preparations to build an Arc for the flooding downtown. Don't tell me this is normal!" She took in my appearance, my onesie, tinted hands and face, and the panic in it as I looked her over. Her blonde hair was piled on her head, and her face was still pretty even void of makeup and lack of sleep. Her silk pajamas were far more sophisticated than mine. If I had to guess, I would say she was probably early thirties, and though it was late, she seemed to have a pleasant disposition that went with her thick southern accent. It was too bad I wanted to shove her out the door to keep the horrid creature that loomed over us at bay.

"Those, my dear neighbor, are Palmetto bugs and very common in these parts. Look forward to skin-eating no-see-ums, mosquitoes, lizards, bullfrogs, snakes, and, of course, alligators."

"Noseyums?"

"NO-SEE-UMS. Oh, you'll know," she said with a wink.

"Of course," I whispered back in sheer terror.

"You'll get used to it."

"Uh huh."

"Lemon juice if you have any, and a sugar scrub should ease that fake bake up a bit." I studied my hands in defeat.

"Do you want to take this with you? You know, back downstairs?" I said as I offered my broom to her.

"No thanks," she muttered before she moved past me with quickness and stomped the kitchen floor. I pushed out an eager thank you as she pulled a paper towel off of my kitchen bar and ended my battle.

"I'm April," she said as she gripped my door handle, my problem bug murdered in the paper towel she held in her hand. I loved her instantly.

"Alice," I said with a sigh.

"You'll get used to it. Welcome to Charleston."

It was the first time I'd hated the words, but still, I smiled and thanked her again before closing my door. I wasted gallons of water trying to rub the all too obvious spray paint from my skin. I stood in front of the mirror three cold showers later and let a few tears stream down my face. A look at the clock had me utterly defeated—4:00 A.M. I was screwed. I pulled my covers tight around me as I scanned my walls for any lingering friends of the recently departed. But they were still *my* walls. And the bed I was in belonged to *me*.

I smiled as I drifted off.

It was the *best* day of my life.

I waited twenty minutes in the parking lot and cursed my stupidity. I'd never been stood up. The irony was that it wasn't even a date. I rolled my eyes as I started my Jeep and began to leave when I saw her blue Prius pull into the drive. She had her baseball hat on and was slumped in her seat.

"You're late."

"Yeah, sorry. I had a rough night. I can't do...whatever it is we were supposed to do today. I, uh...didn't have your number so I drove down to tell you."

I frowned as I looked down at her. "You could at least look at me when you ditch me." *What the hell was that, Rafe? You pussy!*

I saw her exhale in defeat as she looked up to me. Half of her chin was tinted dark brown and so were her ears. I pressed my lips together to keep from laughing. "What happened?"

Her eyes narrowed as she looked up at me. "I had an incident with a chemical."

"Looks like the worst fucking spray tan in Charleston."

She sighed as she straightened in her seat to turn her key. "I'll see you around, Rafe."

Still in our cars, I looked down at her with a smile. "I can see the bikini strings tied behind your neck."

"It was a stupid move. I can't go anywhere in public. You have no idea. I look like I haven't washed in certain places in twenty years."

"The waves will get it off. Hop in."

"No way," she said with a shake of her head.

"I promise not to bring it up or even look at you funny." She gave me those wide, doe eyes, and I couldn't help but acknowledge the kick in my chest. I raised my palm to her. "I won't. I promise, Lesbian Alice."

"Okay," she said as she grabbed her bag and threw it in the back of my Jeep. She stood outside the passenger door, her arms crossed, and looked at me expectantly. I gave her a sideways glance.

"Whatever," she muttered as she opened her door and climbed in.

The open air seemed to sooth her on our silent ride to Folly Beach. She had a thin sweatshirt on that hung from her shoulder and cut off shorts. I loved the shape of her small frame as it sat next to mine. Without thinking, I pulled the hat from her head and shoved it under my seat. Her blonde locks flew around her face as she looked at me in puzzlement and then gave me my first genuine smile.

Andy's words hit me in that second.

You aren't ready for the real.

Jesus, he was beautiful. His hair was loosely cropped around his crown, but he still had plenty of length to run fingers through. It was messy and thick and slightly wavy. His tank accented his insane build. The top of his shoulders were sculpted as if he were some sort of gladiator pre Jesus, and the rest of his upper torso was just as etched. I was tempted to rip the cut on the side of his shirt to see more. I let my eyes drift up to his face just as he glanced over at me. I realized I'd smiled at him and as he smiled back at me, I felt a hint of something as my pulse kicked.

Our eyes diverted, his to the road and mine to take in the sun dancing over the water. I couldn't help but to remember how good it felt to be desired in his eyes for that brief moment in the bar.

I'd been hit on in the past. I'd had sex, and had no intentions of remaining celibate. It had been almost three years aside from my close encounter with a pilot last year who'd suddenly come up with a wife.

Hopes obliterated, I kind of shut down after that incident and sex hadn't mattered as much. As I looked back over at Rafe, his tall frame taking up the majority of the cabin, his muscular arm was braced on the door and his other large hand on the gear shift, I could only think of his lips and skin and what they may feel like if they touched mine.

He oozed confident sex appeal, and by the manner he came on to me at the bar, I was more than confident he could deliver. Maybe a night with a skilled lover was just what I needed to get me out of the slump I'd been in.

"Rafe," I said in a whisper.

"We're here," he said as he parked the Jeep.

"Read my lips. No."

"Listen, Alice, I'll have you harnessed in. I won't let a thing happen to you."

I clenched my thighs together as the driver of the boat looked over my half-bronzed, bikini-clad body. His expression as he observed me bordered on laughter. I looked a total mess in my solid pink, two-piece swimsuit. Rafe had refused to let me keep my shorts on, and I'd stupidly agreed.

"Rafe, I can't do this. I'll scream the whole time!"

"Feet in," he barked as he pulled the straps up my legs and clasped them around my body.

"Aren't you a pilot, woman?" he snapped as he cupped my face and brought us nose to nose. Wide-eyed with panic, he waited on me to calm down a bit before he spoke gently.

"You've got this. Thirty seconds in the air, and if you hate it, I'll bring you down."

"Right into Jaws's mouth."

"Alice"—Rafe chuckled—"I've got you." The driver started the boat and began whipping through the waves as Rafe egged me on with encouragement while he sat me at the edge of the boat, making sure I was properly strapped in. I'd never Googled parasailing. I had no idea how safe or unsafe it was. I knew absolutely nothing about it, and I *hated* that fact.

"Okay." I pulled the last of my Red Bull into my mouth and crushed the can before throwing it at his feet. I bowed up to Rafe in my harness, fists clenched, teeth gritted, with a quick, "Let's do this." Rafe howled with laughter as I threw air punch after air punch in front of him to psyche myself up.

"What in the hell are you doing?" he asked, incredulous.

"Haven't you seen Rocky?"

"Oh, Jesus," Rafe mused as he checked my gear one more time.

"I'm going to make this my—Oh my GOD!!" Rafe pushed me just as I was lifted and rocked me back with a wink. As soon as I began to rise, a stream poured from between my legs. There was no stopping it.

I peed when I was nervous, excited, or scared.

Like a dog.

I peed.

And I was pretty sure I'd just slapped Rafe in the chest with it. I looked for and saw his reaction as I hovered above, screaming like a banshee, and he poured bottled water all over himself. I didn't care how scared I was. I was never coming down.

Agonizing minutes later and after fighting a bout of humiliation induced nausea, I focused on finding my center. Once I'd managed to open my eyes, I sighed in awe. The sea was beautiful as the blooming sky lit up the water in oranges and yellows. I floated above, completely confident as realization struck of what a baby I'd acted like. Rafe gave me a thumbs up, and I shot it right back as I drifted in the air above him. My confidence slightly restored, I took in my surroundings in new appreciation. I shouted down an "I love it" that I wasn't sure he could hear, and a silent thank you to the clouds above and the sea below for the show they gave me.

Like all good things, my ride came to an end. I couldn't look

Rafe in the eye as I was lowered back to the boat. My whole face flamed and it was from more than the result of my first hour in the sun.

"I'm sorry," I said quickly as he freed me from the restraints. "I should have warned you."

"About what? Your R. Kelly moment?"

"Yeah, when I get really nervous—"

"You give golden showers? Some men subscribe to that. I'm not one of them." I kept my eyes averted. How could I ever look at him again? Rafe chuckled as I quickly scrambled for conversation. "So are you going next?"

"Yeah, I'll see you in a bit."

I looked up to see Rafe enter the water on a surfboard fastened to his feet and a bar clutched in his hands. Seconds later, he was jumping waves as he caught the wind with his kite and gained at least thirty feet in the air. "The wind is killer today. He'll be at it all afternoon," the boat driver said as he handed me...a beer.

Great.

Instead of trying to find ways to entertain myself, I sat mesmerized by his skill as he floated above before he crashed down, coasting on wave after wave.

In the boat, we followed a graceful and determined Rafe as he ripped through both air and water. Pretty soon, others joined him, and I realized the show had just really begun. A circus of colorful kites and air acrobatics floated around me, but my eyes focused on Rafe. I fell into a dazed stupor. Rafe was completely in control, dancing over the curtains of water with ease. I was nursing my third beer by the time he let himself land and whipped his hand in the air in a round up way. He pulled himself onto the boat as water dripped from his ridiculously defined torso and arms. I took in every solid inch of him in appreciation. The driver, whose name was Marc, grabbed Rafe's board from the water as Rafe dismantled his kite.

"God, that was phenomenal," I said as he popped a beer and sat next to me. "You are *truly* gifted at that."

Rafe seemed taken aback by my comment as I gushed on. "You looked so...good, just like a... just so skilled, so in control. I loved watching you. I wasn't even bored like I thought I would be," I said with a wave of my hand, "but I wasn't, not for a single second. I could watch you all day."

"Thanks," he said with an amused grin.

"Yeah, dude, you totally rocked that," I said as I tilted my beer back, and without too much thought, grabbed another from the cooler between us.

A few minutes into the boat ride back, Rafe turned to me. "So tell me about your last relationship," Rafe said with a smirk. "You said you were single now."

I stiffened in response, his arm slung around me casually.

"It was a long time ago."

"We have about fifteen minutes to dock," he chided.

That was a lot of lying to do in fifteen minutes. So I began. "Ah...I, well, he—oh, she was...crap." I had no choice but to look him in the eye. "I'm not a lesbian."

Rafe nodded with a smirk as my face flushed. "You knew that."

"I did. So, I'm out of the Pride party this weekend."

I pointed to the air above us with my next declaration. "On a technicality only, *and* because I have no gay friends...yet."

"The parts of you that aren't orange are now pink," Rafe said as he looked me over, ignoring my threat.

"Blush and bashful. My colors are blush and bashful," I said in my best southern accent. I went on to explain. "It's a line from—"

"Steel Magnolias, I know. I *do* have a mother and sister."

I gave him a smile I knew to be my biggest, and I swear I could hear him mutter 'shit' under his breath.

5

This woman was insane, but the kind of insane you gravitated toward. There was nothing generic about her. She didn't hold back on anything, not her wrath, her opinion, or her compliments, which she gave freely. I watched her as she sank into the ocean once we docked and came out soaking wet. Her body was a mix of color but still completely alluring, even with the mess that her skin was in. Her shoulder length, golden hair was dripping wet as she put on her shorts and slipped on her sweatshirt. I was fantasizing about wrapping her arms and legs around me and sinking into her.

God, I wanted this woman.

And she'd made it clear she didn't want me, which of course made my dick even harder. We packed up my Jeep as she turned to me.

"Beer...I can do beer now...and parasailing!"

I couldn't help my grin. "That's a lot in a day."

"Best day of my life," she declared. "Thank you, Rafe." She took a long look at the water and turned to me with a smile that stole my breath. "God, I love it here!"

I chuckled as we closed our doors and I started the Jeep and put it into gear.

"I don't know why good days have to end. It's so sad. Criminal, don't you think?" She gripped my hand on the gear shift and squeezed it once before she let it go. "I guess so we appreciate them more or whatever."

"Guess so," I said, having the most honest conversation with a woman I'd ever had. She was completely raw to me, nothing about her guarded. I was starting to think I really was the prick Andy spoke of and that she may be *too* real, which made me more of a prick.

I studied her as she soaked in the scenery and I soaked in mine. I was staring *at* the real, and at that moment, nothing in my life aside from ball had been so appealing.

"I came here to have nothing but good days," she declared absently, staring at the marsh as we crossed over the bridge onto the connecting island.

"And where you're from, you didn't have good days?"

"Huh." She wrinkled her nose. "My mother was the definition of oppressive. Happiness, smiles, excitement, it was all a foreign concept to her. She was serious and...strict."

I looked over at her and saw a sad smile. "She was just way too intense." Alice lifted her hands in the air through the top of the Jeep with a sinister smile. "SO I ESCAAAAAAAPED!"

I couldn't help my light laughter as she closed her eyes with her hands held up...all the way back to the bar.

"I think I was a little buzzed," she said as she unbuckled her seatbelt and checked her phone. "Thank you for an awesome time."

"You're welcome," I said as I took her phone and texted myself a hello with her number. "For the next time you want to cancel on me."

"For days like this, *never*. Except next time...I won't be so nervous."

"Good to know," I said as we both grabbed her bag from the backseat. Our hands connected, and I rubbed my thumb over the top of her soft skin as she exhaled and lowered her head.

"Rafe," she protested as I leaned in to claim her lips. She closed her eyes tightly and then looked to me with brown-eyed seriousness. "So far, you're the only person *resembling* a friend I have. I'm going to be at every single home game of yours this year because I promised Dutch I would. Do you really want to do this with me? I mean, I know how this works. You're curious, we have sex, I may like it, I may not, either way, I may like *you* more, and your curiosity will be quenched, and then I don't get to have days like today. You're a ladies' man. Find another lady, and let me have more days like this."

I sat, stunned, fucking speechless.

"It's not that I'm not attracted to you, Rafe. Believe me, I am... *really* attracted to you," she whispered. "But I can't beat days like this, okay?"

"Okay," I said as I let her hand go. Beautiful brown eyes seared right into me in thanks.

She paused before she opened the door. "I may be wrong about you, I think. I thought you were one of those bone-headed, stupid athletes who only cared about baseball and women. But I have a feeling you're worth knowing."

For the second time in a minute, I couldn't say a single fucking word.

"So, okay, I'll see you at the game."

My body felt like it had been dipped in lava. I couldn't handle another second. I tore off my pajamas just as Rocky knocked out Apollo Creed and stood under the cold shower. I had the sunburn of someone being electrocuted. Still on fire, I wrapped myself in my favorite afghan and picked another movie: *Sixteen Candles*.

John Hughes was my ultimate go-to. Never had my world been rocked like it was when I discovered his movies. I'd memorized his whole collection, coveting the underrated *Some Kind of Wonderful* like most women did their favorite pair of shoes. My movies meant everything to me. They were my best friends, my confidants, and my prophetic teachers when life got hard.

There was a question on the board the first day of my human studies class at Cornell that asked: If you could take only one thing from your home as you flee from a fire, what would it be?

I answered my movie collection and odd looks were shot my

way. The professor asked me why I would choose to take something so easily replaceable. My first instinct was to tell him that they'd belonged to my father, and that was some of the significance, but instead I answered, "Jake Ryan."

I cringed when no one got it. I was referring to a movie as old as most of the students in the class.

I sat up that night thinking about that question and wondering if something was truly wrong with me. I'd listened to the other answers of the other students in an attempt to understand. Those answers consisted mostly of computer towers, iPads, and their phones being the number one answer. Others were family photos, childhood stuffed animals, jewelry. Watching the movie that night and with a sigh on my lips, I kicked myself mentally for not having more confidence in my answer.

JAKE RYAN.

The ultimate man.

The prince charming that had it all, but despite the fact that his life seemed perfect, he looked around, sought out and fell in love with the "different" girl. It was no secret why I loved that movie and Jake so much. It had always been my hope for me one day.

Rafe popped into my head at that moment, and I found myself restless at the very thought of him. His perfect body, his beautiful, soul-filled eyes, and Lord, his voice, deep with a hint of southern twang. He hadn't been nearly as shallow as I'd originally thought. Though we didn't say much, I knew he was in there. He'd probably had too many women who gave themselves easily that he had to put forth little to no effort to open up before they did.

I was more than curious, but I knew I was right about his intentions. When he'd given in so easily to my plea to keep things platonic, I knew I was a curiosity for him. I should've been on cloud nine that a man like that would take sexual interest in me. And though I didn't have much experience in dating or sex, I knew things could turn bad for me and fast if I let Rafe touch me because I'd *really* wanted him to touch me.

It would have been a new kind of paradise—a temporary high

for him, a new craving for me. I knew that deep down after just a few hours with him. Or maybe he would be a poorly skilled, tongue slinger with halitosis. The fantasy was always better, wasn't it? At least, that's the conclusion I came to.

But *Jake Ryan* hadn't drifted through the air in front of me like a wet god. Jake Ryan didn't have soulful eyes. Okay, maybe he did, but they weren't *as* soulful. I closed my eyes as I mentally finger flicked Jake to the edge of his pedestal.

This is not platonic thinking, Alice.

Fucking away games. I'd come to loathe them in my downtime. The bus rides always seemed to drag on, and the cities began to bore me after the first few years. While the rest of the team celebrated another win with beers and a group of girls who'd waited at the bar for them, I lay in the stale smelling motel room and stared at the ceiling.

And I thought of Alice. She'd attended every home game last week and only made an appearance once at the bar after. She'd spent the majority of her time chatting with Andy and Kristina and barely glanced at me before she excused herself to go home. I had to fight the urge to get her alone and tried to respect her wish to keep things friendly. Even with the line drawn, she'd barely given me any of her attention. She was fighting it, and I knew it every time our eyes locked.

It took me exactly five minutes to work up the nerve to text her. She made me nervous. I fucking loved that.

> Rafe: What are you doing?
>
> Alice: HI, RAFE!

I chuckled. She never played cool.

> Rafe: Hi, Alice, and you didn't answer my question.
>
> Alice: I'm listening to the recap of the game on WSAP. Congrats on your win. You are soooo talented!

I smiled as the warmth in my chest spread.

> Rafe: Thank you.
>
> Alice: They say you'll get drafted to the majors this year. How exciting!!!
>
> Rafe: Hope so.
>
> Alice: I'm so happy for you. You struck out Jason Tillman! He's the best hitter in the minors.

Another smile she couldn't see. But I could feel her excitement, and it felt good.

> Rafe: He was so mad he broke his bat.
>
> Alice: I heard. I'll buy you a beer when you get back to celebrate.
>
> Rafe: I'll let you.
>
> Alice: So why haven't they promoted you yet? You have some of the best stats in the MiLB.

The woman was doing her homework.

> Rafe: You sure you're new to ball?

Alice: I'm writing an email to Gerry Knight.

Rafe: What? No, Alice, don't do that. That's not the way this works.

She was definitely new to ball. Gerry was the manager of the major league team I was signed with.

Alice: Why not? I'm a fan. Someone needs to spell it out for him. You should have been pulled by now.

Rafe: Really, Alice, don't do that.

Alice: You can't stop this train. I'm kind of notorious for speaking my mind.

Rafe: You don't say? When you go fan, you go all in, huh?

Alice: I kind of do everything that way.

Rafe: Makes me curious...

Alice: Email sent. Did you know that Frozen is a fifty-million-dollar movie, and they didn't bother to put ear holes on the characters heads?

This chick is so random.

Alice: Oh, you meant that sexually...Rafe?

Rafe: Yeah, Alice?

Alice: Just making sure you were there. Did you know that people in Japan who injure walking pedestrians with their cars have to pay their medical bills? Funerals are cheaper. Do you know what that means?!

Rafe: I can't wait...

Alice: That they continue to run over them until they're dead to avoid bankruptcy.

Rafe: What the hell are you doing?

Alice: I'm Googling.

Rafe: That's a thing?

Alice: For me it is.

Rafe: Do you have ADD?

Alice: You would think that but...no. This is my normal.

And I believed her.

Rafe: Tell me more.

And she did. She spent hours texting me random things, mostly trivial movie facts, which I knew were her favorite. I laughed so hard that the couple in the room next to me pounded on the wall a few times *after* they'd had an extremely vocal fuck fest.

We both fell asleep with our conversation un-ended, without a goodnight, or a goodbye. I smiled as I woke up to her last text.

Alice: Do you know that at any given intersection you are likely to catch someone picking their nose, like finger deep? Gag, I'll never look around at a stoplight again.

I coughed out a laugh as I turned on my side, trying to imagine what she would look like sleeping in the bed next to me. I imagined her waking up with the smile she gave me in my Jeep. I was hard in seconds.

So. Fucking. Beautiful.

Rafe: Morning, Alice.

I spent a few minutes imagining her alone in her bed, her phone lying on her pillow, and wrapped my fist around my thoughts.

I had to have that woman.

7
Alice

"Mr. Harp, that was your last chance to fly through. I'm afraid I can't give you the green light for this aircraft." In the cabin of the simulator, I braced myself for the inevitable as I saw the panic race through him.

"Fuck," he said, scrubbing his hand down his face as he looked back at the screen.

"I'm afraid I smell alcohol on you, as well, and have several times throughout our sessions. I'll have to report it."

"What?" he said as he turned his red, pug face to me. "You can't do that!"

"I can and I will," I said as I threw my clipboard down between us. "Drunks *can't* pilot."

"You little bitch. You know nothing about me. I've been flying for twenty-six years."

I shrugged. "And it will remain twenty-six."

"You can't do that. I have a wife and kids to support!" He leaned in, his posture a threat as his voice dripped with warning.

"These planes carry three hundred and twelve souls," I snapped without apology. "If you want to call someone a little b-b-b...itch you need to point that finger inward. You have absolutely no right to gamble with the lives of that many people."

"You don't know me," he seethed.

"I don't ever want to. The level of stupidity running through that brain of yours is enough to make me run in the other direction. You will either sober up, or you won't fly planes."

"I swear to God I will."

"Swear to him in treatment," I said as I looked at him square on.

"You bitch!" Just as he lunged at me, Trey reached in and jerked him out of his seat and pinned him to the door in the cockpit.

"You're a fucking disgrace. Go get cleaned up!" Trey hissed as he looked back in to check on me. When he saw me unharmed, he let the older pilot go. "Get the hell out of here." Trey looked back down at me with concern. "You okay?"

"Fine," I said with a sigh and meant it. "He's a drunk. He slept through the whole classroom session, failed the simulation, *and* takes issue with me? Entitled and disgusting."

Trey slid into the cabin next to me. "You did the right thing."

"I know," I said confidently.

Trey laughed as he looked over at me. "You're something else, you know that?"

I blushed as he scoured my appearance.

"Want to go grab some dinner this Saturday?"

I knew my features were covered in shock as he went on. "I've wanted to ask for weeks."

"Oh, I..." For a brief moment, I thought of Rafe. Rafe who was a self-proclaimed ladies' man. Rafe, who I'd drawn a clear line of friendship with. Rafe whose own best friend inadvertently warned me away from him.

As those thoughts swirled through my head, I gave my answer. "I'd love to."

After work, I found myself at Andy's Brew House. Andy sat next to me as good company and introduced me to some of the bar regulars. Andy was an all-around incredible guy. He and Rafe had come up through the minors together, though Andy was almost four years older. He'd been recognized as Rafe advanced, and they had progressed and played for a few different Single-A teams together. He would never be drafted to the pros but didn't seem discontent about that fact. Andy opened the bar when the two had moved to Charleston with the intention of having a place to call his own when he finished with the minors.

"This is my last year," he said as he eyed Kristina across the bar. "My knees are wearing out, and I'm tired of all the traveling. I'm playing one last season to see Rafe through."

I couldn't help the tug in my chest as I recognized Andy as one of my tribe. He'd been nothing but the perfect gentlemen since I met him. I respected him, and in a way, I'd developed a personality crush on him.

"So have you always wanted to open a bar?"

Andy smiled, his blue eyes crinkled at the corners. "It's funny you ask that, actually. Rafe bought me a brew kit for Christmas one year as a gag. He said I'd sworn I could do better than some of the local brew masters in the area. I think it was a drunken conversation. Anyway, the kit stayed in my closet for a month and then one day, I went for it, and I loved it. Anyway, when I was home, I brewed in my garage and eventually came up with a few recipes, found some bar space here, and the rest is history."

"A gag gift, huh?"

"Yep, funny how shit like that works out," he said as he tapped his glass to mine. "My dream is to get it in stores."

"I can see that happening," I said as I gestured around the bar. "The regulars seem to love it."

"Meh, that's only because it's all I serve on tap," he winked at me, and I noticed just how good looking he was. Andy was more blond than red up top but had a thin goatee of dark red hair around his lips. His eyes were a beautiful, pale blue, and he was all solid man behind his sweet smile.

"Have some faith," I said as I tipped my beer. "I mean, you've got me drinking it."

"I will, doll," he promised. "Bonfire tonight, you up for it?"

"It's a weekday. I have work tomorrow."

"We all do. That's the point."

Later that night, I found myself beachside surrounded by a small group of Andy's most loyal regulars and friends. Someone played a ukulele while Andy tapped a keg of his finest brew. Rafe joined the party and took a seat beside me in greeting.

"Lesbian Alice."

"Bonehead Athlete."

He looked down at me with his trademark smirk. "What brings you out tonight?"

"An invitation, of course," I answered as I held up my cup. "And free beer."

Rafe smelled like heaven as he surveyed the party. Flames licked his perfect profile as he greeted a few others seated around the roaring fire.

"Looking for someone willing to play with you?" I said with a nudge of my shoulder. His eyes roved over me, and I averted mine to the fire.

He leaned in so slowly, I held my breath. "Would you be jealous?"

I didn't hesitate a second as I turned back to answer. "Would you want me to be?"

Rafe's eyes sparkled with thoughts behind them I could only imagine. I'd actually made a small effort tonight in my appearance and wore a black sundress. I'd flattened my hair and put on some mascara and lip gloss. Rafe stared at my coated lips for endless seconds before he looked up to me.

"I'm pretty good at fucking," he said under his breath as mine again caught in my throat, and I swallowed hard. "It's not something I *play* around with."

"A professional with *all* of your balls," I murmured as my mind drifted with thoughts of the space closing between us.

"Really, Alice?" he whispered as his breath hit my bare neck.

"A sure thing with your big…bat."

"Curious?" he quipped as he studied my lips before he stood to make his way across the fire toward Andy and a group of guys huddled around the keg.

"Remember, no glove, no love!" I shouted after him as he looked back at me and shook his head. I watched as he took a red plastic cup and poured himself a beer from the keg. I was unable to rip my eyes away from the way his perfect butt filled out his shorts or the arms that bulged beneath his t-shirt. As if he could sense me focused on him, Rafe looked back at me and caught me staring. I smiled in an attempt to recover some of my senses, and he did the same. My smile vanished when a perky brunette with a high pitched voice practically moaned his name in greeting and covered him with her intimate posture. My eyes narrowed as he smiled at whatever suggestion she whispered to him and he slapped her butt while he deadpanned at me.

My eyes narrowed and then rolled as I ripped myself away from the situation and took off walking down the shore. Heart pounding, I breathed in deep as I watched the waves roll in and leave their foam residue. A handful of seashells later, I decided my bed was calling and made my way toward the bonfire to say a quick goodbye. I looked up just as Rafe approached me.

"So was today the best day of your life?"

"Every day," I chimed happily. "I'm heading home, so I'll see you at the next game."

Stopping me, Rafe gripped my hand and opened it up to start rummaging through my seashells. He pulled a solid orange, pristine shell from the pile and put in his pocket.

"Hey! That was my favorite."

"My day wasn't as good so I'm taking a piece of yours," he said as he took a step forward and pulled a strand of hair from my mouth.

"This city, this place is beautiful. Did you grow up here?"

"Yep."

"Well, you're one *lucky* man. I mean, I love everything about it. I just don't think you know how lucky you really are."

"Am I?" he said as he inched forward and took my free hand in his.

"Absolutely," I went on nervously. "I mean, so much beauty at your fingertips."

"I agree," he whispered as he brought my hand slowly to his lips and placed a sweet kiss on the back of it before he let it go.

"What was that for?" I said, my legs Jell-O as he looked down at me with intense and greedy eyes. I was suddenly so turned on I was clenching my thighs.

The man was fire.

"It was for the seashell, of course."

"You know good seashells are hard to find, and by the way, you *took* it. I didn't give it, yet you give your lips so freely in exchange."

"Yet?" he mimicked as he took another step forward, and I was forced to look up at him. "Is there something else you want in exchange, Alice?"

Your big bat.

"Well, of course not," I practically sprayed out as I stared up at him.

"You sure?" he said as he inched closer. "I'd be happy to oblige."

Feeling powerless, and my resolve slipping along with my will to keep my dress on, I put up my best fight.

"I'm sure you would. You know," I piped as I mustered up my courage and best shot at southern twang, "you're the definition of a southern gentleman, Rafe. I bet you take the dishes out the sink before you pee in it."

Rafe burst into laughter at my personal rendition and favorite line from "Steel Magnolias". I was pretty sure he didn't place it. I gave my inner Ouiser high five.

"You doin' anything tomorrow afternoon?"

"Not really, no," I said as I looked over to the water and pushed my foot through the sand.

"Good, I could use some help," he said as his eyes alone covered me in goose bumps. "I'll text you."

"Rafe, come on, baby, naked poker!" the girl who had staked her claim on him earlier shrieked from somewhere near the fire.

Rafe lifted a brow in question.

"Not a chance in Satan's hell," I said as I nodded toward the party. "That's all you, playboy."

The air between us whirled with tension, much like the sea breeze that surrounded us. I was under his spell, and he full well knew it. "Shame," he said as he stared down at me. "It would have made my day a whole helluva lot better to know what color your panties are. And, Alice, I *meant* that sexually."

"Better not keep her waiting," I said as I took a step back and broke our connection.

"I know what color her panties are," he said dryly.

I studied him hard as he put his hands in his pockets. "I'm not sure what you want me to think of you, Rafe."

"I'm pretty sure I just want you to think of me, Alice," he said in a whisper as he turned and walked back to the party.

I spent a majority of my day staring at the Google animation in my office. They really were inventive with those letters. Today was Earth Day and the O in Google was a spinning mother earth, reminiscent of Mrs. Potato Head with those gloved white arms and large features. One of the Ls morphed into a squirrel gathering nuts while another of the letters planted a tree. The fact that designing things like this was actually someone's job baffled me. I bet that person sat in their office in Mountain View, high on a pot brownie from lunch, and smiled all day every day. They probably went home and had sex on a pile of money with their husband or wife and picked out tomorrow's work outfit of lazy beach wear, just as excited to show up as the day before. I peeked around my screen to see my class full of new pilots answering a questionnaire I'd decided to pass out in lieu of introducing myself. A few of them looked up at me as I squared my shoulders, redirecting my gaze to the screen and pretending to type.

You can't hide every day.

But I can today.

I'd agreed to meet Rafe at an address by text in a few hours. He told me to "Come in something I could get dirty in."

The man had darn near stripped me of my confidence last night. I wanted him in the worst way, and I could at least admit to myself at the moment I did not want him to see last night's panties of the stage-five clinger who'd ogled him right along with me last night. My lip curled in distaste as I thought of them together, and yet he'd made it clear he wanted me...sexually.

"Pig," I muttered under my breath. I must have been blind when I thought there was more depth to that man. True colors are often the biggest slaps in the face. He'd all but told me he was dominant in the sack last night and little else. Maybe with Rafe what you saw was what you got. At least I had a date with a handsome Trey to look forward to.

I breathed a sigh of relief as the pilots filed out one by one, and I plastered a smile on my face as I said my goodbyes. Tomorrow, I would do better; today, I just didn't have it in me. I looked to the sky out of my window as I watched a plane descend into the nearby airport. There had never been a time in my life when I didn't want to be a pilot. I'd never second guessed that decision. The choice to be an instructor had come later, and I doubted it daily.

I decided airtime would be a temporary and quick fix and scheduled myself some airtime for the following week. It would cost a small fortune, but it was more than necessary.

I needed a reason to keep going.

I pulled up to the address hours later in blue jean shorts, a white tank, and sneakers. It had taken me the better part of half an hour to find the place with my drunken GPS. Every direction I looked at was a sea of grass and trees. The house sat nestled in acres of land that desperately needed some TLC. The grass was overgrown. I spotted Rafe to the left of the large country home, gassing up a riding lawn mower. I approached him as he shut the lid of the rider and looked at me with a satisfied grin.

"Thanks for coming," he said as I looked around the house and back to him.

"What're we doing?"

"Isn't it obvious?" Rafe said as he grabbed my hand and led me to a small shed at the back of the property. Rows of flowers and bags of mulch sat on the cement floor along with all the tools a gardener could possibly need.

"It is now," I said as I gave him a puzzled look.

"You two got what you need?" I jumped as I turned to see the face that matched the familiar voice.

"Hi, Dutch!"

"Hi, Alice," she said as she took a step forward. "Thank you," she said as she looked anywhere but at me, "for helping with this."

"My pleasure," I replied with enthusiasm to try to help with her discomfort.

"If you need anything, Rafe, just holler," she directed at Rafe before she turned to me. "You too, missy." She began her walk back to the house, which I assumed belonged to her, and for the first time, I noticed her limp. I turned back to Rafe in question.

"She lost her leg to diabetes last year. And you know about her husband, Herb?"

"Not really, no...I mean, I know he passed, but I don't know what happened," I said as I surveyed the land and the amount of work it needed. It was several hours until sunset, but the job was daunting.

"He died having a stint put in his heart. One day he was here, the next he was gone. He had a massive heart attack on the table. She refuses to leave this house, except to attend ballgames, so I help her when I can. She can't manage it herself." I looked back to Rafe, who was now bare chested, and looked completely edible in his beige cargo shorts that seemed to be a wardrobe staple of his. His hat was flipped backward and the only thing more alluring than his ripped chest was the hopeful smile on his face.

"So you up for this?"

"I don't have a green thumb, but it *is* Earth Day," I said as I grabbed a pair of gloves. "I'll take the entrance."

"Anything will help," he said as he fired up the lawn mower and stuck his ear buds in. "Thanks, Alice."

For the next three hours, I found myself enjoying the task. The cool air and welcomed sunshine on my face brought me out of my pity party concerning my career choice. Once I'd cleared the weeds from the walkway and thoroughly aerated the dirt, I began the task of strategically planting flowers. I looked up every so often to find Rafe had made amazing progress cutting what had to be several acres of grass. He seemed to be enjoying himself. Every once in a while, I would catch his eyes on me, a nod or a smile of comradery shared between us. Once finished, I showered fresh water on my newly planted flowers in preparation of the mulch.

"That looks incredible," Rafe said behind me as he cradled his arms around me and put his hands beneath my hose. I could smell the mix of his soap and sweat as he surrounded me without actually touching me. Temptation once again reared his ugly head, and I was, for once, ready to just give in.

"I was thinking we could place some walkway lights," I said as I looked over my shoulder into his hazel eyes and then back to the newly planted, delicate bushes.

"I like that idea. It's about time for a break. Hop in the Jeep."

I gripped the hose and began to spray off my legs, but Rafe snatched it quickly and began to spray me off. He held the hose low as he washed the dirt off of my caked knees and then suddenly aimed it directly at my chest. I screamed out in outrage as the entirety of my chest was soaked, and my nipples showed up to the party as the perkiest of guests.

"You jerk," I seethed as Dutch walked outside with two large bottles of Gatorade. We both thanked her as we took the drinks and downed them greedily.

"We're off to find some things, Dutch. We'll be back shortly."

"Really, you've done enough," she said as she looked around appreciatively. "Wow, you two have really...wow."

I smiled with pride as I surveyed the grass and the entrance. It really looked like a different place. It felt amazing to be a part of the rare and full smile that graced Dutch's face. I looked over to Rafe, who seemed to be thinking the same thing. Dutch and I had been cozy enough as friends at the games, but seeing her in her element was completely different. Silent and feeling accomplished, we both piled into his Jeep and made our way through the country roads. Rafe turned up the radio and began to sing along with the music as I looked over at him with a grin. He squeezed my knee as he sang directly to me with emphasis on every word. His expression, his touch on my knee, the twinkle in his eyes, it was surreal. When the song ended, I looked at him in question.

"Dutch is a friend of yours?"

"You could say that," he said as we circled a roundabout and he parked at Lowe's.

"She's been there rain or shine for every single game." He looked away briefly. "She loves the game and the team."

"She's your biggest fan."

"And I'm hers," he said as he turned to me. "Let's go."

A while later, our cart was filled with solar lights that complemented the walkway. Unbeknownst to Dutch, I'd purchased a porch swing that would be delivered later that week. I could see the appreciation in Rafe for the gesture as he looked over at me.

I shrugged it off. "Now that she's got a view, she needs a good seat."

Outside of Lowe's and back in the Jeep, Rafe grabbed my hand and laced our fingers together and didn't let go until we got back to Dutch's house. Once we'd placed all our finishing touches and did a little clean up, Rafe turned to me.

"Follow me out. I'm taking you to eat."

"Rafe, I'm filthy!"

"It won't matter at this place."

My stomach growled. "Okay," I agreed as we said our goodbyes to Dutch, who seemed overwhelmed by our gesture. I could've sworn I saw tears fill her eyes before she quickly made her way back down her walkway and into the house.

"Maybe I should go after her. She seems upset."

"Dutch is a *very* private person," Rafe warned. "She's just happy, I promise," he assured as he pushed my wayward hair off of my shoulders. "Come on, I'm starving."

I followed Rafe closely in my Prius as he took the back roads. I reveled in the feeling of a hard day's work and smiled as I recalled the look on Dutch's face and came to the conclusion again that there was more to Rafe than he let on.

Rafe Hembrey had depth *and* a giving and beautiful heart.

Rafe stopped outside a one-story, wooden house on the marsh that had a simple sign written in white and blue that read Peggy's Fish Camp. I got out, still reluctant, with my hair in a tight, dirt-filled bun and covered in a day of sweat.

"Come on. It's fine, I promise," he urged as he gripped my hand and pulled me reluctantly inside. Once there, the smell of fried fish wafted through the air, and my stomach began to growl again with neglect.

"Let's get you local and out of your Google-filled tourist trap," he chuckled as we sat at a table covered in newspaper.

A lady with short, spiky, bright red hair made her way over to greet us.

"Hey, Bullet! Kickin' ass this year, aren't ya?!"

"Hey, Sue," he said with a wink and a smile. "Trying to."

"Ain't no tryin' to it. Ray, the boys, and I will be there this weekend."

Rafe pulled out an envelope from his pocket. "I was just about to ask you if you'd been yet."

Sue pulled the tickets out of the envelope and gave him a huge, toothy grin. "God, you're an angel. Thank you. So who you got wicha?" Sue turned her attention to me, completely unaffected by the total mess I was.

"This is Alice. She's new to town. We just left Dutch's, fixing up the place a bit."

"Nice to meet you, Alice," she said sincerely.

"Likewise," I said with a matching smile.

Sue looked down at Rafe with a dimmer expression. "How is Dutch?"

Rafe paused briefly. "She seems a bit better." He gestured over to me. "Alice has been keeping her company at the games."

"Really?" she said as she looked at Rafe with unbelieving eyes. "That is something."

"She's something," Rafe said as he looked over at me. I suddenly felt uncomfortable as Sue cleared her throat.

Rafe looked around the restaurant filled with wooden picnic tables. "Peggy in tonight?"

"No, she wasn't up to it today. She hit eighty-nine last week, but wouldn't you know she still comes in every day or so. I'll tell her you stopped by. She'll be upset she missed you."

"Tell her I'll be back after we sweep Myrtle."

"Will do. What you in the mood for?"

"The usual." As an afterthought, Rafe looked at me. "Do you like flounder?"

"Never had it," I said honestly.

"I've got you," he said as he nodded at Sue. Sue looked between us, a smirk growing into a smile on her face before she made her way back behind the counter. Minutes later, Rafe and I sipped on delicious sweet tea and munched on perfectly cooked and odd shaped hush puppies. I'd eaten half the bowl without apology as Rafe stared on at me.

"Thank you again for helping."

"Anytime, and I mean that," I said through a mouthful of perfectly fried, breaded goodness. "I like your life," I noted as I looked around the cabin of the small restaurant. "Your friends seem incredible and completely supportive. It must be a good feeling to have so many people in your corner."

"I can't complain. Most of them have watched me throw balls my whole life."

"Surely, you can't think it's just baseball." Rafe stayed silent as I continued shoving hushpuppies in my mouth. "You have this charisma, this genuine strength, patience, and tenderness when you speak to people. It's admirable."

I picked up a bottle of tartar sauce and squeezed it over a hushpuppy and felt the air whoosh out of the bottle as I sprayed us both in the mayonnaise/relish concoction. A large clump of it landed directly in my eye, and I stood up suddenly, forgetting the bench behind me, and fell backward, landing hard on my butt. I began choking on the bread that remained in my mouth and heaved as I tried to breathe around it.

Rafe was at my side seconds later as laughter spilled from his lips. Sue rushed to us with a tray full of freshly cooked fish and an "Oh shit, honey, you okay?" It took Rafe a solid minute between laughing and scraping me off the floor to get me seated at the table. I wiped at my eye furiously with a napkin from the dispenser, and when I could see clearly, I looked to Rafe, who resumed his seat at the table, his eyes fixed on me, his lips twisted into a half grin. His face was dotted with tartar sauce, and there was a large clump of it on his ear and embedded in his hairline. He looked over at me as I adjusted my newly sore butt in the seat and tried to shake off some of the embarrassment.

"Sorry," I said as I looked at the table below us filled with perfectly cooked, golden fish.

Rafe lifted his shirt, revealing an edible chest, and wiped his face. "You owe me another shirt."

"Yeah," I said as nervous laughter spilled out of me. "Put it on my tab."

Rafe and I ate greedily, and when the last bite of delectable fish was gone, I twisted sideways on the bench and sipped my tea.

"That was delicious, thank you."

I knew I'd made the right call when I'd asked Alice to help me. What I didn't expect was the amount of heart the woman had and how freely she gave it. Without so many words, and zero protest, she'd gone straight to work with me to help Dutch, and even gone above and beyond. I spent the majority of the day watching her work tirelessly, covered in sweat and sunshine. When she briefly paused in her work, her gaze always drifted to me, and her smile sucked the breath from my lungs. More than once I thought of ending the charade we played as "friends." There was something between us. Even a field away, I could feel the need on both our parts to bridge the gap. I wanted to freeze time when she looked at me the way she did. She was doing a poor job of hiding her attraction and more than once the asshole in me had wanted to call her on it, but I didn't want to scare her. She'd felt comfortable holding my hand, and I didn't want to fuck that up. Just the feel of her tiny hand in mine made me feel invincible. It was addicting in the best way.

She'd given me the best compliment of my life right before she'd landed on her adorable ass, and I was still choking on the way it made me feel.

As we observed our quiet surroundings, I found myself grasping at straws to keep her with me a little longer. I suddenly understood it when she said it was criminal for good days to come to an end. She said she admired me in a roundabout way. I wondered if she even knew the power of her words, of what just a simple look from her or a smile did to me.

"Alice, let's go take a bath."

Her eyes widened as she looked over at me like I had two heads.

"Trust me?"

I looked over at her smudged in dirt and mayonnaise as she gave me a careful nod.

"Let's go."

She followed me out to old man Thompson's pond a quarter mile away from the camp, and I saw her pause just outside her driver's side door when I made my way toward the dock, shirtless. Without a second thought, I lost my shorts and kept my boxers on as she joined me.

"Rafe, are we trespassing?"

"Yes and no."

"Care to elaborate?" She slid her flip flops off, and I grabbed the keys from her hand and tossed them onto her discarded flip flops. It was late, and I could see the exhaustion start to creep over her face as her headlights began to dim in the distance.

"Just a dip," I said as I scooped her into my arms and ran toward the water. She screamed in surprise as we flew into the pond. I freed her just before we hit the surface.

When we surfaced, she looked over at me with a grin. "Cold."

"Come here," I ordered as she hesitated before she paddled my way. I pulled her tight to me and heard her suck in a breath. "I have to keep an eye on you; you're a dangerous woman on your own."

"I've been doing just fine." My eyes narrowed, but I doubt she could see.

"Well, we can't be too careful," I whispered as her breath hit my skin. I was fully hard as she kept her small hands wrapped around my neck.

"I highly doubt this is for my safety."

"Well, you know alligators and all." Suddenly, she was clinging to me in a way that had my heart pounding.

"Rafe Hembrey, get me out of this water now!"

"Calm down, there are no gators in this water."

Of that, I was not entirely sure.

"Old man Thompson? That sounds like a name you pulled from your butt. Do you even know whose land this is?"

"Use to swim here when I was a kid. He's a friend of the family."

"You sounded *so* southern just then," she said with a chuckle.

I looked down, curious. "What's your preference?"

"I like a man in a suit and tie, maybe a little more built than you, and my man would never drive a Jee—"

I held her head under water for mere seconds, and when she resurfaced, she was laughing.

"Seriously, you suck," she choked out as I gripped her tightly to me.

"Which part do you want me to start on?" I asked as she stiffened in my arms. "I could start on those pretty pink lips of yours. I'm pretty sure I could suck on them all night. I could suck this neck," I said as I dipped my head, and without thinking, she tilted to the side to give me access. I smirked though she couldn't see it as I whispered along her neck. "I could start there and move down to those cherry sized nipples of yours."

"Rafe," she said breathlessly.

"Or I could move further down and suck on that pussy you're trying really hard to keep from me."

She went completely still, our mouths a breath away from touching.

"That's so...vulgar."

"I bet if I checked right now, I have you wet, and it wouldn't be the water's fault."

"It's late, Rafe. Thank you so much for everything." She pulled away from me and made her way to the dock while I cursed and followed her. I'd been every type of nice I knew how to be with this woman, and nothing had worked. Undeniably hard and losing my patience, my dick cursed me as I climbed onto the dock next to her.

"Crud, we don't have towels," she said as she sat soaking wet and glanced over at me. I was sure she could see the bulge in my pants and chose to ignore it.

"Where's your head at, man?" Andy asked as he took a bite of his sandwich and threw a scrap of bread crumbs away from the table. Eager seagulls snatched it up and remained waiting for their next handout. We sat out on the deck overlooking Shem Creek as Andy ate. I sat back with a beer I wasn't drinking.

"I don't know lately," I answered honestly. I'd never been anything but truthful with Andy. He had taken me under his wing my rookie year, and once he realized I didn't need the guidance and could handle myself, it became something else, though he was still quick to step up with sound advice when he felt the urge.

"They'll call."

"It's not that," I said, looking over the water as a speedboat parked at the dock and a cute girl in a bikini paddled in the distance on a surfboard. She was stacked from top to bottom, and I couldn't help but notice the blonde hair whipping around her shoulders. She looked a lot like Alice, though everything with tits did these days. "I'm restless," I said simply. Alice had been heavy on my mind since she showed up to the first game and purposefully ignored every fucking signal I'd given her. I'd agreed initially to keep this friendly, but every time I saw her, I became more convinced it wasn't possible. Last night, I'd damn near lost my shit on that dock. I'd come on too strong and got my ass handed to me. No matter how I approached her, she wasn't having it.

"You're worried about your future, and it's about fucking time."

"Just because I don't vocalize every thought in my head doesn't mean I don't think about it."

"What are you thinking about now?"

I looked at him dead on. "Alice."

Andy threw the rest of his sandwich the way of the birds, which caused an all-out war amongst them and a glare from the diners at the table beside us.

"You'll hurt her," Andy said with certainty.

"It's not your business."

"She's not interested in you."

"Because *you* told her not to be."

"Girls like *that* deserve the best version we can give of ourselves. You honestly think you're ready for that and all the damned pressure of waiting...playing?"

"Not your call," I snapped as Andy stood and placed a few twenties on the table and started to walk away. I slammed my beer down and followed him.

"What the fuck is your problem, man? You like her, too?"

Andy paused midstride down the steps to reach the parking lot and then kept going.

"I'm not your bitch, man. Don't take your shit out on me!"

Andy did stop this time and reared his head back with a laugh before he turned to me. "You're still fucking clueless."

"What the hell is that supposed to mean?"

"You're a fucking narcissist when it comes to women, Rafe. You want Alice? Go for it. Maybe she'll give you the medicine you deserve."

I looked down at Andy, who shoved his hands in his shorts and walked away without his usual complimentary parting bird, which to him was considered a nicety. Something was up, and it was unlike him not to share. I looked on after him, my hands over the railing of the two-story, creek-side restaurant. I saw a crowd gather as the girl I'd seen on the surfboard repeatedly screamed in the distance.

I walked over to see that the girl I'd admired minutes before was, in fact, Alice. She was standing on her surfboard in the middle of Shem Creek without her paddle and shrieking at the dolphins surrounding her. I made my way over to her as she balanced herself on the board. Hundreds of eyes watched for her next move while suggestions flew through the air.

"You're going to have to swim, honey."

"A boat will be by in a few minutes."

And then mine. "What the hell are you doing, Alice?!"

Skin clean now from her disastrous can tan, a solid brown tint lit her skin and she looked absolutely gorgeous in her pink bikini and terrified out of her mind.

"RAFE!" she cried as the crowd looked at me.

"Just jump in!" I said, waving to her as another dolphin playfully nudged her board. I took the steps down to the dock two at a time and raced toward her.

"OH GOD!" she said as she clenched her thighs together. It took everything I had to keep from laughing. If she peed now, there would be no stopping it.

"They aren't killer dolphins, sweetheart," I urged. "Just jump in!"

"I...can't." I saw her begin to shake as her lower lip trembled. She was truly terrified and more people were gathering. I set my phone, wallet, and keys down and jumped in then swam her way.

"Rafe!" she said in shock as I approached her. "It looked so easy," she said with a shaky voice. Stacks of restaurants filled with patrons watched on as she looked down at me.

"What the hell, woman? All you had to do was jump off."

"Just...I...there are dolphins in here! Earlier, I saw an alligator!"

"Sharks, too, and yet you rented a surfboard and paddled your way through marshland and ocean into the most populated creek in Charleston."

"Rafe, get out of the water!" she screamed with clear concern for me. If I wasn't worried about the growing crowd, I would have laughed.

"Sit down on the board, Alice," I commanded. She moved slowly as her perfect little ass lowered to the board and stayed put while I swam and tugged her in.

"I'm so embarrassed."

"Up a creek without a paddle," I huffed out before I grinned back at her with a wince. "Too soon?"

She narrowed her eyes at me as onlookers cheered for the big, yet unnecessary rescue. Alice damn near kissed the dock as soon as I pulled her on.

"I'll never do anything that stupid again," she assured.

"What made you go and do that alone your first time? You could have drifted out with the tide." I pulled her board in as I scolded her.

"I just...it looked so fun. And like good exercise," she huffed. "I can't move. My arms are so sore. I have no idea where I left my car. I'm so screwed."

"How long have you been in the water?"

"What time is it?"

I picked up my phone and glanced at it. "Three o'clock."

"SIX HOURS!"

"Jesus," I said as I scrubbed my face.

"I'm in so much pain," she choked out as I pulled her to me. "I can't move."

"I've got you," I said as I scooped her up into my arms and the onlookers cheered. "You are something else," I said as I walked through the small patch of sand between the dock and the restaurant parking lot.

"My board," she said as she looked after it on the dock.

"I'll go back for it." When I set her into the Jeep, I caught her wince. She'd been vigorously rowing for six hours. I would not envy her when morning came.

When I'd secured her board on the top of my Jeep, I climbed in with her.

"I don't know where I am," she said as she looked at me, completely lost, her voice hoarse.

"You're with me, you're okay," I said as I squeezed her thigh in reassurance.

"Free" by the Zac Brown Band began to play as I put the car into gear and we took off.

"My car. It was a row of houses with a boat dock at the end. I don't have my phone. I don't even remember the name."

"That's Lucky's lot. I'll call him and tell him we'll be after it in the morning."

"Wait...what?"

"You can't drive if you can't feel your arms. Where to?"

"Oh..." She rattled off her address and I began to drive.

"Beautiful song," she noted as she sank further into her seat, pain all over her face.

"Reminded me of you," I said without thinking.

"Really? A song reminded you of me?"

"Yeah," I said, closing my eyes briefly at my slip.

"So you've been thinking about me?"

JESUS. This woman had no filter, no concern for other's comfort as she pushed for easy answers to hard questions.

"Yeah, I was. You talked about your mother, and then I heard this."

"Oh," she said as she crisscrossed her arms and rubbed her biceps. "That's nice."

Minutes of silence followed as she listened to the words. I knew that was what she was doing.

"My hero," I heard whispered as I looked over at her and caught her smile before her eyes closed. At that moment, she was the most beautiful woman I'd ever seen in my life.

I loved her praise, and if that made me a narcissist when it came to her, so fucking be it.

"We're here," I heard Rafe whisper as he opened up his driver's door. I was exhausted out of my mind and felt the chap of my lips. I tried to move but couldn't. Tears of pain pooled in my eyes.

"Me and this town I love so much are a disaster. I keep getting inspired to do things and end up humiliated. I almost peed in front of a live audience today because a few dolphins wanted to make nice."

I chuckled as I opened her door and gripped her to me.

"Rafe, I can walk. Just give me like...two days."

"I've got this."

"Everything hurts," I said as tears rolled down my face. "I mean, I think I'm dying."

"Next time you decide to do something *inspiring*, text me first. Which floor?"

"Third," I said with panic. "Besides, you started it," I whispered tearfully. "You looked so amazing on your board. I wanted something like that for myself. I wanted to look good doing something athletic."

"Oh, trust me," he said as he effortlessly cleared the last floor and eyed my chest below his chin before he gently set me on my feet, "you looked fucking perfect."

I swallowed hard as his comment hit me in all the right places. I opened my door with Rafe hot on my heels.

"You don't lock your door?"

"I didn't today, thank GOD!" I made my way to the bathroom and began sorting through my drawer. Without looking, I took a scoop of lip balm smeared it over my blistered mouth before I limped back into the kitchen to thank Rafe.

"Are you thirsty? What can I get you?"

"I think the question is what can I get you? You look liked you just sucked off an elephant!"

I quickly brought my hands to my lips and realized just how much lip balm I'd smeared on. Nervous laughter took over as I stood there, barely able to keep my legs planted.

Our laughing slowed as I grabbed a paper towel from the counter and began wiping at my lips.

"What happened out there?"

"It was like the dream that you went to school naked, you know? I dropped my paddle, and I was already in survival mode at that point. My brain was fried. I was headed for the dock, and then it just slipped into the water. When I reached for it, I saw the fin. It scared the crap out of me. I mean, I know these things dwell in the water, but I'm the type who is better off not actually *seeing* them. I grew up in Ohio. We don't have sharks, alligators, and dolphins in Ohio. Anyway, I panicked, and when I looked up and was surrounded by people, I froze."

"I get it," he said as he started looking through my cupboards.

"What are you doing?"

"Some serious aftercare," he said as he grabbed a Ziploc bag and shoved it under the ice dispenser. "Go lie on your bed."

"Pardon?" I asked, my eyes wide.

"Alice, go lie on your bed." His tone was commanding, and I found myself quickly doing what he said.

"Got anything with menthol in it? Vicks?"

"I have Icy Hot in my bathroom," I called out as I lay on my bed, completely unsure of what to do. I thanked the Lord the sunblock I used had worked, and I wasn't burning on the outside as much as I was on the inside. I'd gotten lost in the water, completely clueless on time. And I'd probably been dragged by the tide for miles through that marshland. It had been wonderful...until it had turned into a nightmare.

"Extra pillows?"

"In the closet," I said as he walked into my room with several ice packs, Icy Hot, and several dry rags.

"Rafe," I said, staring up at the ceiling, "thank you. That was humiliating, and it could have been so much worse. Thank God I didn't pee."

Rafe positioned several pillows underneath my arms and legs and set the rest of the supplies next to me on the bed. He handed me three Advil, which I swallowed with the cup he'd brought from my bathroom before he pushed me gently back to the bed. Before I could go on in my appreciation, his hands were on me.

I looked into his eyes as he massaged my shoulders first and began working his way down to my bicep. His huge frame towered over me as he sat beside me. He licked his perfect lips as golden colored eyes peered down at me. Every ounce of fight I had withered as he touched me.

"So what were you doing at the creek?" I asked, trying to ignore my hard nipples and the heat building at my center.

"Eating lunch with Andy."

"Oh? Where was he?"

"He took off. I think he's pissed at me for some reason and won't come clean."

"Well, ask him," I said as he grinned down at me.

"I did, and he's not happy about me hanging out with you, either."

"Why not?" I said as my breath hitched when his hands began to massage my sides, drifting from one side of my stomach to the other.

"Because he thinks you're too good for me. He thinks I'm shit for women."

"Oh," I said as I got lost in his hands. "Well, have faith, Rafe. If a fourteen-inch seahorse can be monogamous, I'm sure there's hope for you."

I gasped when his fingertips lingered just above the tip of my bottoms, and his fingers skirted just beneath the hem.

I looked up to see Rafe's eyes smolder as my lips parted. His hands never stopped, but his brow quirked up slightly in question, and so I began rambling.

"Before it got terrible, I really lo...loved it."

"Uh huh."

"I didn't do enough research, I guess," I said as he massaged my right thigh with amazing skill and then concentrated on my left.

I kept my eyes fixed on his Adam's apple as his hands seduced me into a puddle.

My eyes began to droop in both arousal and relaxation.

It was only when Rafe spoke that I opened them again. "I spotted your movie collection. VHS, who has that anymore? And they're all as old as you are."

"Movies are everything," I said as I began to slip away again due to his amazing touch.

"They are, huh?"

"Absolutely. One movie, one song can change *everything*."

"Really?" he said as he began to work on my calves. My skin felt sticky, and I knew I looked a mess, but my body gave into his touch, and it didn't matter.

"Haven't you ever seen Purple Rain?" My voice was a near moan at that point. "His career was in the toilet, and he was on the rocks with Apollonia. He even pimp slapped her through that whole movie. He plays one song and poof, everything is instantly better."

Rafe chuckled as he began to work his magic on my feet.

"All women deserve one movie moment in their life. I truly believe that," I murmured.

"Are you willing to be pimp slapped to get yours?" My eyes opened wide. He was so close. Hazel fire stared down at me as I inhaled his features. His hair was a mess, his t-shirt still a bit damp from his jump, and I could see every defined muscle in his chest.

"You should take your clothes off."

Rafe's brow lifted again as he gripped the Icy Hot roller and began to circle my arms with it.

"I mean, I have a washer and dryer if you want to toss them in."

"Relax, Alice," he whispered as he placed the Ziploc bags directly onto my skin. "Rotate these fifteen minutes on and off. If it gets to be too much, use the rags to buffer the sting."

I looked out my window to see it was still light outside. "You can stay...with me, you know, if you...want to."

"I have a game in a few hours."

"Oh crud, I forgot!" I said as I tried to lift up and he stilled me. "I'll let Dutch know."

"Okay," I whispered.

"I'll call Lucky's and make sure they don't tow your car."

"Thank you, Rafe, really...so much."

He pulled a blanket over me before he stood. "I'll be back to check on you."

I started to drift off as exhaustion took over. "Go get 'em, Bullet."

I felt his knuckles drift over my cheek and opened my eyes with a sleepy smile.

"Did you win?"

Rafe nodded and licked his lips as I melted into the bed. I smelled his clean skin and realized I'd been asleep for hours. He was freshly showered and dressed, and I had the sudden urge to pull him to me until I felt the burn...everywhere.

"Oh God. Oh...GOD!" I shrieked as I felt the unrelenting throb in my body take over.

"I brought you this," he whispered as he held out a small yellow pill in his hand. "It's a muscle relaxer. It should help a lot." Without another word, I greedily took the pill and swallowed it, along with three more Advil that looked like tiny dots of debris in his large hand.

"You need to shower in hot water. Think you can handle that?"

"I'm on fire," I said as I tried to sit up. There wasn't a spot on me that didn't burn. Sore wasn't the word for the way I felt.

Rafe helped me stand, and again I found myself looking up at him. His features screamed masculine. His eyes roamed over my chest and then lingered on my neck before they met mine. "I've got it now."

"Okay," he relented. "I brought some food. I'll be in the kitchen."

"Rafe, thank you," I called after him as a single tear slid down my cheek. Never in my life had I felt so cared for.

Rafe stood in my doorway, and I could tell my emotion made him slightly uncomfortable. He took a step toward me and faltered as I made my excuse.

"It just hurts," I said as I made my way toward the bathroom without looking back. I stood in a hot shower, trying not to scream out. When it ran cold, I slipped out, unwilling to move too much, and let myself air dry. Minutes later, I wrestled with my boy shorts and a long t-shirt, which seemed like an act of God to get on. I met Rafe in the kitchen, and he looked me over with approval.

"Nice shirt."

It was a vintage Star Wars tee and was my absolute favorite.

"Thanks," I said. "I wanted to be Princes Leia when I was little and then decided on Molly Ringwald."

His lips pursed in a smirk.

"I wanted to be Rocky and The Karate Kid, too." His smirk turned into a smile as I continued. "For Halloween, of course. But I never got to trick or treat."

Rafe looked down at me with a mix of amusement and a look of "Are you done yet?"

"I'm going to start kickboxing in a few weeks, so *take that*, Mom," I rattled on nervously. Rafe looked over the counter and then back to me before I could say anything else.

"I figured southern comfort food. Fried green tomatoes, fried chicken, mashed potatoes, that sort of thing."

I looked over the counter and nodded. Though I was

embarrassed and in too much pain to think about eating, I couldn't wait for the medicine to kick in so I could sleep through it. Also, I desperately wanted to keep his company.

"You must be exhausted," I said as he looked down to me before he piled our plates ridiculously high. "You didn't have to come back."

"If there's one thing—" he paused as he scooped some mashed potatoes on our plates "—I know, it's muscle strain and aftercare. Go pick a movie. I'll bring it to you."

I selected the *Outsiders* and pushed the tape in. Rafe looked like a giant on my oversized couch. His appeal was overwhelming as I tried to keep my eyes averted. After the opening credits rolled, and out of habit, I began to speak along with the dialogue. Rafe turned to me, curious, as I winced in apology.

Food worked as a muzzle as I ate the most delicious chicken on the face of the planet while I sat next to Rafe watching one of my favorite movies. I fought hard to stay awake against the pull of the muscle relaxer. I didn't want to miss a minute of it. I watched Rafe more than I did the movie, and when he caught me, he would simply smile.

Right before I dozed off, I put my hand in his. It was the best day of my life.

I studied her small hand in mine as she nodded off, her legs tucked underneath her and her head resting on my shoulder. She looked so perfect, not a hint of makeup, nothing but an old t-shirt and high shorts that exposed most of her bare thighs. I wanted nothing more than to wake her just so I could see her eyes again. I pulled her hand toward my mouth and kissed it as she sighed in a sleep stupor. That sigh did me in, and my cock jerked beneath my jeans. I was harder than I'd ever been in my life.

"Stay gold, Ponyboy. Stay gold."

I looked up to the screen and back to Alice as she slept and once again scooped her into my arms. I stared at her for a brief moment as her lashes fluttered against her cheek and her sweet plump lips drew breath. Once I had her tucked in bed, I pulled out another movie and lay on her couch, thinking of only her. She was alone here, that much I knew. Aside from Andy, I was too. All my friends had either left Charleston once we graduated or had married off and were living their lives. I was on the road more often than not and barely had time to keep the relationships I had.

My mother only called for a handout and my father, well...*fuck him.*

I knew exactly how Alice felt, except Charleston was home for me, and she'd been brave enough to come here alone. She needed someone and I wanted to be that someone for her. But deep down, I knew it would be close to impossible.

Andy was all that I had and a few fair-weather friends at the bar. But lately, Andy seemed so pissed off at me, I didn't know how to talk to him anymore. He was dealing with his own shit, which I assumed had to do with Kristina. Alice came along at a perfect time, despite what Andy said.

We needed each other.

I wondered if I could handle my attraction for her and keep my hands away. Touching her earlier had felt so fucking right and had tested every single part of the man in me. If I was honest, she seemed fine with being alone.

In truth, I needed her.

Every time she looked at me, I wanted more of it. Every time she opened those perfect lips to speak, it was like Christmas. There was just something about her I couldn't shake. Maybe it was her innocence, her honesty, or maybe it was just *her*.

"Fuck," I mumbled as I grew harder at the thought of her sprawled out on the bed in her bikini earlier. She'd let me touch her, and she'd been turned on, I could tell.

She hadn't done a thing to lead me on, and yet I was fucking consumed with thoughts of her.

I tossed and turned on her couch as she tortured me asleep in her bedroom.

"Good morning," I said to the most beautiful man imaginable who lay shirtless and sleeping on my couch. His hands were behind his head as if he was on display. I felt myself grow hot and leaned down to whisper to him again as I studied the hard lines of his body and then the smooth, etched planes of his face. His lips were so perfectly full, top and bottom, I could only imagine what they felt like.

"Morning, Rafe," I whispered a little louder as I leaned in further. I saw the smile that crept over his lips as he opened his eyes.

"How are you feeling?" he asked as he gave me a smirk when he realized how close I was. Like a mad scientist in love with a lab experiment, I was completely bent over him and realized what a fool I looked like. I stood up with a wince. "Better but worse?"

"Sounds about right," he said as he grabbed his shirt off the floor. I grimaced at the loss of the bare sight of him.

"I want to buy you breakfast for...all that you've done. Or I can just catch a cab to my car."

"I have an early meeting, but I'll take you to your car."

Disappointed, I sighed. "Okay."

Rafe looked up at me and then down as he towered over me. "I've wanted to ask you a question all night."

"Oh?"

"Yeah, what the hell happened to your wall?"

After a silent drive filled with sideways smiles between Rafe and me, I thanked him again as he got out and started to unhook my board from the top of his Jeep.

"How the hell did you get it here?"

"I bought it from the shop inside. Want to hold onto it for me?"

"Sure," he offered, leaving it where it was.

"Okay, so I'll see you tonight?"

Rafe was in front of me now as I held my keys in my hand, my back to my Prius.

"Tonight," he whispered as his head descended and I held my breath. He placed his lips next to my mouth and briefly touched the corner. Everything that was sore began to tingle.

"Thank you," I said as his body pushed in further so there was no space between us.

"Friends, right," he said as a statement, but it seemed like more of a question.

"Right. Good luck tonight," I said as he slowly backed away and nodded. I sat in my Prius as I thought of the feeling of his brief kiss, his gentle way with me. He was laying it on thick, and I was gullible to every move he made. His touch was calculated and had thoroughly seduced me. He was breaking my resolve with every minute we spent together.

I spent the whole drive home wrapped in confusion.

Three innings in, Dutch and me stared at Rafe as he wound up and threw another crappy pitch. I shook my head as Dutch sat back with a sigh. "His game is completely off tonight."

"He was fine this morning," I said aloud. Dutch looked at me quizzically. "*Not* what you're thinking."

"Not my business, but something's wrong."

We saw Andy stand from his catcher's crouch and walk over to the pitcher's mound. Rafe shook his head as Andy spoke to him.

Andy left the mound after what looked like a heated exchange, and after another inning, the Swampgators were down 2-0. I stood as Rafe made his way off the field and through the dugout. No one seemed to notice or even bother to stop me as I took the steps and hit the field to follow after him. I found him in the dugout hall, pacing.

"Rafe," I whispered as he stopped his trek and looked behind me and then moved his eyes over me so slowly I became consumed by just his stare. "Is everything okay?"

A series of slow heartbeats followed before Rafe gripped and threw down his hat between us as he moved toward me. I saw his jaw twitch as fear crept through me but remained standing where I was. He looked furious as I waited for what I was sure was his wrath.

When he reached me, no words were spoken. My body was lifted by his in one sweeping movement as he shoved me against the wall. His lips crushed mine in an unforgiving kiss as I shrieked out in surprise before I buried my fingers in the soft, sweaty threads of his hair. He opened me without invitation and tasted every part of my mouth. His invading tongue made me gasp and moan into his. Our mouths molded, gave and took, and I felt the tension in his body as he lifted my legs higher and he ground into me.

He kissed me senseless, and when I thought he'd had enough, he kissed me some more. When he finally pulled his lips away, I opened my eyes to meet the lust mixed with anger in his.

"Rafe, what's wrong?"

"Nothing's wrong."

"You're off your game."

"I think so, too," he breathed out as he pulled my bottom lip and sucked it gently.

"Your pitching is awful tonight," I said as his hand slipped beneath my t-shirt. I arched my back and gave him more access. He moved his thumb over my nipple on top of my bra, and I cried out.

"Alice...shut up," he groaned as he gripped my hair and twisted my head while he sank his teeth into my shoulder.

"Rafe," I said, driven by pure need.

"Friends my ass," he said as he hovered above me and slowly let my legs hit the floor. "We were never meant to be friends." When he ripped himself away, his eyes bore into mine.

"How did you get back here, anyway?"

"No one was watching. I'll go." I turned to leave, completely confused between his anger and his unbelievable kiss.

"Alice," he said with regret as I looked back at him. Every bit of his body language showed remorse. "We okay?"

"Yeah," I said with reassurance. "You're just frustrated. You've got this."

"That's not why I kissed you," he said firmly.

"Rafe, you're up," I heard barked behind me. I turned to see his pitching coach glare at me. "Lady, you can't be back here."

"My apologies," I said as he scrutinized me. I heard heated words between them as I made my way out of the dugout and winced as "piece of pussy" flew out of the coach's mouth. I'd been categorized as a distraction from Rafe's game at that moment. I hurried back to my seat as Dutch eyed me.

"You can't do that."

"I'm aware," I said as my cheeks heated. Andy eyed me from the dugout as he took the steps to the field. I smiled at him, and he did not smile back. I mouthed "Sorry" to which he nodded as Rafe took the plate. His first pitch had Dutch clenching her first at her sides. His second got my attention. I watched his posture, and he didn't seem rattled at all. I'd been thoroughly kissed. The kind of kiss a woman begs life for. The kind of kiss that keeps the sexual imagination spinning for months, even years.

I watched the umpire close his fist as the batter struck out, and I couldn't help the smile on my face as Dutch eyed me with suspicion.

"What did you say to him?"

"Nothing prophetic," I said as Rafe threw another solid pitch.

Rafe might not be rattled, but the man had my head spinning.

"Good game, Rafe," Jon, my manager, complimented as I toweled off. I looked at him and could see the lecture coming, or at the very least, a tongue lashing. It was rare that my manager ever approached me outside of his office. I took it as a good sign.

"It wasn't her."

"You can't afford to—"

"I've played too many seasons for this," I said as I pulled a shirt over my head and deadpanned, "It's not the girl."

"You're being watched, Rafe."

"Nothing new," I assured. "I'm good."

"Fair enough." He spit out the black sludge from his curled lip. "Briefing is canceled tomorrow. Get with Rod about the reschedule."

I nodded and didn't bother to ask why. He managed his way. I played mine.

With a rare free day ahead, I immediately thought of Alice and texted her.

Rafe: Meet me at Andy's tomorrow at seven.

I then looked at the message below it.

Unknown: Son, I need to talk to you.

I threw my phone in my locker and showered. When I told Jon it wasn't Alice, I'd meant it. My father had texted me hours before my game. In all my years, nothing had ever tripped me up on the field except for Martin Hembrey and his bullshit.

He'd played his role, too, but unlike my concerned manager, my father had played for himself. Martin Hembrey was the sole reason I wasn't playing major league baseball. The man had bred me to love ball, live it, breathe it, but he hadn't given me the talent or the tenacity. He hadn't played the games for me but took credit for everything, anyway. Like my mother, he took and took until one night I gave back. The result of that cost me the first few years of my career.

No, it definitely wasn't the girl that had me off my game. It was the girl who had saved it.

I'd tasted her, and now she lingered everywhere, my lips, my tongue. She had me so hard up, I stayed semi the rest of the game. I wanted to bury my face between those legs and hear that moan that sounded like a song for me. I wanted to lick every inch of her and then lose myself so deep inside she'd forget to breathe. And then I wanted to fuck her back to life stroke by stroke.

I'd always been loyal to my game, my attention never swayed, ever. Kissing Alice the way I had with several innings left to pitch was the first time I'd ever betrayed my first love, and it felt fucking amazing.

I knew I'd never pull another stunt like that again. I knew that those watching hadn't missed her leave the field or the improvement in my throwing after. If I was being watched, and I knew I was, let them see. Let them all see.

I slammed my locker door and made a beeline for my car. I forwent my usual visit to Andy's bar for a new reason.

My tastes were changing.

I tapped the bar for another round as I waited on Rafe, unsure of what he could possibly want from me. We hadn't spoken since our kiss last night, which was odd because we usually texted until one of us passed out. I wasn't sure if his text invite for a drink was a means to an end or a chance to explore our chemistry. I was up all night touching the places he hadn't touched.

"You've been drinking a lot of that horrible beer lately," I heard as he took the stool next to me. His scent lingered between us as I turned to greet him. "It's an acquired taste," I said as I took another sip to try to hide the obvious perk in my presence at his arrival. He was dressed in jeans, a dark t-shirt, a reversed ball cap, and had never looked better. "You called this meeting. I'm all ears."

He gave me a sideways glance. "You in a hurry?" He motioned to Kristina behind the bar.

"I kind of am. I have a date," I said as I braved a glance in his direction.

"Not anymore," he countered with a clear tick in his jaw. "Text him now and tell him you got held up."

"Why would I do that?" I asked, shocked as I noticed the sudden stiffness in his back. All the humor vanished from his face.

"You know damn well why," he barked as he gripped his beer without breaking eye contact with me. He was close, his lips pure temptation.

"Well, I've been here almost two months and haven't been on a date, so, no, Rafe, I won't cancel."

He smirked and pulled away from me. "The hell you won't."

"I'm not your toy. There are at least twenty women in here that will go without dinner and good conversation to let you play with them."

"What if I want to play with you?" he said as his finger slipped through the belt loop on my dress. His fingers splayed on my hip, and he dug them in possessively.

"I would have to say tough. I have a date."

"Fair enough," he said, leaning back in his seat. "I'll make a deal with you, or rather, a wager."

"A wager?"

"This is a sure thing for me," he said as he motioned for Kristina.

"I'm not following," I said as he turned to me, his eyes full of mischief. "And I'm pretty sure you're already cheating."

"Now, Alice," he said in an odd sounding, singsong voice, "hear me out. I'm going to order a shot. You take it the *way* I instruct you to, and you can go out on a date with..."

"Trey."

He rolled his eyes. "You take this shot I'll let you got out with Trey."

I looked at him defiantly. "I don't need your permission."

"Humor me," he said as he whispered over at Kristina. She gave me a look that said "Oh shit, sister" and began to gather bottles.

"Fine," I said. "One shot and I'm leaving."

"Ah, but here's the kicker," he said as he took the slip of a light scarf from around my neck and tied it behind my head. "You have to actually be able to *take* the shot."

"Rafe, cut the crap," I barked. "Why do I need to be blindfolded for a shot?"

His breath was at my ear as he lingered and placed a kiss on my cheek. "Secret southern ingredients, baby."

"Whatever," I rasped out as he put the glass in my hand.

"Now, once you take it, you have to swish it in your mouth for fifteen seconds, not a second less, and then swallow. If you do that, then I'll not only let you go on your date with Trey, I'll *pay* for it."

"Rafe, I have to drive," I said, suddenly worried about the shot's potency.

"I promise it's harmless."

"Fine, can we do this now?" I didn't know what my real issue was, it may have to do with the fact that I felt he liked me, and I now wanted him to admit it. I couldn't stand the constant wondering, the incessant thinking about it. I wanted him to verbalize it like an adult. This ploy to keep me away from a date was childish. Well, screw him. I had a perfectly fit pilot ready to let me know he liked me in a mature way. Without hesitance, I lifted the glass and began to swish the liquid in my mouth.

And then hell unleashed it's fury on me as the longest fifteen seconds of my life began.

My first sensation was a sour burn on my tongue, quickly followed by the presence of something solid. Something that should not be present in a liquid shot. Cottage cheese? I swished as I held my gag in and smacked my hands over my mouth to keep from spilling a drop.

"Holy shit, Rafe, she's going to do it," I heard a bar regular named Will shout as I became aware I had an audience. The count was at an unbearable six, and for a second, I thought the concoction would bulge out of my mouth and through my fingers.

"Spit it out, Alice!" Kristina pleaded as she ripped one hand from my mouth and put an empty plastic cup in it.

"It doesn't get better," Rafe whispered, his voice unsure, which only fueled me to keep going.

In my mind, I'd thrown up a hundred times, and yet as the count wound down and I thought Rafe nothing more than a barbaric pig, I ripped off my blindfold and looked right into his eyes as I swallowed in an exaggerated gulp.

"FIFTEEN!" The crowd shouted in unison.

"Here, honey," Kristina said as she handed me a fresh beer. I took it gratefully as I downed half of it and got several pats on the back as a few people dispersed. Rafe kept my eyes, his full of ice as he pulled his wallet out of his back pocket and threw a couple hundred on the bar. "Have a nice dinner."

I looked down at the bills and left them there as I pushed myself away from the bar. "A simple I don't want you to go, Alice, would have been enough," I whispered as I stood in front of him and saw his eyes roam my light blue dress. I was more dressed up than any other night he'd seen me. I had a dusting of bronzer on my newly tanned face and had applied mascara and a nude lip gloss. My dress was cut in a V in the front and showed my molehill of cleavage. I felt pretty. The way Rafe was looking at me made me feel beautiful, but in a way, he'd just ruined it.

I waited all of the three seconds he deserved and walked out of the bar as my chest sank a little. I made it to my car and jumped when I heard him close behind me.

"I don't want you to go, Alice."

"Why?"

He turned me around to face him. His eyes held the honesty I was looking for, his voice was thick with sex. "Because I want to kiss you, Alice, and then I want to drive you home—to *my* home—and make you come while you say my name in a way and in a tone you've never used before."

"That's all?"

"That's all I've got," he said as he took a step forward.

"You'll hurt me."

"I don't want to."

I knew he meant that, but still, they weren't the words I wanted to hear. My head was at odds as I voiced my body's decision.

"I'll let you kiss me...and take me to *your* home. And we can see what happens from there on *one* condition.

"Name it."

I stood there staring at him and wrapped up in the desire that thrummed between us. I slowly lifted my phone from my purse.

Alice: I'm sorry, Trey. I can't make it tonight.

I swished the cement mixer made up of Bailey's and lime juice in my mouth until it curdled and grimaced as the whole bar watched on and laughed at me in my misery. Thirty seconds, she'd given me thirty *fucking* seconds to her fifteen, and so far I'd failed...*twice*. Looking over her small frame, I stared at the divot between her perfect tits.

Motivation.

I wanted this woman, and I wanted my head between those beautiful breasts.

"Twenty-five, Rafe," Kristina said as she looked over at Alice and mouthed "You are my hero." Alice ate it up as the countdown ended. I held the now completely solid shot in my mouth and closed my eyes as I swallowed. The bar cheered as a slow smile built on Alice's face. I'd won her. I dipped in without thinking and kissed her right there for everyone to see. And it wasn't just any kiss. It was similar to the one I'd given her last night, full of promises I intended to keep. Alice protested as she tasted the aftermath of the shot from hell and then sank into our kiss. The bar roared as I tasted her completely. I slid the bills I'd set out for Alice Kristina's way and took Alice's hand and led her out of the bar. Alice looked up at me with wide, brown eyes. We paused in front of my Jeep.

"Nothing will happen that you don't want to happen. I just want to be alone with you. Okay?"

Oh, it *was* going to happen. I'd make sure of it. We'd cross the friend line. There was no going back, and deep down, no part of me wanted to. He'd made no promises, absolutely nothing had changed. He was still a playboy, and he still wanted sex, and I was still sure if he touched me, if we remained intimate, my heart would get involved. That's who I was without a shadow of a doubt. Everything about our new situation screamed disaster as I scorned myself mentally to stop what was about to happen.

That kiss, the way he tasted me, spoke to every part of the woman who'd been void of kisses like that her whole life.

Tonight I would let her free to explore.

I looked over at Rafe as he stroked my leg with his fingertips and faced forward, his jaw set. He was completely turned on. He wanted me.

He wanted *me*.

Oh God, how I wanted him, too. The stroke of his fingers made it hard for me to concentrate on my task. I held my phone at an angle he couldn't possibly see.

I had research to brush up on.

According to the internet, there were only a few key erogenous zones on a man

Obviously, the penis. God, I was about to see Rafe's penis! I cleared my throat.

Then there were the mouth and lips, neck, scrotum, perineum (aka taint or magic button), and ears. As I looked over at Rafe, I decided that if our friendship was going to end with sex, I would be the best he'd ever had. I kept my phone hidden as I quickly watched a two-minute silent video on oral etiquette. I glanced over nervously as I darted my eyes and researched on my phone. My whole body flushed as my blood boiled with need. I mentally prepared myself for the steps necessary to give a blowjob fit for a porn star.

Step One: Completely unhinge jaw like a snake.

Step Two: Suck and slurp like your life depends on it while you clamp your lips hard around the edge of penis.

Step Three: Bob on penis enthusiastically until you almost choke to death while you keep eye contact and cup the scrotum.

It looked doable...and kind of sick. I'd never been on the giving end, and still, I wanted to try it...on Rafe.

Oh God.

I was about to have sex with a far more experienced man, and I knew without a doubt I had to somehow blow his mind. My cheeks heated as I reached my hand over as he drove and started to massage his neck. Zone one. His eyes on fire, they perused me thoroughly as his fingers drifted a little higher up my leg before he turned back to face the road. I raked my fingernails through his hair and then slowly moved my pointer and thumb to his ear and massaged the lobe. He hissed through his teeth, and I saw it as encouragement. After a few minutes of lobe stimulation, I slowly moved my hand down to his chest and heard his exhale as his fingers brushed over my sex.

"Oh," I moaned out as Rafe floored his Jeep.

"Alice," he pleaded as I moved my hand underneath the hem of his shirt and rubbed as single finger along the edge of his jeans. He was noticeably hard, and I studied the evidence before I covered it with my hand and squeezed. Rafe coughed out an incredulous bark as he turned to me with surprised eyes.

"Alice, you have to stop."

"I don't think I will," I murmured as his hand slipped into my panties and he found me soaked for him.

"Fuck...I'm going to kill us both," he groaned as he pushed a finger inside me and my head tilted back on a gasp.

"Alice, spread for me," he ordered as I did what I was told and was rewarded with another mind blowing stroke of his fingertips. My whole lower body began to shiver with awareness as he elicited nothing but sensation.

"I'm going to bury my tongue right here," he said as he pushed another finger inside and my legs began to shake. I covered his hand with mine as I fell into a stupor. When he was forced to stop at a light, he withdrew his hand and leaned over and pulled my protest into his mouth as his tongue silenced me. I was on fire, lips and tongue not nearly enough. Rafe pulled himself away as his eyes pierced me.

"In five minutes, I'm going to make sure you understand just how much I didn't want you to go on that date."

"Rafe," I moaned as my body buzzed with need.

"I want you. I want you," he repeated as the wind blew through our open window and lifted my hair. "You are so goddamned beautiful, Alice."

"Rafe," I whispered and pointed. "The light," I urged as he turned to face forward and floored it. We made it the rest of the way back to his place in silence, undeniable sexual tension brewing between us. Time stopped as he pulled up in front of a townhouse and got out of the Jeep with an order for me to wait where I was. I sat restlessly as I thought of the way my body burned under his touch. Panic ripped through me as I thought of all the things that could go wrong.

As he rounded the car and ripped open my door, he pulled me out to meet his lips, and all rational thought fell away.

He kissed me long and hard as he gripped my legs and wrapped them around him as he walked backward toward his door. On instinct, my body began to grind against his. Rafe tore his lips away once we were behind his door and fisted my dress. In one sweeping movement, he pulled it away from my body. I stood in my bra and panties as he kicked the door shut behind me and gazed over my form. He'd already seen me in next to nothing, yet I couldn't help the small amount of anxiety that raced through me. He saw it whisper over my features.

"We can stop right now," he said with a voice filled with sex, "or I can deliver on my promise."

I unhooked my bra and let it slip down my panties as Rafe cursed under his breath. Seconds later, I was spread across his couch, his mouth on mine, his tongue a tool of worship. He backed away from my lips and landed hot, wet kisses down my chest as his finger found me again. I gasped as he took a nipple into his mouth. "I've been dreaming about this," he whispered as he devoured one nipple and then the other."

"Feels so good," I murmured as he looked up at me with paralyzing eyes.

His mouth drifted down as he gently pulled my legs over each of his shoulders. Rafe dipped his head, our eyes locked, and darted his tongue out exactly where I needed it.

"Yeeesss," I hissed as he circled me over and over with his tongue. I reached down and thrust my hands into his hair as he guided me into an unparalleled state. I was so gone.

I'd never had this type of sex, never been on the receiving end of a kiss like the ones he'd given me. I was too focused on what he was doing to give back and then it struck me. I was supposed to blow *his* mind. I lifted on my forearms and just as fast he pressed me back down flat with one hand. It was a silent order as he spelled out a sonnet with his tongue. Minutes later, I felt the sensation of falling and burst into flames as I moaned out an orgasm. It seemed to last forever as I trembled and shook beneath his mouth. His tongue never stopped its thrusts as his fingers pushed into me at a faster pace. He twisted them as he worked me to a frenzied peak again and pushed me over. Covered in a thin veil of sweat, I looked down at him as he kissed my soaked sex with the same gentle tongue he'd tasted my mouth with. Gently, he took one last sip and stood.

Barely recovered, I watch Rafe undress. I sat up to admire him. His long torso was etched with solid muscle, his stomach cut on the sides with beautiful indents. As he pulled down his jeans, I reached out to him greedily and gripped the solid muscle between his thighs in my hands. Every single part of him was beautiful.

Blow his mind, Alice.

I wet my lips and simply went for it. Seconds later, I heard his deep moan of appreciation as I tasted and sucked him just as thoroughly as he did me. I cupped zone four and pushed on zone five as I heard praise and curses drip from his throat.

Research really does pay off.

"Alice, Jesus," he whispered as he gently pulled my head away after several minutes of unrelenting worship. I looked up to him, no longer afraid, my desire for him my guide. I lay back, legs spread, unashamed and fearless as he kept me captive with his eyes and fitted a condom he'd pulled from his wallet. Shadows danced from the large windows of the living room over our bodies just enough so we could see every part of the other.

He hovered over me, our eyes locked, as he gently pushed inside. Inch by inch, he filled me until I cried out in a mix of pain and pleasure. I gripped his butt and kept him seated as I took a deep breath. Rafe captured my exhale with his tongue and began to move as I fell into rhythm with him.

Clutched together for several minutes, we both basked in the undeniable feeling of our bodies until Rafe pulled back and bit his lip as he watched my reaction to him. Unrehearsed, I let myself go as he pushed inside so impossibly deep I had no choice but to let him know.

"Rafe...you're so deep." I gasped as another sensation overtook me. It was one of intimacy as he swiveled his hips and sank in further. He pulled back just enough and then thrust in hard so the friction was overwhelming.

Dizzy with lust and bubbling with feelings, I begged for release as he soothed me with his body.

"Come with me," he said as he beckoned me to obey. I fell apart with a loud cry as Rafe buried himself and gripped my hair. He tilted my head back as he let go, his eyes glued to mine as he spilled over.

Minutes later, we remained naked and wrapped in each other's arms on his couch as his head lay on my chest and his fingers drifted over my skin. I feathered mine through his hair as he kissed me lightly on the side of my breast and then underneath it and continued over my stomach.

"Alice," he whispered as neither of us moved in the quiet house that was only interrupted by the sound of our breathing. "I want you to be mine."

"It was the sex," I whispered back with a small smile he couldn't see.

"No, it was the blow job," he chuckled as I smacked his head.

"We'll see."

Rafe lifted his head and looked at me with a frown. "We'll see?"

"Yeah, I think I'll take a page from your playbook."

"I don't have a playbook."

"Then I'll think one up for myself."

"That's totally fucked up," he said with a grin. "Challenge accepted."

"Have you ever even *had* a girlfriend, Rafe?"

"Of course, plenty of them."

"That's reassuring."
"What about you?"
"No."
"Never?"
"No."
"But you've had sex."
"Twice with the same guy when I was twenty-one. It was anticlimactic the first time, and I was equally disappointed the second."
"What happened?"
"We had sex."

Rafe looked up at me with a frown. "No boyfriend, not even in high school?"

I grimaced at my revelation. "It's not like I didn't want one. It was just...impossible. You have to be seen to be visible, right? My mother was too much to deal with to try. I was asked out a couple of times, but could never date." I didn't mention the fact that I was holding out for Jake Ryan. He would never understand.

A few minutes of silence passed.

"Rafe?"
"Yeah?"
"Why me?"

"It could only *be* you," he whispered as he lay back down and we both drifted off.

The next morning, I woke up to a very playful Rafe.

"Wake up and let me see them." His deep voice pulled me into the room.

"See what?" I said, slightly agitated, sleep still beckoning me to cooperate. Suddenly aware I was in bed with a man, a beautiful man, with Rafe, my eyes flew open.

"There they are."

"Rafe," I said on a smile-filled whisper.
"You were hoping for someone else?"
"God no."

His smile turned more endearing, and I realized he was fully dressed in gym clothes and covered in sweat. "It's almost eleven. We knocked you out good."

I stretched and then realized I was bare breasted. I pulled covers over me and clamped my mouth closed in fear of morning breath.

"We knocked me out?"

"Yeah," he said as he lifted a brow and gestured to his crotch. "It was a team effort."

I giggled like a four-year-old as he leaned in. "You. In. My. Bed," he said on a deep groan. "I should lock you in here." He stood and opened a dresser drawer and threw a Swampgators t-shirt at me. I pulled the shirt over my head. "Don't move. I'm going to take a shower and then undress you again."

"Okay."

"Wow, we made you agreeable, too."

"Stop referring to your junk as another entity, Rafe. It's creepy."

"We'll shut you up again soon."

He pulled off his shirt, revealing his perfectly cut chest, and then dropped his shorts and boxers to reveal himself fully hard. My mouth watered as a blush crept through my chest and my cheeks flamed. I was staring. God, *that thing* was inside me. Rafe smiled but said nothing else as he left the door open behind him. I did get out of bed as he showered and grabbed a shot of toothpaste from his tube and cleaned my mouth. I ogled him behind the bubble glass. I couldn't make out much but a perfect butt and concentrated on that as I rinsed. I splashed cold water on my face and was just about to resume my place in the bed when I saw the open drawer full of t-shirts.

Andy's words hit me like lead to the stomach.

"Every available woman in Charleston has the t-shirt."

I knew I would eventually be jerked from the dream state I was in but had no idea how soon after I'd be pulled back into reality.

I'd just gotten my answer.

Pain seared my every limb as I choked back a sob.

Feeling sick, I pulled off the disgusting souvenir and shuffled to the living room to find my dress.

I found my cell and ordered an Uber. Four minutes.

Anger boiled through me as I made my way back into his bedroom and paced, the shower water still running. I channeled my inner Ouiser and quickly gathered the shirts from the drawer and called out to Rafe.

"I'm making you breakfast."

I didn't hear his response as I ran into the kitchen and set the t-shirts on the counter. There was at least a dozen. Putting my plan into motion, I heard my Uber arrive by the honk of its horn. I took a look around the living room to make sure I hadn't forgotten anything and briefly admired Rafe's taste. It didn't seem like the home of a playboy. Suddenly, I was saddened it was the last time I would see it. When I was sure I had everything that belonged to me, I closed the door but knew a huge amount of my pride remained behind.

10

I rinsed off quickly, the only thing on my mind was Alice and her lips. I wanted to drive every moan possible from her body and watch her eyes as she came. Those beautiful brown eyes did things to me I couldn't explain and didn't want to. Her stare was like a drug, and I couldn't wait for my next fix. I was leaving today for a four-game series in Savannah and wouldn't be back for another two weeks. I wondered briefly if she would make the drive down to attend a game and stay with me after. I wanted her there, and the thought made me smile. Being inside her had set my soul on fire. I couldn't remember the last time a woman had quenched my thirst. And this woman...this woman was *everything*. She'd completely rocked my world last night with her skill set. I almost didn't believe her when she'd told me she'd only slept with one other man. I would erase that asshole from her memory. She'd denied me when I'd asked her to be mine, and honestly, I was up for the chase. It was all I had done since I'd met her, anyway. I looked forward to it, and as soon as I walked out of the bathroom, it was game on.

I was toweling off when the awful stench of something burning hit me, and I called out to her.

"You okay in there?"

Seconds later, the alarm went off, and I hustled to the kitchen to see the shirts on the counter and one smoking on the stove.

"What the fuck?!" I looked around the living room. "ALICE?" But I knew it was pointless. She was gone. I pulled the ruined t-shirt from the stove and ran water over it before I silenced the alarms. I stood confused in my kitchen as I thought of what she could possibly be thinking when it hit me.

"Fuck."

I looked down at my phone in the back of the sedan and sighed. "Hi, Mom."

"Alice, how are you?" I rolled my eyes. Her tone seemed indifferent, as if the call was obligatory.

"I'm fine, Mom."

"I'm well, thank you for asking."

"I apologize for not asking. I'm distracted."

Just then, a beep interrupted our call, and I ignored it when I saw Rafe's name. I looked at my phone just as the driver pulled into the bar parking lot.

Rafe: Call me NOW!

I hadn't said a word to the driver aside from the address but knew he was paid so I exited the car and got into my Prius. It was only fitting I took the drive of shame in last night's clothes while I spoke with my puritan mother.

Rafe made you feel this way. Don't forget that.

"What's distracting you?"

"Work, of course," I said with a dry tone—a tone acceptable to her. Any sort of excitement or animation on my part had always been deemed unnecessary. The woman was allergic to happiness.

"Well, I'm sure you'll handle it. You've always been a smart girl."

"Thank you." A compliment was a nice change of pace. So I asked her genuinely, "How are you, Mother?"

She spent the better part of twenty minutes telling me about church, about a small bridge club scandal that involved...she lowered her voice to a whisper *"infidelity* with one of the player's husbands with another's wife."

I listened halfheartedly while mentally kicking myself for letting myself feel for Rafe.

He'd been so gentle, so completely perfect. I let a single tear slip down my cheek.

Friendship over.

Alone again.

I ended the call with my mother and decided to hit the store before I went home. Carbs and movies had to fix this. I had nothing else. I pushed my cart down the aisle in last night's dress, completely dazed. I had only grabbed a box of Twinkies and was sure I'd spent an hour just circling the store.

"Hey, you," Kristina greeted me from out of nowhere. "You must live close." She eyed my dress and gathered her conclusion which, unfortunately, was the right one. She saw my face fall as I nodded my head in agreement and then let the budding tears fall.

"I'm such an idiot."

Kristina quickly looked around us and moved toward me. "No, you aren't. You're just a victim to his charms like the rest of us. Come on," she said as she put my box of Twinkies in her cart and began grabbing everything I would have, had I been in the right state of mind.

"You're coming with me," she said as she grabbed two bottles of wine. "We'll make it a lazy 'Fuck Men' day, and hang at the pool."

"Where's Dillon?"

"With his grandmother, thank Jesus. I was going to do this

alone, but now I have you."

"I won't be much for company. I don't have a suit," I said as she pulled a few bags of assorted chips and threw them in the cart.

"I've got you."

Pain seared through me as she looked on at me with sympathy. I shrugged my shoulders. "I thought I was onto something."

"We all do," she said as she pushed the cart in front of her and me along with it.

An hour later, I floated in a large inflatable pool in a borrowed bathing suit with a plastic cup of red wine in my hand. Despite my circumstances, I smiled at a perfect looking Kristina who looked stunning in a silver bikini as she danced around her yard, picking up toys as Lana Del Rey sang about her heart.

"Thank you," I said as she looked over at me with a smile.

"Girl, I'm not a fan of too many women, especially the ones that come and go strictly to become part of the club or marry into it. I knew you weren't one of those. And by the way you had Rafe looking at you…I was sure…"

I winced.

"Anyway, I know you're good people, even if you did threaten to eat my son."

I shot up in my float. "I was joking."

"He's a kid so he took it literally. I'm pretty sure I could hire you to come over and scare him into cleaning his room."

"Sorry! I'm not really that good with the little people."

"Neither am I, and *I'm* a mother," she said as she joined me in the pool with a cup of her own. She lay back and looked up at the sky. "This is the life."

I looked around her backyard. It was definitely a fitting playground for a little person, complete with a bike, a sandpit, and multiple water guns.

"I bet you're an awesome mom."

She looked at me, her hand over her eyes, shielding them from the sun. "I try really hard."

"I can tell you are," I said with certainty.

"It's not easy, but worth it at times. I didn't see my life turning out like this, that's for sure. A bartender and a single mom. I imagined it much different."

I nodded because I understood it, at least the career aspect. As far as my romantic life went, I'd never really had any expectations. Rafe had given me a piece of something I now craved, and I felt like he'd taken it away just as easily. I wondered why he even bothered calling me and still I cringed at the thought of not speaking to him again. I'd left my phone in my purse inside Kristina's house but was dying a little with each second that passed.

"Every available woman in Charleston has the t-shirt."

I wouldn't be that woman for him, though technically I'd already *been* that woman for him. I refused to let him look at me the way he did other women. I wasn't a "piece of pussy." But just the thought of being another insignificant fling had me in knots.

Hours later, and after drinking more wine than I ever thought I was capable, I found myself in a conversation with her that had me revealing everything about myself.

"Wow, that strict."

"It was a nightmare. I was home by eight-thirty on prom night. It started at seven."

"That's a shame, girl. But here you are now, living it up."

"True," I said as I lay back on the float, my head spinning slightly. "A little too much maybe."

"You want to tell me about it?" she asked, her voice mournful as if she understood exactly how I felt. For a brief second, I looked on at her, curious if she'd ever been in Rafe's bed. She read my thoughts.

"No, we've never hooked up."

"Sorry."

"It's fine," she said as she pulled our floats together. "Andy has a thing for me. Rafe wouldn't lay a hand on me. I'm kinda getting over...someone." A brief silence followed. "Andy is perfect, you know...but the heart wants what it wants."

Shocked by her admission, I looked over at her beautiful face and thought the world a screwed up place if a girl that beautiful whose insides seemed to match her outsides couldn't have the man she wanted. If that was the case, I held out very little hope.

"It's funny you say that because last night I could have gone on a date with a man worthy of my time and instead I blew him off for Rafe."

She nodded as if she understood, and I reveled in our budding friendship. "What did he do?"

"He gave me a t-shirt."

"I'm not following." I told her everything, aside from the sex. As she listened and laughed about the fact that I peed on him, she held her hand up when I got to the part about the shirts and what Andy had said.

"Wait, you said there were how many?"

"At least a dozen."

"Were they green with white writing?"

"Yes."

"Oh girl," she said with wide eyes. "I think you may have jumped the gun."

I lifted to straddle the float.

"Rafe coaches little league on his Saturdays at home. I just ordered those shirts. He's passing them out next week."

When I really thought about it, the t-shirt had been a little snug. "Oh...crud."

Kristina smiled and winked. "Let him sweat it out a little. You're the type of girl he *needs* to work for."

"You think so?" I said as my heart leaped into a steady stride.

"Absolutely. I saw the way he looked at you, kissed you," she looked away briefly and cleared her throat. "He's into you."

I groaned at her admission. "And I just screwed it up."

"If he gives up that easily, he's not worth keeping."

A few minutes later, I looked over at Kristina, who sipped her wine. "Thank you for today."

"Anytime, girl, that's what friends are for."

I couldn't help the pride-filled smiled that crept over my lips.

Hours later and mildly sober, I sat on my patio looking at my messages. He'd only sent one more text.

Rafe: Just let me explain.

I thought of Kristina's words and to ensure I never felt that way again, I would make him work for it.

Alice: Explain.

The bubble started immediately, and I couldn't help my smile.

Rafe: First of all, you are crazy as shit for starting a fire in my house, but I'll forgive you because I kind of like you jealous so I'm willing to overlook it. Second, I coach a little league team on Saturdays. I don't pass out t-shirts to the women I have sex with. I want you, Alice. I asked you to be mine last night. What part of that don't you get?

Alice: I'm sorry I overreacted.

Rafe: So we're good?

Alice: Yes.

Rafe: I'm on my way to Savannah now. I planned on spending the morning making you come and feeding you like a queen, but you

screwed that up.

My face burned with embarrassment.

Alice: Raincheck?

Rafe: Oh, I'm going to get my hands on that ass of yours, I promise.

Alice: Text me when you get there?

Rafe: I will, and you owe me another shirt.

Unknown: Son, we need to talk.

It was the fourth text in a week. I could only curse my mother as I dialed her.

"Hey, honey!"

"Mom, have you talked to Dad? Did you give him my number?"

Silence followed as I blew out a breath of frustration.

"You know he's truly proud of you and you cutting him out of your life like that—"

"Was my decision," I snapped. "He's never been a father, and you know it. He divorced you years ago, he left you, and you're still siding with him. Why?"

"He's a good man, Rafe."

"No, he's a self-serving asshole that abandoned you and damn near ruined my career. You need to get that through your head,

Mom."

"Things used to be good, Rafe."

And she was right. When my father posed as a supportive coach and mentor throughout high school, things were good, until he got greedy and accepted a bribe.

"And things are fine now. Stop filling him in on shit that is none of his business! If he wants to watch my career, he can do it from the sidelines."

"It's just that this is your year. I wanted him to know that."

"Exactly, Mom, my year!" Frustration rolled off me. "I gotta go."

"Rafe, hon—"

"I may have forgiven you for going along with it, but I haven't forgotten. It's either him or me."

She spoke quickly. "It's you, Rafe," she sniffed. "I'm sorry."

"Mom," I said on a sigh. "I have to go."

"Okay, honey. Good luck tonight."

"I don't have a game tonight."

"Oh, well, good luck at your next one." I ended the call. She was just as self-serving as he was. She never had an interest in showing up for a game, just the bragging rights, along with my father who'd been far too involved in every aspect of my budding career. He'd taken a one hundred-thousand-dollar bribe from the Racer's scout to get me on their ball team, and damned near broke my pitching arm to make sure it happened. It wasn't until one of my high school coaches brought it to my attention that he'd accepted some money that I realized the implications of what he'd done. Senior night after my last game, he'd come out to the mound to congratulate me. Furious with the fresh information of his betrayal, I broke his nose in front of my class, high school coaches, and several reporters. After months of scout visits to my house, and hours of arguing, we were in a deadlock about my future, and he'd taken it upon himself to make sure I went in the direction he wanted. I washed my hands of him on that mound. The next morning, I held a press conference stating the facts and knew by coming clean I purposefully finished the relationship with my father as I denounced him publicly.

It was the worst day of my life.

Endless practices, games, and a bright future of ball and my father had thrown everything into a pile and lit it on fire.

He was my mentor, my driving force, and it was only after I went to play ball in junior college that I realized how truly devoted I was to the game itself. My love for ball had little to do with my father, and when I finally got my head straight, I realized I'd always played for me.

After the press conference ending our relationship, I left the house and never spoke to him again. He divorced my mother shortly after for siding with me but later told me in a text she'd agreed to take the bribe with him. I almost disowned her as well when everything was falling apart, and she told me "Everything would have been fine had you gone along with it."

I had to let it go. She was hurt, and he was the cause of all of it. Our family had been torn apart by a rash and greedy decision. I still loved my mother, but I would never look at her the same.

Once in Savannah, I checked into another stale motel and scrubbed my hands down my face as I lay in bed, my thoughts on years of endless ball games. I'd ignored every possible offer after senior night and just resigned myself to being under the radar. My situation wasn't uncommon, but I never thought it would happen to me. I turned down six-figure offers to simply pitch college ball and get my head together. Now, all I wanted to do was advance to the majors, something that could have happened long before now if he hadn't pulled that stunt and I hadn't let it screw with my head.

Even if I forgave him, I wouldn't know how to act around him. That shady shit had completely shifted the way I thought of him. There is no doubt in my mind if I would have signed and played well, I would've taken care of both my parents as much as I could financially.

I'll never understand why they couldn't have just waited.

I'll never understand why neither of them loved me enough to keep from stripping me of the future I'd worked so hard for.

My thoughts drifted to Alice as my motel door opened.

"What the fuck?"

"Fucking perfect," Rodriguez said as he threw his gear on the floor.

"You aren't staying."

"If we don't, Jon will know it. Suck it up, Hembrey."

I wouldn't put it past Jon to pair Rodriquez and me. Sometimes, he really was a bastard.

"Fuck you," I said as I shifted to sit on the bed.

"You know," he said with his hands fisted on his sides, "you're the one who fucked *my girl*. Shouldn't *I* be the one to pitch a bitch about sharing a room?"

"Well, you're right about one thing," I said as I stood and grabbed my packed bag. "You pitch like a bitch." I pulled the door open.

"Think about it, Hembrey. If he finds out and we split rooms, you won't play."

I was only pitching every fifth game as it was, and I needed to keep my stats up. "I can afford to miss a game," I spit out sarcastically.

"A Ranger scout will be at this one," he pointed out.

"Fuck." I paused, still at the door, and looked over my shoulder. "Why are you helping me?"

"I'm next," he muttered under his breath. Rodriguez would be moved up to starting pitcher for the Swampgators if I made it to the big show. Though I gave him shit, he was a decent pitcher. One of the best in the minors, actually.

I shut the door and resumed my spot on the bed. After an hour of watching the Rangers play, I looked over to Rodriguez. He wasn't much taller than me, and his feet hung off the full sized bed as he stared at the screen, indifferent.

"I didn't know she was your girl."

He didn't move his eyes from the game as he replied. "But you knew she was *someone's girl*. The big fucking engagement ring she had on gave you that much of a clue."

"It was her decision."

"And she's no longer my girl. Now shut the fuck up before you remind me of how pissed off I was."

"You can fucking try," I quipped with venom. Maybe it was thoughts of my father that triggered me to say the wrong fucking thing. Maybe it was my restlessness or guilt. Either way, with my next words, I knew what I was asking for. "Don't worry. She meant shit to me. In fact, I don't even remember her name."

An hour later, two bruised knuckles (mine), two black eyes (his and mine), and a busted lip (mine again), Rodriguez and I sat in an utterly destroyed hotel room. We'd both swung with our weak fists to save our game arm and did a poor job of landing punches. It would have been funny if I wasn't so fucking remorseful about it.

I looked over to him as he nursed his eye with ice from a dirty bucket. It was on the tip of my tongue. Simple words that could make the tension between us slightly better. I'd given him far more room to take me than I was comfortable, but I knew I deserved it. As he stretched his hand and studied the broken skin on his knuckles, he seemed satisfied. That was enough for now.

I decided to concentrate on Alice instead.

> **Rafe:** You're the only fucking thing good about my day, and you nearly burned me alive if that's any indication of how bad this day was. I want you here. I want you mine, Alice. What do I have to do?
>
> **Alice:** Make it worth my while.

I groaned and ducked as Rodriguez gave me an odd look.

Rafe: You'll make a pussy out of me yet.

11
Alice

"All I care about in this goddamn life are me, my drums, and you," I voiced along with Watts as I watched the movie *Some Kind of Wonderful*. The feeling in my chest almost matched the one I had every time my phone pinged with a new message from Rafe. He was wooing me by text, and I was letting him. I was tempted to drive down and surprise him, but I didn't want to assume anything and seem like a stage-five clinger. I still owed him a proper apology, but it seemed he'd all but forgotten my arson outburst. I had, in my defense, soaked the shirt in water so it would smoke. But the fact that he still spoke to me after that crazy outburst still left me stunned. I meant it to be the end of us. Surely, he had a groupie in every city just waiting for a chance to pounce.

Any other guy would have run the other way, I'm sure. Then again, what did I know?

I sighed happily as I packed a bag for the beach and another text came through. It was of Rafe. Well, not Rafe exactly. It was a picture of his ball pants and his bulging and pronounced "teammate." The one who'd helped to knock me out. It wasn't graphic, just a flirtation, but I'd almost wished he'd sent the real deal. I was already flushed with thoughts of our night together. I'd never sexted so I went all in.

Alice: I want it everywhere, between my breasts.

Rafe: Holy fuck.

Rafe: Alice?

I glanced at my kitchen counter and went a step further.

Alice: I want you to come in my mouth.

Alice: I want to cover it in Nutella and lick it off.

Rafe: Are you fucking with me?

At work the following week, I frowned as I looked at the progress of the pilots. Half of them had failed the written spec examination about the aircraft. And it was the easiest part. I knew that reflected poorly on me as an instructor. I looked around the room at the tired, long faces and sighed.

This is so not what I'd hoped it would be.

"Gentlemen, if you learn to fly this aircraft, you are twice as likely to see a pay increase or get a better offer from a competing airline. That is the last incentive I will give you to do *your* job."

I barely got a reaction and looked over to Trey, who eyed me with curiosity. I'd hastily dismissed our date to have a night of sex with Rafe. It seemed I had more than one sincere apology to give, and as soon as class ended, he was quick to approach.

"I'm sorry," I said in a low tone. "I had something come up." I was lying, and that was not okay. "I got...involved with someone."

"That fast?" he asked as he stuck his hands in a black pair of chinos.

"Yes, I'm sorry."

"No, I'm sorry I didn't ask you sooner. I'm pissed about that fact, actually." I looked up to see he was close. He was truly a good looking man. Trey had full, kissable, lips, and boyishly handsome features. Even with his face lit by the dull lights of the classroom, he was quite alluring. If I wasn't so wrapped up in a ballplayer full of "charm," Trey would be ideal. Still, I could never ignore the way I felt with said ballplayer around. My heart was already declaring itself faithful.

I want you to be mine.

"I'm not doing well at this," I said as I motioned to the empty classroom in an attempt to change the subject. "I'm not doing well at all."

"Alice, it's not your job to motivate them. It's your job to make sure they can fly the plane."

"And I'm failing."

"One week and you'll have a new batch of pilots. I have to say, this was a tough room. And you didn't fail. I'm not failing."

I gave him a smile. "Thanks for that apple."

"Anytime, teach." He paused in the doorway. "If you change your mind, you have my number." I nodded again as he gave me a heated look. "I hope you use it."

I answered the phone with a smile. "You won."

"We did. I wish you were here. I pitched—"

"A perfect game. I really wish I was, too." I sat on the beach that Saturday, counting down the hours until Rafe came home. He assured me he wanted me in his bed tomorrow night when he got there. He'd even told me where he hides a key, so I assured him I would be waiting.

"You could've come." Rafe's voice was as deep and soothing as the ocean I was staring at.

"You didn't invite me." I smiled as I realized he wanted me there just as much as I wanted to be there. Still, my current view was a great consolation.

"Something wrong?" My smile deepened because he was becoming in tune with me and my tones.

I'd spent the better half of my day thinking about my career choice and wondering if I should stay. Trey was right. I had a new class of pilots coming and "a tough room" didn't even begin to describe my current one.

"It's just...my job. It's not what I thought it would be. I think I'd be happier flying."

"So then fly."

"It's not that simple. I don't want to give up just because it's tough. I have a contract with Boeing for a year I have to see through. It's just...I feel like they *hate* me."

"Just a bunch of arrogant assholes, huh?"

"Maybe I'm not cut out to be an instructor. I just don't think they *like* me."

"*I* like you."

"I know," I said with a sigh. "There's that."

"And it's not changing. Tomorrow, Alice," I heard the need in his voice and my stomach knotted with excitement. Just as I was about to respond, I felt the sting in my legs as I smacked my hand on my thigh and looked at it, sure I'd just killed a mosquito. The next sting came as I stood and looked below me for an ant pile.

"Yeah, tomorrow, Rafe—Ouch!" I said as I twisted my body, looking for any sign of life and got nothing.

"Alice, what's wrong?"

"I don't know. I think I sat in an ant pile at the beach."

"There are no ant piles at the beach."

"HOW...OW, Oh my God," I jumped out of my skin as I swatted around me like I was being attacked by a swarm of bees.

"Alice, what the hell is going on?"

"Rafe, something's biting me! I have to go." I hung up and began swatting furiously at the air around me as one soft pinch after another ravaged my body. Onlookers stared at me as I furiously waved my hands around me to ward off the unseen enemy. The sun was setting, and the sand was cool on my feet as I grabbed my bag and made my way toward my car, enraged by the disruption of my Zen. Realization struck as I remembered my neighbors warning.

No-see-ums!

God, I had crappy luck. I fought the invisible killer sandflies the whole way to my car and turned on the AC full blast, still feeling the sting of their harmless bite.

Alice: Just the darned no-see-ums. God, that was awful. Seriously, this state should come with a warning.

Rafe: Hang in there, baby.

Alice: Baby?

Rafe: Be mine, Alice.

My heart hammered at his term of endearment. I'd told him, but I wasn't sure if he knew just how many firsts he'd really given me in just a few weeks. We spoke for hours every night, either by text or phone. Endless hours of talking with Rafe had somehow made him able to read my voice, my thoughts. I'd never had that type of connection with a man, *ever*.

Our conversations were always entertaining. I smiled and sighed so much. He alone made up for the years of my youth as a teenage girl who'd missed out on the fun parts. He was quickly becoming etched inside of me. His voice, his words, his way of letting me know just how much he wanted me, it was surreal and beautiful and all mine.

Though my week had turned to crap, I had someone to look forward to, and I'd never had that. I quickly texted Rafe a picture of Nutella.

If he didn't think I was serious, then he would definitely know when he got home.

12

"Alice?"

Her car wasn't in the driveway when I got home, and I'd almost jumped in my Jeep to get to her place when I noticed my bedroom light on.

"In here," she said as she called from my bedroom. My heart hammered as I threw my bag down and quickly made my way to her. I stopped at the door, expecting to see something over the top: candles, lingerie, and soft music playing. Instead, I burst out laughing.

Alice was laid out on my bed, her hair a soft mess splayed around her shoulders. Her hands caressed her bloated stomach, and she had empty snack pack wrappers all around her.

"I ate it all," she groaned as I stared at the empty jar of Nutella. "And you're late."

I made my way across the room as she lifted to kneel on the bed. I quickly scanned her version of lingerie: boy shorts and a t-shirt that read "BIG BANG."

"Cute," I pointed to her shirt as I pulled her to me and ravaged her mouth. She fell quickly into rhythm with me and then pulled away. I was seconds away from being where I wanted to be most. "God, my stomach," she moaned.

"Really?" I said as my dick twitched in disappointment.

"Give me an hour," she said just as disheartened. "I got to Googling, and I just ate...a lot. I'm sorry."

"I have something," I said as I went to my bathroom and threw two antacids in a cup of water. I handed it to her, and she drank greedily. Suddenly, her hand was over her mouth as her eyes grew wide.

"Do it," I said with a chuckle. Alice quickly turned her head and ran toward the bathroom, but I blocked her.

She dodged my hungry hands and dashed out of the room with a burp slipping out the size of one of Booger's from that movie *Revenge of The Nerds* she'd made me watch with her. I laughed, following after her as she ranted. "Oh my God, oh my God, oh my GOD!" She stood in the living room, her hand on her stomach, as I stood entertained in the corner. "Don't look at me, Rafe!" Another loud burp and she clenched her thighs with hysterical laughter.

"Don't you dare pee on my floor!"

"Leave this room!"

"This is my house," I said with a chuckle.

Another burp had her shaking her head, her face beet red with embarrassment. "You knew I wouldn't be able to stop it!"

"Feel better?"

She nodded as I approached her. "I'm so disgusting."

"You're fucking hilarious, and *I* find that sexy."

She looked at me, *really* looked at me for the first time since I walked into the house, and smiled. I closed the gap between us. "I missed you," she said with a hiccup, her brown eyes sincere.

"The feeling is mutual," I whispered before I tugged her bottom lip in my mouth and sucked gently. She hiccupped again, and I stepped away.

"What were you Googling?"

She gave me wary eyes as she pulled away slightly. "Please don't ever look at my browsing history. You wouldn't understand," she said with wide eyes. "It's a sickness."

I grabbed her hand and led her back to my bedroom and stared at the catastrophe on my bed. "Well, you're a slob. Looks like I don't have to feed you tonight." She gathered the wrappers from my bed and threw them in the trash and then wiped my bed free of crumbs. I studied the Nutella jar and shook my head in disappointment. "Not even a teaspoon?"

"I, uh..." She hiccupped again. "I'll make it up to you." I pulled my shirt over my head with my fist as I saw her eyes rake my body, and then rid myself of my shoes and shorts. Her gaze drifted from between my thighs to meet my eyes.

"How?" I said with a quirked eyebrow. I saw her pause as her wheels turned. God, I loved that she was so sexually innocent and yet so damned eager to please me. In my head, all I heard were the words on repeat.

Be mine. Be mine. Be mine. Be mine. Be mine, Alice.

"Get into bed, Alice."

Her eyes bulged. "Rafe, I really do feel sick."

"Come here," I said as I looked at the clock. We'd had a last minute meeting that ran long, and I had rushed home instead of texting her. She'd probably been waiting for hours in my room for me.

I pulled and tucked her into me as I turned off the bedside light. She sighed in my arms and ground her ass into my throbbing cock.

"Alice," I hissed as she giggled.

"Sorry," she said, amused.

"No, you aren't. Go to sleep."

"Did you know that a movie theater manager in Seoul Korea cut out all the songs from the Sound Of Music because he thought the movie was too long?"

Alice chuckled hysterically as I held her tighter to me and joined in.

"Tell me more," I whispered as I moved her t-shirt and placed a slow kiss on her shoulder.

"Judy Garland received thirty-five dollars a week for her role in The Wizard of Oz, but Toto got one hundred and twenty-five a week."

"That's fucked up."

"Right? And Ariel—" she yawned "—from the movie Little Mermaid was originally supposed to be a blonde."

"Interesting."

"Do you like blondes?" Her breathing picked up. "I mean, what's your preference?"

"Alice."

"No, I mean, really, what *is* your preference? I can handle it."

"My preference is...Alice."

"God, that's sooooo lame."

"Fine...brunettes."

"Great," I heard her huff.

"You asked." I turned her over on her back and rubbed her belly gently with my hand.

"Better?"

She nodded as I kissed her deep before I grinned down at her in the dark. "I'm an ass man, too," I said as I cupped her chest and heard her breath intake. "But when I think of touching you, all I want to do is run my fingers over these." I feathered her nipples through her t-shirt as she met my slow kiss. I delved into every surface of her mouth, her moan evidence of a job well done. I pulled her to my chest and waited for her breathing to even out before I let sleep take me.

I don't know who moved first, or who kissed who, but in the late hours of morning, I found myself being ravaged by Rafe, and I'd never been hungrier. Come to think of it, I think it was me who pressed back into him repeatedly, asking for the hard length that remained underneath his boxers. I vaguely remembered cupping him in the middle of the night with his name on my lips in a soft moan. He may have reached for me then and groaned my name as he pushed his hips up to give me better access. And if I think really hard, I can remember dipping my hand into those boxers and rubbing my thumb over the tip of his silky head.

I was becoming a bold sex goddess. Well, one that burped like a man, but Rafe didn't seem to mind.

He undressed me slowly, and his hands roamed my body with the same gentle way he always seemed to have with me. I succumbed to him without any protest as he turned me on my back, nipped and softly kissed every inch of exposed skin. My body arched as he sipped and sampled between my legs. His tongue was slow, exquisite torture, but welcomed by my fever-filled moans. I clutched him to me, pumping my hips as he gripped my butt and lifted it to slide his tongue back and forth over my audibly slick center. All of my nerves fired as he licked and sucked, and I detonated in a long, blissful orgasm before he slowly made his way back up.

I lay back as he opened his nightstand drawer, fit himself in a condom, my hands gliding over every hard surface of him. I could feel the ripple of his stomach, the strength in his arms, and the curve of muscle on the sides of his neck.

"Rafe," I whispered as he cradled my face and kissed me with so much force, everything built between us burst the moment he fit inside me.

"Jesus, you were made for me," he whispered as he pushed into me farther, my body tight around him. I could feel every slow grind of his hips, every movement mattered. It was a dream.

"It's not a dream, Alice," he pushed out as he hovered above me. I hadn't realized I'd said it out loud. "This is us."

Completely consumed but dying to express something... anything, I cupped his neck.

"Rafe?"

He slowed to a stop, my voice enough reason to alarm him. I withdrew my hips and reached between us, slowly pulled his condom off, and began stroking him in worship.

"What are you doing?" His whisper was needful and urgent.

"If I'm going to be yours, this is the way I trust you, right? And you can trust me. I'm covered."

Everything inside me felt adored. I wanted to be closer, *feel* closer to him, and this was the only way I knew how. Rafe remained above me and stilled for several moments.

"You can trust me," I whispered as I lifted up to place a soft kiss on his mouth. Rafe lined himself at my entrance and rubbed his swollen head between my lips. In the dark of the room, and without being able to fully read his expression, I began to backtrack.

"Never mind...I just thought—" I was cut off by his eager mouth as he buried himself so deep a tear escaped my eye. He held my face in his hands as he pushed into me, his thrust and kiss blew all my walls to hell. My lips remained parted with cries for him. I took his strokes, needing more as he continued to take all that I had. Wrapping my legs around him, he sank further, deeper, as soft words were murmured between us.

"So soft, so beautiful."

"I missed you."

"I can't stop thinking about you."

"Please don't stop."

"Alice...God, baby, you feel so good."

We worked together, fire and air in perfect sync until we both came, sweat covered and completely sated.

Hours later, in a sunlit room, both of us covered from the waist down in his red sheets, we ate Cocoa Puffs naked in his bed. He'd had me bare for hours, a happy hostage. It was the best kind of sex imaginable. I couldn't get enough, and the growing evidence below his part of the sheet between us said he felt the same. He looked me over, my hair a matted mess, my nipples drawn tight, and bruised from hours of teeth and tongue. I was now a super fan of sex and was never going back. I briefly wondered if they had a giant foam finger for this sport.

"I've wanted this since I met you, stubborn woman."

"Naked Cocoa Puff consumption? Aiming high, aren't you, Bullet?"

He leaned over and deadpanned, "Smartass."

"I am," I conceded as I took a huge mouthful of cereal and grabbed the box between us to pour more in my bowl before I pulled the box away from his eager hands. "You can't eat too much sugar."

He reached for it again, and I threw it behind me, and it smacked his wall.

"You're kidding."

"Nope."

"Also," I said as I chomped another bite, "you have got to stop shaking off Andy's signals."

"What?"

"You're doing that a lot—"

"Are you fucking serious?"

"Don't you trust him?"

"You're *really* going to do this right now?" he asked, incredulous.

"This will help your issue," I said confidently.

"My...issue."

"You're lacking in confidence and a little sportsmanship, Rafe." I put the bowl down, and he stacked his onto mine with a loud thunk on his bedside table.

"You really are doing this. *You're* giving *me* ball advice?"

"Rafe, I'm just trying to help!"

"Thanks," he said as his eyes went cold.

"And your dugout manner with your teammate Rodriguez is appalling."

"What the hell did you just say?" His eyes narrowed, and for the life of me, I could not shut up.

"Everyone else congratulates him when he pitches well, and you just stare him down."

"This is professional baseball, Alice. We don't have to high five each other for doing our job. Jesus, you're really unbelievable."

"You're a very poor team player at times, and it's noticeable."

"I can't tell if you're serious right now, Alice."

"Dead serious," I said as I gathered the covers and held them to my chest in defense. Rafe swatted my hands away, and the curtain fell down.

"Then you're a jerk." He gripped the cotton between us and wadded the sheet up with his hands and threw it on the floor, leaving us bared to the other.

"What?"

"You're a jerk, Alice, *and* a class-A nerd who never grew out of it."

I blinked.

And blinked.

And blinked again.

My mouth moved before I had a chance to think it through.

"That really hurt."

"And you have no idea how to play it cool."

"That's because I don't pretend to be something I'm not, ever," I snapped as I stood to search for my panties. "Not even for you.

Though, I did do three hundred hours of research on the game of baseball to help with *your* game this season."

"So now that we're *fucking*, you get to dole out advice on my game." He remained in bed, his eyes dull as if he were bored. He might as well have slapped me.

I blinked again as I pulled on the rest of my clothes.

"You don't *f...fuck* me Rafe, and you know it."

I walked into his living room and called an Uber. Four minutes.

"Three hundred hours?" he scoffed behind me as he leaned against the wall with a sheet gripped around him. He was livid and sexy as hell.

"Yes," I answered as I slipped on my sandals.

"I've spent thousands! Oh, and I play the game for a living."

"And you're *still* in the minors, Rafe. You've got a slight reputation for being hot-tempered. Maybe it wouldn't hurt to listen to a *nerd*." God, that word hurt.

"Touché. Do you always bite the heads off after you mate, Ms. Mantis?"

"I'm just being honest," I declared with my hands on my hips. "I told you I was new to this!"

"Clearly, you've upped your game in the last few weeks."

My phone buzzed in my hand, telling me my Uber was outside. Kristina had dropped me off at Rafe's last night to throw him off that I was there and waiting for him. I was thankful I didn't have to wait long to make my escape. "Good day, sir."

"See, a total nerd. *No one* says that, Alice."

"I just fucking did," I spat as my voice shook with embarrassment and hurt. I couldn't look at him. I was angry and tears threatened.

"Wait...did you just cuss?"

"Goodbye, Rafe."

"Goodbye?" he parroted as he slammed his front door shut when I opened it. "No, Alice, that's not the way this works."

I turned to him with malice as he clutched his sheet loosely around his waist. I tugged at it hard, disrobing him, and as he bent down to retrieve it, I made my way out of the door and slipped into the sleek sedan. I rattled off my address and saw no sign of him in the drive.

Minutes later, a text from him came over. It was a picture of a praying mantis with no head. The tagline read "Was it good for you?"

When I didn't respond, I got another.

Rafe: Too soon? It was a fight, Alice.

The next text came immediately after.

Rafe: At least let me know you got home safe.

Fifteen minutes later, I answered.

Alice: I'm home.

What the fuck just happened? Damn it, I couldn't win with her! She'd called me out while my balls were still freshly unpacked, when I was my most vulnerable, naked and in bed with hopes of remaining that way until pre-game briefing. I was sure if she'd brought up my game any other time, my bite would have been much worse. Who in the hell did this woman think she was? And why couldn't I stay pissed enough to push aside my want of her?

We had over a hundred games left in the season. I had to keep my game sharp, and she was in my head, under my skin, and I wanted more.

I wound up and fired the ball into Andy's waiting glove.

"Too much, Rafe," he barked as he punched his fist in the

leather.

"Yeah, got it," I nodded, more determined than ever to keep my shit in check.

I read the ball clock with my next pitch: ninety-seven. I winced as Andy cursed. We were just screwing around on the field as we waited for the others to arrive. I wound up again and followed his signal.

"One-oh-two, Rafe. What the fuck!"

With a groan, I hit the dugout. Andy was fast on my heels as I drained some Gatorade from the dispenser.

"What's up with you, man?"

"I could ask you the same." I looked at him skeptically as we watched the rest of the pitching roster cross the field and head toward the manager suite.

"I've got a lot of shit going on."

"So do I," I shot back. I looked at my best friend and saw a clear rip running through him. In the four years he'd been my catcher, we'd formed a no bullshit friendship. We'd started out in a league together in Savannah and had moved together since, me fresh out of junior college as a rookie and Andy, never getting the recognition he deserved, had remained stagnant until we did well together. We fed off of each other. My pitch got sharper, and his batting average improved, so we'd moved on, both hoping to be exactly where we were now in Double-A, back in Charleston, and ripe for the picking. Except now, I was ready for major ball, and Andy ready to hang up his glove. They could pick either of us up at any time, but Andy was satisfied with his career. He was happy with his bar and didn't want to leave it. In the rare instance I'd found myself able to trust someone again after the fiasco with my father, Andy had been that someone. The distance he was putting between us was purposeful.

I spoke first. "This is on you, man, until you come clean."

"I don't like you very much right now," he said through gritted teeth.

"Suit yourself," I snapped as I crushed my paper cup and threw it in the trash can.

Andy called after me with contempt. "You're going to go up in flames if you let her get into your head."

"I can separate the game, both of them. I don't need you harping on me like my old man did. I got rid of him, remember?" The threat was there as Andy took a step back and ran his hands through his hair. I took an aggressive step forward to defend the first piece of happiness I felt good about in far too long. "There's not a goddamn thing wrong with wanting to be with a woman while you have a career in ball. She's helping my game not hurting it. If I'm on fire, it's *because* of her."

"So you're in love now, huh?" Andy said with a smug grin. It was the first time I wanted to wipe it off with my fists.

"I'm living my life. I'm a professional athlete, like you. If I fuck up, it's *on me*. If I do well, that too is on me. If you really give two shits about me or my career, you'll do the one thing nobody else in my fucking life has ever done and respect that. Respect me and my decisions."

"Fine, you're right. I'm out," Andy said, making his way back to the locker room.

"Just like that, huh? We have briefing, Andy," I barked after him.

"*You* have briefing, hot shot. I have a fucking business to run."

I threw my glove at his back and just as quickly he flew at me. I took his lick and barely remained on my feet. Lip bleeding, I looked at my best friend, my fists curled at my sides.

Andy eyed my lip with regret. I could take a punch way more than I could handle his next words. "She loves you, man. She's *in love* with you. Of all the fucking men in the world to compete with, Kristina loves *you*."

I felt the weight of the world land on my shoulders at that moment. I thought of Alice and how it would kill me if she'd fallen for Andy and never looked my way. I took a step forward. "I've never laid a hand on her, man, and I never will."

"Do you think that matters?"

It didn't, and I knew the truth of it in that moment. "I won't come to the bar again. I'll stay away."

"You think *I* want that?"

A few moments of silence followed as I stared at Andy and knew it was ruining him.

"I don't know how to navigate this play, Andy. *You* are my wingman. She's a friend, sure, but it's never been deep."

We both stayed silent for another minute until Andy spoke up. "And Alice?"

I didn't even hesitate. "Deep."

Andy surprised me with a smug smile. "I called that one."

"Yeah, you did, and I'm thankful you checked me on that, but this..." I scrubbed my hands down my face as management barked our names behind us. "I don't want to lose your friendship, man."

I'd surprised both of us with my honesty. I wasn't one to spit it out so easily. It was a growing change in me. It was a change Alice brought out in me.

"Good for you," Andy said, trying his best to hide the bitterness in his voice.

"All right, so you coming?" I asked, my lip throbbing. The son of a bitch could throw a punch.

"Nah, I need to get my head straight."

I nodded and turned to go to the meeting.

"Just give me some time, Rafe." I paused briefly then nodded again as I made the walk down the hall.

Jon looked behind me as I closed the door and made a quick excuse for Andy. "Emergency."

He nodded but not before he noticed my lip. He knew better, but ball was business, and he got back to it.

An hour after our meeting wrapped, I got a text from Kristina. I swallowed hard. I didn't want to engage at all. This was one fucked up position to be in. I mean, sure, we had a friendship, and I coached her kid's little league team, but our relationship had never been intimate. I'd never saw her that way, especially after Andy had shown interest.

> **Kristina: Alice is stranded on 526. Her car broke down. She texted me, but I'm already at the bar for a shift. Can you go?**
>
> **Rafe: What exit?**
>
> **Kristina: Just past the airport.**
>
> **Rafe: I'm on it. Thanks.**

I paused with my fingers over the text. I thought of all Kristina's and my interactions over the years and couldn't find anything to indicate anything other than friendship than a lingering kiss on New Year's Eve last year. I thought maybe it was just the alcohol or my imagination. Kristina knew me and well. I suddenly felt the guilt of pulling her into my wager with Alice and kissing her at the bar like I had that day. Though I had none of *those* feelings for Kristina whatsoever, I knew that had to have been hard for her if she had them for me. Even if she'd said a word, I wouldn't have pursued her, and she knew it. That's probably why she kept silent.

The girl I couldn't keep in my bed was stranded on a busy highway and was all that I wanted to concentrate on. I pulled up fifteen minutes later, thanking Christ it wasn't rush hour. It was the difference between minutes and hours. Alice had her hood popped and was waist deep in the engine of her Prius.

"What the hell are you doing?"

She froze, and I heard her mutter "Oh great" as she kept busy with her inspection. Jesus, she was a tiny woman who packed one hell of a little body. She was dressed in slacks and heels, and that's all I could see as she buried her head in the engine of her clown car.

"Give me your phone. Turn on the flashlight, please," she held out her hand, and I gave it to her as I studied her sweet ass bent over the hood.

"If you're going to just stand there and stare at my butt, you really aren't of use here."

"You called for help."

"I called Kristina for a ride and company while I waited on a tow."

"I'm of use," I said as I moved her seat back and sat in her tiny car. "My little nerd's car."

"I heard that."

"Good."

"Rafe...just go away." I looked around her cabin and picked up her phone. I turned up the volume and listened for a few moments to her John Hughes Flicks playlist.

"You really are stuck in the '80s."

"Indefinitely, now eff off before I bite your head off again."

"You have to mate with me first. Those are the rules, and it was a fight, Alice," I called out as traffic buzzed by.

"Rafe, I have a degree in aeronautics. I'll figure out what's wrong and fix it. You can go."

"Planes aren't cars, baby, and if that were the case, you would have it figured out by now."

"Don't call me, baby!"

I turned her key and grinned from ear to ear in silent knowledge and then made my way toward her, deciding it was too dangerous to continue to argue on the highway.

She pulled her tiny body from under the hood to peer up at me. Her beautiful, brown eyes trimmed in dark black lashes would be my undoing. Her golden, honey colored hair slipped from a loose bun, and she had a grease smear on her nose. No woman had ever looked so beautiful and so pissed off.

"Just what exactly are you so mad about?" I said as I took a step toward her.

"Which part?"

"This is a two-part fight?"

"Three," she barked back. "You suck at handling critique, you called me a...nerd *and* you said we were just f-f...screwing."

And then she *really* looked at me. "What's wrong?"

"Heavy day," I said. "And you aren't so innocent in this. You tore down my game. You don't do that to a man when his pants are down."

"I was wrong," she admitted openly. "I'm sorry. I need couth... tact when it comes to giving my opinion. It's a flaw of mine."

"You have no flaws, Alice," I said as I took another step forward and wiped the grease away from her nose with my thumb. "And you're right, we aren't just fucking. This thing between us is more than that. And, Alice, let's go ahead and put it out there. You *are* a nerd, but I love that about you. Can we do this somewhere else? Like maybe a place where cars aren't whizzing by us at eighty miles per hour?"

She barely hid her smile and huffed as she looked at her engine. "I don't know what's wrong."

"You're out of gas."

Her perfectly plump lips twisted. "What?"

"Sometimes the solution is the most obvious."

"Oh God," she sighed as she tried to walk around me, but I pulled her through my arm and away from traffic as she took a seat in her car and saw the evidence for herself.

"I'm out of gas! Jesus, what is *wrong* with me?"

I chuckled as I shut her hood and reached in and pulled the key and Alice from the car and loaded them into my Jeep.

"We'll gas her up, get her to your place, order Chinese food, and watch The Karate Kid."

Alice smiled with tears in her eyes as she turned to me. "I hate my job."

"I know, and I'm sorry."

"I don't know what to do. I have a new class. They're even worse than the last."

"So your day was heavy, too?"

"The heaviest," she said as I laced our fingers together and kissed the back of her hand. "I've got you."

    She turned to me with the same confidence. "I've got you, too."

13
Alice

"Lift your right hand."
I rolled my eyes, and Rafe pinched my sides.
"Do it."
I raised my hand as I straddled him, naked.
"I, Alice Boyd."
"I, Alice Boyd."
"Do solemnly swear."
"Do solemnly swear," I said in a dull monotone.
"To praise the penis of Rafe Hembrey."
"To prrraise," I burst out laughing as Rafe licked his thumb and stroked my exposed nipple, eliciting a moan from me. He raised his brow as I sucked in air. "To praise the penis of Rafe Hembrey."
"Keep your hand up, baby."
"It's up," I said as I looked down at my golden man with golden skin and rich dark hair and eyes. It was by far the best night of my

life.

"I promise to love, honor, and cherish his penis and only his penis."

"Are you serious right now?"

"You called my penis Jake Ryan."

"It's the highest of compliments, I swear."

"Say it!"

"I promise to love, honor, and cherish Rafe's penis and only his penis."

"I will not under any circumstances title it without written consent from Rafe Hembrey."

"I will not, this is ridiculous—Rafe!" I shrieked as he pinched my nipple. "I will not under any circumstances title it without written consent from Rafe Hembrey."

"I will pleasure it fully and often."

I smacked his chest as he looked up at me, a change in his tone, and a hopeful lift in his voice. "Say it, beautiful."

"I will pleasure it fully and often."

I waited for more, my hand held high.

"Rafe, what's the end?"

"No end," he said softly, "no end, Alice," before he brought my mouth down to his.

In the dark, with only whispers between us and little else, I kissed Rafe's chest and folded my hands over it.

"Tell me about your family."

"Nothing to tell," he said quickly.

"Your dad?"

"Estranged," he answered. I could feel his discomfort.

"Why?"

"Some other time, okay?" I nodded into his chest.

"Your sister?"

"Harmony was ten years older than me and married right out of high school, so I don't really know her that well. She moved to Utah with her husband years ago. We don't speak often."

"And your mother?"

"We're cool."

"Rafe..."

"She'll be at a game sometime. I'll introduce you." I frowned though he couldn't see it.

Rafe ran his fingers through my hair with his question. "What about your dad?"

"He left me a stack of movies when I was five, and that's all I know about him. He didn't actually *leave* them for me. I took them and hid them from my mother before she had a chance to throw them out."

Rafe nodded and gripped me tighter to him. "He called me mimic because I looked just like him. I remember a day at the zoo, that's about it. His loss. I don't lose sleep over it."

Rafe pushed my hair away from my face and leaned in with a whisper. "Definitely his loss."

14
Alice

"Baseball is a mental sport," Dutch explained as I looked over at Rafe, who was pitching a home game. "The reason players don't get drafted out of high school is because they need the time to develop the mental skills, the decisiveness. On average, each player needs to get their reaction time as quick as two seconds." Rafe looked behind him as his opponent attempted to inch his way to second base. He threw a warning shot to the first baseman and nearly took him out.

"I'd say ninety percent mental and ten percent skill. Rafe was born to pitch, but his reaction time has to be as sharp as his arm." Just as Dutch finished her sentence, the umpire let out a "Striiike."

A voice sounded as new arrivals sat down behind us. "You don't even like baseball."

"Give it a chance, Hil. Drink your beer."

"Fine, but we came here for a second honeymoon. This is *soooo* not a honeymoon. We could have brought Mallory along to this, and I wanted all activities on this trip to be *very* un-kid friendly."

I looked over to Dutch who grinned back at me. The woman was hilarious. I glanced back at her with sympathetic eyes and saw she was a beautiful redhead and her husband was nothing short of a stunner with paralyzing, deep blue eyes and colorful tattoos that covered his arm. He wasn't aware of my eyes on him as he turned to his wife with a grin.

"Are you saying you want to sex me?"

"Jayden!" She hushed him as if *he* was the one being inappropriate. He toyed with her and projected his voice much louder as he went on. "Because, Fishnipple, if you want my body, all you have to do is say so!"

I burst out in laughter as I had no choice at his pet name for her. Even Dutch was having a hard time keeping her composure.

"I'm sorry," the woman said as she looked down to me, horrified. "He kind of has no filter."

"I'm not the one throwing a fit that we aren't getting it on in a hotel room," he defended with a sly grin as she slugged him on the shoulder and he gave me a wink.

"I kind of have that same no filter problem," I said with a grin. "Where are you two from?" I questioned as Rafe whipped out another strike to end the inning and the Hornets took the field.

"Just a few hours upstate. Spartanburg," she answered. "I'm Hilary Monroe."

"She prefers Fishnipple," blue eyes muttered.

She turned and gave her husband the evil eye. "And this hot mess is my husband, Jayden."

"Nice to meet you. I'm Alice, and this lady here is Dutch." Dutch grunted nicely in greeting and barely gave them her attention.

Three innings later, Hilary had spilled and inhaled enough beer for the four of us. I'd had to clench my thighs together more than once as Jayden and Hilary went back and forth. Hilary, clearly drunk, looked at her husband with loving eyes.

"I would go to allllll the baseball games with you."

He grinned at her and sighed. "I better get you back to the hotel."

Hilary looked around her, glossy-eyed, but still present. "The game isn't over."

"There are three pounds of crab legs, two bottles of champagne, and chocolate croissants waiting in our suite."

My heart clenched as I watched Hilary's face contort as if she were going to cry, and then she flung herself in his lap and began to kiss him sporadically all over his face.

"Yep, you're completely drunk." He shook his head as he stood and put his wife over his shoulder. She laughed hysterically as she slapped his butt.

"Wait!"

Jayden paused. "Yes, Mrs. Monroe?"

"Turn around." Jayden did as asked as Hilary's long hair hit the top of his thighs and she smiled at me, her face reddening with the blood rushing to it. "Alice, it was so nice to meet you!"

"Same here. Bye, you guys." I laughed as I watched Jayden climb the stadium steps easily with Hilary in tow and stared after them until they were out of sight.

I want that.

I looked back over to Rafe in the dugout and caught him eyeing me. And for a brief moment, I convinced myself I may already have it.

"Alice, we have to go."

"I'm almost ready!"

I sat on her couch and screwed with my watch as I looked around her condo. She had no pictures of family hung up, none of friends, either. She'd told me enough about her life back in Ohio, but a large part of me wanted different for her. I scanned an old year book underneath the coffee table and didn't see one signature. It cracked my chest a bit to see she'd been so fucking alone. Didn't anyone see her? How could the world have ignored a woman so funny, so full of life, so completely beautiful?

"Okay, let's go," she pushed out nervously as she rounded the couch and stood in front of me. The crack in my chest expanded to the point I couldn't breathe. Alice stood in a long, black cocktail dress that tied around her neck and accentuated every curve of her body. Her perfect tits pressed into the top just enough to make my dick twitch. As my eyes rose to her red painted lips, I damned near came. Her lashes were painted a thick black and her eyes looked deadly sexy.

"You're fucking beautiful," I whispered as I walked over to her and gripped her delicate neck. I wanted all of it gone, the dress on the floor, the lipstick stain on my cock, her neatly pinned up hair a sweaty fucking mess. I moved to untie her dress and heard her protest.

"Rafe, no!"

"I was kidding," I lied.

"No, you weren't and we don't have time," she said as I kissed the sweet spot between her shoulder and her neck. "So you're telling me," I pushed out as my dick grew unbearably hard, "no?" I used one finger and slid it from her neck over her tight nipple and past her waist as I nipped at the soft skin below her ear. I began to lift her skirt as her chest rose and fell and her neck tilted slightly.

"Yes, I'm saying no." She reared back from my lips, her mouth still close to mine, her red lips my undoing. I knelt down before her and lifted her skirt to her waist and pulled her panties down to her thighs. I smirked when she unknowingly gripped her dress and held it up to help me out. I slid my finger between her thighs and found her wet. She looked down at me with lips parted as I brushed her clit over and over in beckoning.

"Rafe," she hissed as she closed her eyes and opened them to watch me, fascinated.

With one hand, I spread her and leaned in to slowly lick her.

"Oh my God," she whispered as her legs began to shake.

"Still a no?"

"No."

"Okay," I said as I backed away and she gripped my hair tightly and brought me back to her soaked center. "No, not no. Yes!" I dove in, tongue and fingers, until she could no longer handle it and her legs gave out. Quick to react, I gently placed her on the floor and resumed my lapping. Her taste, her moans, her pleas all fueled me to keep going, so I did. I licked her a thousand times, and if she wouldn't have come, I would have stayed buried and tasted her a thousand more. I made my way up her body as she lay defeated beneath me, a thin sheen of sweat on her forehead.

"I'm a mess now. Thanks a lot." I went in to kiss the ruby red lips that started it.

"Don't you dare, Rafe!"

"Didn't I just teach you *not* to say no to me?"

"No."

Not the answer I wanted so I kissed her until I got it.

Forty-five minutes later, I grabbed a glass of champagne for each of us as I made my way to our table. I always got invited to different events around the city and had always turned them down. Alice had seen the invitation on my counter to this one in particular and asked me about it. When I saw the hope in her face, there was no fucking way I could say no. Alice did that to me. Whatever got her excited, whatever made her happy, became my next move. I was in unchartered territory and it was through sheer fascination of her.

The woman was a tumbleweed when it came to her next move.

I'd caught sight of a ukulele in her bedroom last week and had a horrible time not breaking down hysterically as she awkwardly strummed it while I showered. She was doing everything in firsts and seemed to have no limits. If she was curious about it, she wanted to experience it, and I found myself jealous of all the time I had to spend away from her. My last two-week stint away, she'd reported that she went on a nine-hour road trip alone to D.C. just to see the cherry trees blossom. I would have been uneasy if I hadn't gotten a dozen photos every three minutes with a "Did you know!" text. Half of them I'd saved to my phone and studied over and over until I could make it home.

Jesus, I was in deep.

She'd already planned a deep-sea fishing excursion while I was at my next series of away games. The thing was, I wanted to do these things with her, and she seemed unaffected to go alone. I wanted to protect her, from whatever, and she seemed to not want or need any protection for herself. I set down the glass of champagne in front of her as she chatted with Andy at our table.

"Doll, you look beautiful," he said to her with a wink.

"Thank you," she said with a slight blush. "And you," she said as she looked up to me with a grin and grabbed her champagne. "I'm off to the ladies' room."

"Don't get lost."

I meant that *seriously*.

I looked over to Andy as he scanned the crowd and then looked back at me.

Our relationship remained changed despite our tussle in the dugout, and I'd been using Alice as a buffer. If I went to his bar, Alice was with me. I tried to do it on the nights Kristina didn't work, but Alice had insisted we go a couple of times to keep her company. It was starting to wear on me and so was Andy's indifference. I felt the anger start to build as he sat without a word. Fed up and ready to wash my hands, but knowing it would hurt Alice to leave, I spoke up, anyway.

"Fuck you," I said under my breath. Andy's eyes shot to mine.

"Seriously, fuck you." I stood to meet Alice when Andy gripped my arm.

"Chill out, man. I was just about to eat shit and apologize."

I pulled my arm away and gripped his shoulder. "You keep eating that shit."

"Alice has been talking about this all week," he warned.

"I don't know why I haven't told her...this bullshit is between you and Kristina. I was better off not knowing."

"I can say it in Spanish if you didn't get it the first time. I'm fucking sorry," Andy pushed out. "Sit down, cabron."

"He just called you an ass," Alice pointed out to me as she sat next to Andy with a wide smile.

"And what do you think of me?" I asked seriously but with a playful wink.

"Honestly?"

Shit.

"Is there *any* other way with you?" I asked sarcastically. She laughed. I studied her neck and the whisper of blonde hair around her shoulders. Andy leaned in, enthralled, and I was sure he was waiting for a punchline only Alice could deliver. I braced myself. She studied me closely, and I began to regret my question.

"I think you're the most beautiful man on the planet. I think you're a superior athlete. I think you play dumb a lot to keep from having to explain yourself. I think you're passionate and considerate. I think you're an amazing lover. I think you're all heart on the ballfield and have a guarded heart off it." I swallowed hard as I realized the whole table was listening. She looked around and noticed as well, and I felt her slip in her resolve only slightly as she downed the rest of her glass and looked dead at me. "I think you're incredible, Rafe Hembrey." She continued to stare at me for a reaction as I sat completely...fucking...stunned.

"Excuse me. I think I'll go get another champagne." She moved to get up as Andy and the rest of the men at the table followed suit. I fumbled to keep up as Alice turned back to look at me with a smirk and eye roll. "But, you are no gentlemen."

My chest expanded in that moment, and was full of her—full of Alice.

"If you *aren't* in love with her," Andy said in a whisper as we resumed our seats and we both watched her walk back to the bar, "you're a fucking idiot."

Oh God, what did I just do?

There should be some sort of electric muzzle or shock system available for women who have no filter. I'd just practically told Rafe and a table full of men that I was in love and damned close to worshipping him.

And it wasn't far from the truth.

No matter how much I wanted to be that cool, calm, and collected woman at times, I just couldn't swing it. At the bar, I ordered champagne. I stood with my glass and stalled for time. Maybe he'd already forgotten about it, or maybe he wouldn't even care.

"Want to dance?" a tall man in a tuxedo jacket with a red tie asked. It only took a moment for me to see it was Rodriguez, Rafe and Andy's teammate. I was relieved at the invitation. Any time I spent away from that table was a blessing.

"Yes, thank you," I agreed as I took his hand. Rodriguez had the perfect athletic build and moved gracefully across the floor. I followed pretty awkwardly, but he was patient. Canopy lights graced the high ceilings of the hotel ballroom, and aside from the candlelit dinner tables, the room was littered with red and yellow balloons. The fundraiser was put on to raise money for the little leaguers of Charleston to upgrade the current sports complex. It seemed the whole team had been invited and quite a few had shown up. I was so busy studying the room around me that when Rodriquez spoke up, I almost jumped.

"What were you doing alone at the bar?"

"Just getting some champagne," I answered absently. When the crowd parted slightly, I looked toward our table and caught a glimpse of Rafe. His eyes were cold, deadly, and his fists were clenched on the table. Andy was rapidly speaking to him in his ear.

"I...better get back to my date."

"Let Rafe sweat. He deserves it, I promise." I looked up to see a genuine smile on his face. "And why is that...?"

"Benley," he answered.

"And why is that, Benley?"

"Well, I was going to get married, but now I'm not."

I looked back at Rafe, confused, and then at Benley. He seemed nice enough. I didn't get that vindictive vibe from him at all, yet I knew something was up. Rafe stood suddenly as Andy gripped his arm, still speaking to him urgently.

"I don't understand. Why would...oh."

"Yeah," he whispered as he looked down at me. "She wasn't as innocent as I thought. But you seem...different."

Suddenly, I knew the reason Rafe treated Rodriguez like a disease. It wasn't poor sportsmanship. It was utter human stupidity.

"I am different," I snapped as I studied Rodriguez closely. "You want to ruin his night, possibly his relationship. I'm not an idiot. This isn't my battle."

Rodriguez gripped my hand and kissed it as Rafe approached. "You deserve to know what type of man he is," he said, and for the first time, his accent came through. He stared down at me, thick black hair, dark eyes, and began to move again.

"What he did, is not who he *is*," I whispered to an unaffected Benley. "Just like what you're trying to do *now* probably isn't you." I looked over to Rafe as he closed in, blinding fury written all over his face. "I think you've made your point."

I pulled away from Benley and stopped Rafe only a foot away.

"Dance with me," I implored as Rafe stared past me at Rodriguez with murder in his eyes.

"Rafe," I said with my hand on his chest. His face remained stone as I pulled his arm around my waist and clasped our hands.

"Rafe," I begged in a low whisper. He finally looked down at me with the same hatred in his eyes as he began to move and gripped my hand tightly.

I felt him began to relax as he broke eye contact with me and started to roam the room with his stare.

"You're dancing with me. The least you could do is look at me," I scolded as his posture remained tight.

Still furious, he glared at me and I let out a deep breath. "Fine, we won't dance." I let go of his hand as he pulled me tighter to him and regripped my fingers.

"Let it go, Rafe," I muttered as my whole body tensed at his grip on me.

"What the fuck did you think you were doing, Alice?"

I slowed my feet, stunned. "What?"

"You knew I didn't like that son of a bitch so you were...what... trying to play matchmaker? Kiss and make up?"

"No, I—" My face went up in flames as my anger grew. "He asked me to dance, I said yes. I didn't know you didn't like him. Well, I did to a degree, but I didn't know why."

He lifted a brow, his jaw set as he looked over me. "I saw the look you gave me when he told you. I saw that fucking look."

"So, I looked at you?" I asked, baffled. "You screwed a man's fiancée and *I'm* the bad guy?"

Rafe gripped my hand and led me off the dance floor. Andy was waiting with my purse.

"Take her home," he hissed and Andy nodded.

"What?" I asked, confused. "No," I protested as Rafe began to walk out of the ballroom. Andy followed close on my heels as I went after him. I caught up with him in the parking lot.

"The hell he will, Rafe. You brought me. You're taking me home!"

Rafe stopped in his tracks, his keys in his hand as Andy spoke up. "Alice, doll, listen to me. It's no problem." I glared at Andy and turned my attention back to Rafe. I circled his stiff body and faced him head on.

"Alice," Rafe insisted, "just let Andy take you home."

"No."

"Fine, get in," he said, pushing past me and opening the door.

"Night, Andy," I whispered with irritation as I climbed in.

"Rafe," Andy said slowly with a warning in his voice.

"Fuck this," he said as he climbed in and ripped off his tie.

Minutes later, the wind whipping through the Jeep, I kept my eyes on him, undeterred. He was furious. In our time together, I'd never seen anything close to this kind of anger.

"This is your baggage, Rafe, and I haven't even said a word about it. You're so pissed off and blind right now you can't even see it."

He laughed at me in mock. "So tell me what you think of *me* now."

"The same darned thing I thought of you an hour ago. *And* I think you're a total jerk for what you did then and how you're acting right now!"

Rafe turned into my complex at warp speed. "Don't endanger my life because you're an idiot!" I screamed as the Jeep skidded to a stop.

"I see it now. You aren't a poor sport; you're a total, volcanic moron! Cabron!" I hissed as I exited the Jeep a good half a mile from my condo. There was no way I was hanging around to watch him implode.

I heard a curse then a mutter as the Jeep sped up beside me. "He had his fucking hands all over you!"

"Over exaggeration," I yelled back as he slowly rolled next to me in his Jeep.

"You were fucking judging me!"

"I was effin' dancing with your teammate! And what you did to him was horrible, really horrible!"

"I didn't know she was his!"

"Doesn't help your cause, Rafe," I said as I stopped to look at him. "Did she have a ring on her finger?" His silence was deafening. "You're guilty."

"And who the hell are you to judge?"

"Oh, please, you're pissed because I'm right."

Rafe cursed, put the Jeep in gear, and made a sudden turn to leave on the narrow drive. I continued to walk as close to the sparse streetlamps that echoed between the palm trees. It was a warm night and I was already sweating. I heard the Jeep brake again as Rafe backed up next to me and kept it in reverse.

I walked on as I tried to ignore him, but the whole thing was suddenly becoming more comical. I heard Rafe grumble next to me as he followed me down the narrow path to my complex in reverse. I bit my lip to keep from laughing.

"I let him beat the shit out of me in Savannah."

"Good!"

"I thought you might say that." I glanced over at him and he was grinning from ear to ear. I clamped my mouth closed as I stared ahead. "I haven't been that pissed in a long time, Alice."

"Well, good for you, a breakthrough. The Neanderthals will be pleased to have their leader back."

I heard his chuckle as he continued to slowly drive next to me. I could physically feel the tension start to leave us. A car moved past him narrowly and slowed to look at us. I was sure we were a spectacle.

"Get in the Jeep, baby, and let me tell you I'm sorry."

"No."

"Alice, please."

"No," I huffed at the mid-mark, determined to make it back to my condo on heels that would scar me.

"Alice...Goddamn it!" The Jeep came to a sharp stop, and seconds later, Rafe was in front of me. I had no choice but to stop and look up at him. His lips were quirked as his green-brown eyes sparkled down at me. He was amused. I was not. Well, I was, but I wasn't about to reveal it.

"I have a shitty temper sometimes. It's not something I'm proud of. I swear to God, when I saw that man touch you, I wanted to end his life."

"Probably how he feels every time he's forced to look at you."

Rafe let out a breath. "I've dealt with the guilt over that. Alice, if you think I haven't, you're wrong."

"I'm not asking you to pay for your mistakes or even regret *anything*. That situation has nothing to do with me."

"So you don't care?"

"Do you want me to? Do you want me to hold it against you?"

"The look you gave me," he whispered as I stood my ground.

"Was disappointment," I said honestly. "I wasn't going to give him the satisfaction of causing a rift between us. You did that all on your own."

Rafe peered down at me with a look I'd never seen. It was somewhere between confusion and admiration.

"You're a baseball player, Rafe. I *have* to be able to trust you. You have groupies in every city and will be gone more than you'll be here. It's part of being a ballplayer's girl. Combine that with the fact that you are so damned good looking...If I can't believe the person you say you are standing in front of me, I'd lose my mind wondering."

I stood, covered in light sweat, my feet aching as I watched him closely.

"Ballplayer's girl?" He quirked a brow as a slow smile spread on his face.

"I'm going to bed," I muttered as I tried to walk around him.

He swept me into his arms with a quick "Don't you dare throat punch me" and slowly walked to his Jeep. He placed me sideways in the seat and stood between my legs, my dress hiked up to my thighs. I sat silently as his eyes and body language implored me to look at him. I finally lifted my head with a sigh.

"I'm sorry."

"I'm not," I said, still holding a grudge.

"I'm an asshole. I ruined your night."

"You totally did."

"Wow, you really are hell to please."

"I don't want to have bad days, Rafe." I saw his expression soften as he cupped my face.

"Baby, I'm sorry."

I nodded. "Okay," I said as he stroked my chin.

"Here's the thing. I will never be able to handle another man touching you, ever."

"But the truth is, that's up to me, isn't it? Just like it's up to you to make sure that doesn't happen. We can't try to control each other. I'm no expert, but I'm pretty sure that won't work."

I peeled off my jacket as Alice showered off our shitty night—a night I'd ruined by acting like a jealous thug. Andy had stepped up to the plate the minute he saw my temper flare and kept me grounded. I hadn't realized I was capable of the same type of anger anymore until I saw him put his hands on her. Possessiveness of the most lethal kind had raced through my every pore. I was too afraid of my reaction, and even when I'd managed to calm down, it was still severe.

For the second time in my life, I was scared I didn't have a handle on my head or my heart. I wanted her in a way I never thought possible. I was falling hard, and though I'd asked for it, I never expected what I got, and it was a helluva lot more.

The idea that I could get the call to the big club and soon be forced to leave her struck next, and I braced myself on the counter.

I was already jealous of my time away from her, already desperate for her touch, her voice, her whisper, her every day.

Alice deserved so much fucking better than what I'd put her through tonight.

I grabbed a bottle of water from her fridge and spotted a card on her counter. The outside was glittered with a blue and white Happy Birthday, and the inside simply read: From all of us in your Boeing family.

FUCK.

I sat in the stands and couldn't shake the smile on my face as I watched Rafe coach. Kristina sat beside me as Rafe knelt down to talk to Dillon, who was up to bat. Kristina's son looked adorable in his little league outfit, armed with a mini slugger, and eager as Rafe whispered to him.

"He's so good with them, *all of them*," she said as she looked over at me. "Every year, without fail, he shows up to teach these kids everything he knows. It's kinda hard not to fall for him a little."

I nodded, my eyes trained on the exchange between a little boy and his coach.

"I think I'm moving to Atlanta," Kristina said as she watched. "Dillon's father's parents live there, and they've offered to help me get settled. They've been begging for years for me to bring him, and I need a change."

My heart cracked at her announcement. "You really want that?"

"Yes, I think I need to try somewhere new. I can go back to school while they watch him. I couldn't afford to do both here."

"Kristina, I could help."

She flung her hand dismissively. "I love you, babe, but you have your own man to concentrate on. It's not that far, and I'm not sure if it's happening, but I'm thinking about it."

"Crap," I whispered as I turned to her. "I'll hate it here without you."

"I'm just thinking for now. Besides, aren't you happy here?"

"Sure." I looked over at Rafe as he encouraged the tiny players. I'd never felt so amazing, so completely powerful, yet helpless at the same time. In the past few weeks, I'd felt Rafe's distance. We'd spoken less every day he was on the road. My texts went unanswered more than once. When he'd arrived home last night, he'd been more than quiet. He'd been withdrawn and refused to admit it.

"You're falling for him," Kristina noted as I turned to her with a nod.

"It's obvious?" I asked as I slid my sunglasses over my eyes. Right at that moment, Rafe looked my way and gave me a small smile, which I returned.

Kristina nudged my arm. "He's just as obvious."

"I don't think that's what that is, Kristina."

She looked over at me with worry etched on her face. "What's wrong?"

"I don't know yet."

Rafe gently pitched the ball a few times as Dillon swung away. Kristina and I hollered out words of encouragement. Dillon's bat connected and the ball flew centerfield. Stunned, he turned and looked directly at his mother with a glowing and unbelieving smile. Kristina stood and waved frantically. "Run, buddy!" Rafe watched the ball go midfield then began to wind his arm, encouraging him to run. Dillon darted from one base to the next then slid into home plate. Rafe was already there to pick him up and pat him on the back.

"Wow," I said as I watched their exchange then turned to Kristina.

She wiped a tear from her eye and looked over at me with light laughter. "PMS," she said in excuse.

As the game ended, Dillon ran up to us, and Rafe followed closely but kept his distance…from me.

"You did good today, buddy," he called after Dillon, who took his Gatorade and drank it down with greed.

I took a step toward Rafe and felt him tense, so I remained planted. Kristina hovered over Dillon, and for a moment, the space between the three of us felt uncomfortable. I'd agreed to be Rafe's only a short time ago, and he had kissed me in public quite passionately, but in that moment, I felt hurt and rejection I'd never experienced, and it scared the hell out of me.

Silence lingered as Rafe waved a quick goodbye to the rest of the little people and their parents.

"Come on, buddy," Kristina said to Dillon, who looked at Rafe with stars in his eyes. "Let's go get some lunch and ice cream." Kristina turned to me. "Girls' night soon?"

I nodded with my eyes on Rafe, who seemed to be absorbed in his thoughts.

As soon as Kristina was out of earshot, I took a step forward. "What am I missing?"

Rafe shrugged as he began to gather the bats. "Nothing."

"Okay," I said as I picked one up and handed it to him. He took it with a small "Thank you."

"I'm leaving," I said as Rafe snapped his eyes to mine. "I'm just going to go"—I swallowed hard— "visit my mom."

His lack of protest told me so much more than his distance. We hadn't seen each other in weeks. I braced myself as I spoke to him again. "You should know you're a really special man. You have a lot of patience with those kids. I can tell they adore you."

Rafe dropped the bats and cursed as he looked over at me. "Why do you have to be so goddamned perfect?"

"I'm just being honest," I said defensively. "I can see you aren't in the mood for it."

"Baby, no," he said as I crossed my arms in front of me and stared at his cleats.

"What's happening between us Rafe?"

"What?" he snapped.

"What are we doing? Are we in a relationship that's now boring you?"

"Damn it, Alice," he said as he took a step toward me, closing the distance. "No."

"No, we're not in a relationship or no I'm not boring you?" I felt my heart rip as he watched the cars leave behind us.

"We have to talk about this right now?" He was feet away but so distant I didn't recognize him. "I have a lot going on."

"So do I," I said as I commanded his eyes to mine.

His continued silence was too much to handle. I pulled my keys from my pocket and kissed him on the cheek. "I'll let you know when I get back."

Rafe nodded, and I didn't bother to wait on anything else.

FUCK. FUCK. FUCK.

I watched her tiny frame disappear into her car then gathered the bats and helmets to load them in my Jeep. I felt my pocket buzz and saw the call was from Andy. I ignored it. His issue was becoming mine, and instead of letting Alice kiss me, I'd cowered away to keep from hurting Kristina but hurt Alice instead. I'd have been so much better off not knowing her feelings for me. I should've just come clean and told Alice the truth, but her budding friendship with Kristina was important to her. Alice had told me as much. She said she'd never really had a close girlfriend, and I didn't want to take that away from her. Kristina was not a spiteful person. She was, in fact, the stuff that a good and loyal friend was made of, like Andy.

I didn't want to hurt either of them. Kristina, along with Andy, had been my two closest friends for years.

This whole situation was fucked. And to top it off, I'd been pushing Alice away little by little to try to stifle my need for her, and it was only fucking with me that much harder. July was coming, and if I got the call, I'd be forced to leave her, and not for just a two-week stint. As much as I hated to admit it, Andy was right; it was the worst time ever to start a relationship.

I ripped through the waves for the rest of the day, taking out my frustration on the ocean. A plane flew by in the distance, and I briefly wondered if Alice would stick around much longer due to her job being a total disaster. We already had the space lingering between us for me to make a clean break. The road was hard, but if I got called off to the majors, I'd all but vanish from her. She sensed the space but didn't have an explanation, which she deserved.

It was so much easier when I was a bit more selfish, when pussy was playtime and ball was business. The lines were clear. I'd initiated the relationship with Alice. I'd purposefully placed myself as the man in her life. I could never get *bored*. I could never, ever get enough of her, and I owed it to her to tell her as much.

I crested the wave and landed in the salty cool water. I wondered what she saw in me for a moment. I loved the way I looked reflected in her eyes. Whatever she saw in me, I wanted to be that man.

I could try to convince myself all I wanted to, that our relationship was fun, an escape, a way of passing time until the moment I'd been waiting for since I turned eighteen arrived, but it was pointless.

I was in love with her.

If mood was a color, today I was gray. My mood coordinated with the old room I occupied in my house. My mother had called me for dinner ten minutes ago and I couldn't bring myself to go to her. As I lay in bed and mulled over my life in Charleston, I envied the women who could confide in their mothers. The women who could discuss anything with them. It would only help to deepen the relationship. As a daughter, I'd always felt judged by my actions.

Why couldn't I have that?

I briefly thought of calling Kristina to vent about Rafe and his sudden withdrawal and thought better of it. Speculating about it would get me nowhere. I closed my eyes and thought of his smile, his powerful kiss, and about the time we spent together. I'd finally found my Jake Ryan, and suddenly all that mattered was the distance he'd put between us. In the two days I'd been back in Ohio, he'd only texted me once to make sure I arrived home safely. My mind refused to shrug it off as anything but a dismissal.

I was only a few months into my first adult relationship, and I'd blown it somehow. A piercing pain spread through my chest as I thought about what I could have possibly done.

"Alice, I called for you," my mother scorned from my door.

"I'm not hungry, Mother. I'm sorry if you went to any trouble."

"Did you come here to mope? You haven't been pleasant a minute since you arrived."

I blew out a breath of frustration. "Yeah, I haven't," I said through gritted teeth. "How inconsiderate of me."

"What's with the tone?" she said, taking a commanding step into the room.

"Oh, I don't know, Mother. Maybe I hoped for a little different reception, myself," I snapped as I grabbed my suitcase and began packing. "Like, I don't know, Alice, you seem upset. What's wrong, honey? But I guess that's too much to ask."

"You don't speak to me like this," she warned.

"No, I don't out of respect. I respect you, but I can't honestly say at the point I know how to do much else."

"What in the world are you talking about?" she said as she adjusted a framed picture on the wall that could never have been crooked. My mother's ship was leak proof.

"You!" I confronted. "And the way you act as if we're in some partnership to get through our time together. As if I'm not your daughter but some sort of...obligation."

"Alice, what has gotten into you?"

"I'm in love with a man! That tends to drive *normal* women crazy."

My mother stood deathly still. "Your virtue—"

"Got taken away years ago, and don't play so innocent. I *found* your vibrator when I was sixteen." I lifted a brow. "Really went all out with those extra lithium batteries, didn't you?"

My mother's jaw dropped. Years of pent up frustration of a relationship we didn't have leaked out in anger as I stared at her.

"You're a woman whose husband left you. It happens to women daily. Please tell me why you decided to nun up and make my life miserable."

My mother took a step back as she shook from head to toe, her hand on her heart. For a brief moment, I knew I was going too far, but couldn't help my outburst.

"I chose to dedicate my life to God and live as sin free as possible. That happens every day, as well."

"By taking all of the fun out of your life *and* mine? And you aren't dedicated, you're hiding behind him. I'm pretty sure the God I pray to doesn't think smiles and good humor are an abomination.

I'm pretty sure he made the stars in the sky for you to admire, not hide your face behind a book—his book of rules."

"Alice!"

"It's been twenty-five years but allow me to introduce myself. I've never been the prim and proper, normal girl you've so desperately tried to turn me in to. Grade school really sucked for me, like it does most nerdy girls, and high school was equally a nightmare. I didn't change to please anyone *except you*." I shook my head as I confronted her. "Not that you would notice because you were too busy pointing out all the crap I wasn't doing. College sucked as well, Mom." My voice shook with defeat. "I felt guilty for every smile, every sinful thought, every chance I didn't have the courage to take. I was stunted because I let you cripple me into thinking I wouldn't be the woman you raised if I lived for even a second outside of character." I shrugged. "But that's just it. I was playing a role." I pushed the rest of my fear aside as I gave her the truth. "That girl doesn't exist. I'm loud, and opinionated to the point of being obnoxious. I take chances now and live like there's no tomorrow. I drink beer and sometimes" —I widened my eyes— "I overindulge. I go to the beach and watch baseball games. I laugh often, I joke, and I smile." I threw my clothes into my suitcase before I looked back at her to give her a sly grin. "And every chance I get; I praise Rafe Hembrey's penis!"

"ALICE BOYD!"

"I'm living!" I yelled as I snapped my suitcase shut. "And it's wonderful. You hide behind this demeanor of yours but you can't stand some of your friends. I can see it sometimes. And do you know why you can't stand them? It's because they're totally boring!"

"Maybe you *should* go. I did not raise you to speak to me or act like this."

"No, you raised me to believe that fun was a sin, and I'm calling bullshit!"

The air thick with tension, she watched me closely. I shrugged my shoulders and held her gaze. When silence lingered, I decided to make my exit. I wanted to be back in Charleston with my movies and my misery. At least life there had seemed promising at one point.

"Wait," she said under her breath as I passed her in the doorway. Ignoring her, I made my way toward the stairs. I was losing it.

"Alice, wait!"

I stepped into the foyer and shouldered my purse.

"You're right."

Those two words stopped me. "What?" I looked over to see her at the foot of the stairs.

"You're right. I was too strict. I've been dealing with that guilt for some time now, and I know that's why you don't visit often. I'm sorry, Alice."

"Not good enough," I huffed as I looked at her in accusation.

"You're all I have."

"That's not my fault. There's a whole world out there, Mother. Go enjoy it."

"It's too late," she said as she took a step forward, reaching out to touch the lining of my suitcase. "But I'm glad you've found your fun."

"I want to have fun *with you*, Mother. That's all I've ever wanted. It's not too late for you to do *anything*...everything."

"You're so full of life, like your father." I froze as she spoke of him.

"I don't want to know anything about him. I want to know you. His absence didn't bother me, but *yours* did."

I saw a tear fall down her face, followed by another as I went on. "I remember the way you smiled and laughed at him and that's all. I know he was the one who took it away when he left. I have no desire to know him. But that was twenty years ago. You have got to let go and try life again. And I can't be scared—"

Realization hit me like a ton of bricks. "Oh, crap." Right before Rafe had become distant, he'd seemed to want reassurance from me. He'd fought hard for my attention, for me, and I'd all but told him I didn't believe in his feelings for me with that statement about another man touching me. He wanted to know if it was safe to trust me, and I'd been ambiguous about the whole thing...because I was scared.

My mother cried silently as I put my suitcase down. We'd never really done the hug thing, and it was one of the reasons I was not good at the woman thing, but I pulled her to me, anyway. "I totally get it now. I'm in love with Rafe, and if he hurt me like Dad hurt you, I know it would change me. But enough is enough, Mom."

She held me to her as she cried.

"You can't possibly still be in love with him after all this time."

"Oh, that's where you're wrong."

"Really?"

"Yes." She pulled away, her brown eyes the color of mine. Her frailty in that moment silenced me. I'd never seen her so vulnerable.

"Well, it's time to get back on the horse," I ordered. "Now," I said as I pulled my suitcase back into the living room and unlocked it. I pulled a sundress out that would fit her perfectly and thrust it toward her. "Get dressed. We're going to do this together."

"You can't be serious."

"No one changes overnight, but one night can change *everything*. We're about twenty years overdue for a night of fun."

"Oookay," she said with a hopeful lift.

"And, Mom?"

"Yes," she said as she eyed the dress with a small amount of fear.

"No spandex."

"So you're in love?" she whispered as she eyed me, curious.

"Totally, and he's unworthy at the moment. One issue at a time, and tonight is about me and you."

Two hours later, the nerdy girl and her warden mother drank copious amounts of alcohol and danced like no one was watching. My mother looked like a beautiful corpse on the dance floor. She had years of pent up stiffness to work out, but she was trying, and together, we made total fools of ourselves as better equipped dancers circled the floor around us.

It didn't matter. My mother's smile and nervous laughter, which I'd finally learned came from her, made it all okay. And when she got too tipsy to drive, I called an Uber for us both. I sat in the backseat with my drunken mother, a virtual stranger, as she spoke to him.

"You're a nice looking man," she cooed as he looked back at her. He was, in fact, a very nice looking man with sandy brown hair and blue eyes. He looked a few years younger than her, but not by much. "My daughter says I need to get back on the horse. Are you a capable horse?"

I burst out laughing as he eyed her from the front seat and joined in with a chuckle. I looked over our driver and gave him a disapproving eye. "What are your credentials?"

"Abe, I'm forty-eight, divorced, and I just started Uber this week. You're my best fare yet."

My mother, who apparently had no filter after five glasses of wine, looked at him in the mirror. "Well, Abe, I'm Penelope and this is my daughter, Alice."

"Pleasure to meet you both," he said with humor.

"Mom, we need greasy food," I muttered, feeling uneasy from the alcohol. I'd gotten a little sauced up a few weeks ago with Kristina and had discovered a cheeseburger helped immensely.

"I know just the place," Abe said as he turned into a breakfast diner and parked the car. He turned in his seat and addressed my mother directly. "Allow me," he said as he opened her door and we both exited with giggles. I couldn't believe the difference in her, but I supposed somewhere deep she'd always wanted permission to feel again. I wasn't surprised when we ordered another Uber after dining a little loudly in the breakfast house, and Abe pulled up again to greet us minutes later. He'd been waiting. I was sure of it.

On the way home, I watched as Abe and my mother spoke, often crossing the same words or reactions to the conversation, and smiled as I looked down at my textless phone. Rafe and I didn't have that type of connection. We didn't finish each other's sentences, we simply accepted each other's differences, and the dynamic was just as powerful, maybe even more so. If he chose to throw us away, it wouldn't be because we didn't work. In truth, I didn't see anything else working better. I saw no one else but him.

No end, Alice. No end.

My heart was breaking with each minute that passed. I felt a hot tear trail down my cheek. If we were over, I would have the heart scar to prove it happened. Once upon a time, Alice Boyd had an intimate affair with the stuff dreams are made of. Though brief, it had been beautiful and real.

Alice: I am a nerd, Rafe. I totally am. XO

It was the best night of my life.

"Rafe," I heard whispered in a raspy voice as Melo-dee joined me at the bar, uninvited. Andy's bar was home to me in a way, and being amongst my teammates tonight had driven home the point even more so.

We'd completely shut out the Yellow Jackets, and in our victory, the team decided a perfect night ender would be a private party at the bar. Everyone was there, including Dutch, who eyed me with suspicion when I told her the vacancy next to her at the game had to do with Alice visiting her mother. I could see her disapproval and knew without a doubt she thought I was full of shit.

And in a way, I was.

"How's it going, Melo-dee?" I said without looking her way.

"It could be better," she chimed back without regard to my *fuck off* demeanor and uninterested tone. "Your place or mine?"

"You know I'm with Alice. You've seen me with her," I reminded, my voice full of disdain.

"I don't see her here," she said as I turned on my stool to finally look at her. Melo-dee was beautiful with long dark hair and dark blue eyes. Her curvy body was bursting out of her short, red dress and begged for any sort of attention it could get. I had no right to judge her, not in the least, but suddenly she repulsed me.

"I'm not the type," I said as I picked up my beer.

"Since when?"

"Since I met my game-changer," I said without apology.

"Well," she said with a fake pout as she eyed Waters over my shoulder. "If you change your mind, you know how to find me."

"Of course I do," I said as I looked over to Waters, who was already eye fucking her. "Double the latex," I muttered under my breath. I was just about to call Alice when I saw Andy and Kristina arguing in the hall behind the bar. Kristina was crying as Andy shook his head and gripped her shoulders. I stood and made my way toward them when I heard his voice.

"Son."

Oh, fuck no.

I turned to look at my father, who seemed to have aged far more than the years since I'd seen him.

"Who let you in?"

"Doesn't matter. I called, you refused to answer, so I came."

He was dressed in a Swampgators t-shirt, and I could only assume he'd attended the game. His next words confirmed it.

"You're a star. I mean, I always knew you would be, but your pitching now...I'm proud of you."

I barked out an incredulous laugh. "You could've saved your breath for that."

"Give me a fucking chance to talk," he said roughly, a tone I'd become used to over the years. It had zero effect on me as I studied him. It dawned on me then.

"You were an asshole father."

"I deserve that," he said as he looked over at the team. "This is your year."

"So everyone says."

"Mark my words."

"Your words are meaningless. I don't want you here."

"I don't want to be here," he said as he looked at me with dead eyes. "I won't beg you anymore to forgive me for something I thought was right for the family. When you have your own one day, you'll understand."

"There's the door, asshole," I said through gritted teeth.

"I see it. I'm getting remarried. My fiancée wanted me to try to make amends. Her son is a huge fan of yours and wants to meet you."

"Does Mom know?" Fear crept through me as I thought of the state of my mother if she found out the news.

"Not yet."

"Don't tell her. I'm asking you to make this private. Don't do this to her."

"I'm not doing anything to *her*. I'm moving on with my life. She made *her* decision."

"Unfuckinbelievable," I hissed as we stood facing each other.

Andy was by my side seconds later as he addressed my father. "Martin, I think you should leave."

"I'm talking to my son."

"All due respect, sir, this is my fucking bar."

"I've got this, Andy," I said as I looked over to him. "I've got it, man." Andy gave me a simple nod and gave us our space.

"Let's end this here," I said casually. "I don't want a damn thing to do with you or your new family. I hope for that kid's sake you learned from your mistakes, but I won't be around to find out. I want nothing to do with you. I've made that clear. The next time I see you, it better be in accidental passing."

"You can throw us away like that?" There was only a hint of

hurt in his voice.

"No, you can and you did. We're done. There's no going back. My mind won't change."

"Then that's that," my father said gruffly as he looked at me again. "Goodbye, son."

"You sold your son for one hundred thousand dollars," I reminded.

"If it makes any difference, it wasn't worth it." It was the rawest and sincerest apology I would get.

"It doesn't."

I motioned toward the door, thinking of my mother's face the minute she found out about his new wife. It was the only thought that gutted me as I watched him disappear. I turned back to the bar to see business as usual. Melo-dee was in Waters' lap in a slow grind. Kristina, now free of tears, was passing out beers like the thirst quenching dealer she was, and Andy was the only one that looked on at me. I stuck my hand up to my forehead and saluted him in goodbye.

The only person in the world I wanted to see was somewhere in Ohio, and I'd done a bang up fucking job of making her believe I wasn't waiting on her when the truth was, I wouldn't be able to breathe right until she was back in my sight.

15
Alice

I pulled my suitcase behind me like the deadweight it was. I'd taken the first flight out and decided not to hide from my life, or the fact that I may very soon be alone again. Fatigue crept through every muscle in my body as I dreaded the idea of losing my heart and having it given back to me in different shape.

I pushed inside my door and unloaded my bag on the floor of my bedroom.

> **Rafe: Please text me when you get home.**
>
> **Alice: I'm home.**
>
> **Rafe: Fifteen minutes?**
>
> **Alice: Okay.**

I left my door unlocked as I put away the rest of my clothes then decided on a scalding shower. I wanted my movies and my bed. I wanted to escape the pain of his rejection a bit longer before I lived in it. I sighed as I lathered the trip home out of my hair and felt strong hands encase me seconds later. I let out a shriek of surprise and turned to Rafe, who was gloriously naked behind me. I studied him closely as he looked on at me with fearful eyes.

"I love you, Alice Boyd." Before I had a chance to react, his mouth was on mine, his arms locked around me as if I was the only thing he had in his life to hold onto. Completely at his mercy, there was only a flicker of time before he found me wet and ready and he thrust fully inside me. I locked my legs around him as he gave me his love, his heart, his need with each movement of his hips, with each groan in his throat.

"Rafe," I whispered as I burned out of control.

"Let me have this, Alice, please," he croaked as he remained inside me and turned off the shower.

He loves me.

I began to shake with hope as he brought us out of the shower and onto my bed. He hovered above as he looked down at me, my eyes shut tight as I felt all of him.

"Let me see them," he prompted gently as he thrust deep. I opened them as he looked down on me, his face breathtaking. "I love you."

He leaned in slowly and drew my lips into his mouth as I sighed out his name again and again. He made it last as we both gazed at each other, mouths parted. Hearts and body movements in sync, we were completely one as he whispered one last time, "I love you."

"You confuse the hell out of me," I said as Rafe pulled his pants on the next morning.

"I know. I won't do that again."

"What happened?"

"I had some stuff to figure out. I had some decisions to make, I guess."

"You had to decide if you loved me?" I asked with my pillow to my chest.

"That was never a decision," he said as he leaned over and placed a slow kiss on my lips. "When you throat punched me, I'm pretty sure I knew then."

"Come here, I'll do it again," I said playfully as I rose from the bed and stretched with a loud yawn. Rafe admired my naked body as I scurried off to the bathroom to find my toothbrush. "Where are you off to?" I piped with a mouth full of toothpaste.

"I've got a few things to do today before briefing, but I want to take you out tonight, okay? I'll explain everything."

"Maybe," I said as I poked my head out of the bathroom with a wink.

"You're a hard woman to please, Alice," he said as he pulled a t-shirt over his chiseled chest.

"Whatever, I'm so easy. All you did was wash my hair and I gave you the booty."

Rafe paused in the bathroom door. "This visual ought to keep me hard all day," he said with heat in his voice as I rinsed my mouth. He was behind me now, my bare butt pressed against his covered crotch.

I moved to kiss him goodbye and he stilled me. He gripped my hips and ground his hardness into me again.

"Let me see them," he urged as I looked back into the mirror and met his hot gaze. His hands wondered freely, covering my breasts, massaging my back. His fingers drifted to my entrance, and I could hear the breath leave him. I boldly kept my eyes on his as he slipped his fingers in and out of me. Our connection never breaking, Rafe unzipped his pants and thrust inside me hard.

"Every bit of this sweet pussy is mine, do you hear me? This body," he said as he ran his hands along my sides and underneath my breasts, "is mine. Say it!"

"It's yours," I rasped out as he drew back and buried himself where I ended. He moved his hand up to grip my neck and forced my head back. Shocked but electrified, I sucked in audibly as he squeezed slightly.

"The soreness you feel today is me. It's me, Alice, still inside of you, reminding you that you are mine."

"RAFE!" I shrieked as he took me roughly and completely. "Oh God," I mouthed as his pace picked up and my legs began to shake.

"It's time you knew," he said as he pressed my breasts flat on the counter and leaned over me so our bodies locked. "You were made for *me*. You fit *me* like a glove. I want you always to remember that." He leaned in and sucked on my shoulder as his hot gaze burned me. "I love you. I love your body. I love being inside this pussy. You. Are. Everything. My everything."

My orgasm crept up and I let out a long moan as he continued to screw me ruthlessly.

"When I fuck you hard like this, I still love you. Understand?"

I nodded as another fast orgasm hit me, and I damn near lost my mind.

"Say it, Alice."

"Fuck me, Rafe," I moaned and saw a slow, satisfied smile cover his face. He continued his assault, his thrusts punishing in the most delicious way. He stilled as we kept our eyes locked and he spent himself inside me and bit the tender flesh of my neck. Rafe grabbed a towel off of the rack and wiped off and then leaned in and kissed me like we would never see each other again. I was at a total loss for words when he pulled away.

We'd totally just had porno sex.

"See you later, baby. I'll let you decide if you want it soft or hard."

I stood there in shock as he smacked my butt, my lips swollen from his kiss. He winked at me. "Tonight."

Still in a stupor, but determined to have a lot more of what I'd just been given, it only took me seconds to throw on a long t-shirt. I raced after him through the living room and called after him as he passed through the door. "Hard! Rafe, I'll take it hard!

It's yours!" I called out to him as I grabbed the door just before it clicked and screamed out into the hall, "MY PUSSY IS YOURS!" I heard Rafe's laughter as he descended the stairs and passed my new neighbor, who had a leash in her hand and what looked like a mop with eyes that walked next to her. My eyes widened as she gave me a smirk and continued to her door. I shut mine, breathless as I ran my hands down my t-shirt with an embarrassed smile.

I walked into the classroom of pilots and was thrilled to see the new addition. It was a woman, mid-thirties, by the name of Edee. I'd originally overlooked her name and thought it Eddie and gave her a broad smile as I introduced myself. She gave me a confident wink with her greeting, and I couldn't have been more thrilled.

Feel that estrogen, boys?

Filled with a new confidence and excitement of my love's confession and possessive claim to my nether region, I got through class without so much as a defeated sigh. I'd called my mother on the way to work and was thrilled about her news of an upcoming date with Abe. The world seemed right again, but I guess that was love's illusion. Everything good was magnified by the feel of it. I made my way out the door of the plant to find Rafe standing next to my Prius. He was dressed to the nines in dark jeans, a black dress shirt, and shiny, black boots. His hair was void of a cap and neatly combed, and his hands held at least three dozen white roses. He wore his signature smirk, but his eyes searched mine for approval.

God, I loved him.

I walked over with a wide smile and inhaled the bouquet in his hands. "White?"

Rafe towered over me as I looked up at him quizzically.

"The florist told me white meant new beginnings." His eyes darted down to his feet briefly and then back to me. "I need the chance to make up your birthday to you."

"Rafe," I said with wide eyes, "it's not a big deal."

"It was. It *is*."

I gathered the roses in my arms and held them to me. "They're so beautiful."

"You're so beautiful," he said as he lifted both the roses and me inside his Jeep."

"Should we go to my place so I can change?" I had on slacks, heels, and a simple peasant blouse, and felt underdressed.

"You're perfect," he said as he cranked his Jeep and pulled the elastic out of my hair. I held my roses to me as I stared over at him.

"What has gotten into you, Rafe Hembrey?"

He looked at me seriously. "I'm happy. For the first time in a long time, I'm happy. You showed me what it looks like and then you became a reason." My heart pounded inside my chest at his declaration. I felt the same but was completely taken aback by this new side of him. He'd always been good to me, but it was a whole new level of intimacy. He put the Jeep into gear as we slipped through the crowded streets of downtown Charleston and ended up at a restaurant on the outskirts with an unparalleled view of the marsh. Seated outside with a breathtaking view, we dined and sipped wine as daylight dimmed and globe lights illuminated the dock around us. Rafe and I got into a deep conversation about our bucket list as I named off a few things I must do by age ninety-nine.

"Fly with a Blue Angel," I said with a sigh. "I had a chance once but was afraid I'd pee."

Rafe chuckled.

"I want to meet Nolan Ryan," he sounded off in thought. "That man is a truly decent human being and amazing pitcher. He's kind of my man crush."

"Oh?" I said with a smile. "Good to know. Find a four leaf clover."

"Go to Ireland for it?"

"Hell yes," I said with enthusiasm.

"You don't cuss much."

"I was raised not to. It kind of stuck with me."

"I like it."

"Yeah, well...you'll know when I'm serious. It's my verbal exclamation point. You don't get one because every other word you use is eff." I said as I sipped my wine and tossed my napkin on my plate. "That was delicious, thank you."

He gave me a smile and then sipped his beer and replied, "Welcome."

"Rafe," I asked as he looked over the marsh, "what would you do if you didn't play ball?"

He didn't miss a beat.

"Male escort."

I narrowed my eyes as he chuckled.

"I've never known life without it, so I don't think that way."

"What if you hadn't found it?"

"Male escort."

"That wasn't funny the first time," I scorned.

He set his beer down and wiped the sweat from his palms down his pants. "It's always been ball." He looked at me across the table, lost in thought. "When my dad bought me my first glove, I refused to take it off for a week." He chuckled. "I was three, and according to my mother, I bathed with it, ate, and slept with it. It's so much a part of me, Alice, there's never been an alternative future. I still have that glove."

"What will you do when it ends?"

"There's no end, Alice."

I looked at him pointedly. "That's not very realistic."

He gave me an eye roll. "Leave it to you to take the romance out of baseball. Do you tell all jokes and lead with the punchline, too?"

"Sorry," I offered with a wince.

"Alice." He grabbed my hand over the table and tugged my arm until I moved to sit in his lap. I turned to look up at him as he continued. "There's no end because, even when I don't play, I'll still love it. It will still be a part of me in one way or another. I'll be involved somehow. I'll still feel that leather fit on my hand."

"That's beautiful," I said as my eyes glazed over and his lips kept me slightly dazed. "That's how I feel about flying."

"Alice, you have got to get back in the air."

"I know, and I will," I said as I nuzzled his neck and rubbed a hand down his smooth jaw. "Anything else in your future?"

He smirked. "I see a runt in my bed with a killer body and beautiful brown eyes...Wait"—he tapped his temple—"she's muzzled."

"Har har," I said as I fell limp against him and his arms encased me.

"I love you," he whispered, his warm breath at my ear.

It was the third or fourth time he'd said it without me reciprocating, and just as I was about to, he spoke up. "Night's not over. Let's go."

He pulled us from the chair, and I heard the song he'd played for me in the Jeep chime over the speakers.

"It's our song," I reminded excitedly as he pulled me to him and we moved around in a slight dance before he whisked me out of the restaurant. "I've never had a song with a boyfriend before." I laughed as I looked over at him. "I've never had a boyfriend before."

"Free" played through the speakers on the top of the small building as we made our way to the parking lot.

Rafe stopped and looked over to me at the entrance as couples and families made their way inside. "That's a lot of pressure on a man."

"It's sad, I know."

"No, it makes you even more mine." While we walked the short distance to the Jeep, I forgot about everything but my need to tell him how I felt.

"I guess there is something to be said about virtue." I looked over at Rafe, who shined so brightly next to me. "I wish...I wish I would have kept it for you." This stopped Rafe in his tracks as he held his hand on the Jeep door, my door, which he opened for me. My heart tugged hard in that moment. "I guess because I've never loved a man before, either."

I felt my confession hit Rafe as a tear slid down my cheek. Rafe wiped it away with his thumb, leaned over, and drew my lips to his. When he pulled away, I gave him the most honest words of my life.

"You could really fuck me up, Rafe."

He only hesitated a second before he promised me, "I've got you."

"I've got you, too."

Hours later, we lay in the sand, Alice's head on my chest, her body wrapped around mine. I'd never done the romance thing, never had a desire to. I wanted to win every part of her. I could only hope, as cliché as our night had been, she, on some level, appreciated it. I had nothing original to offer except myself, and even then I wasn't sure it was what she needed. She had such high expectations of life, and I wasn't sure I could be the man to meet them. It was only when I'd realized I'd fallen so goddamned hard for her that I really began to worry. She'd confessed she loved me too, and that was all I could really ask for.

We listened to the lull of the waves as Alice remained paranoid about the possibility of the return of the no-see-ums. She twitched in paranoia every few minutes as I laughed at her and forced her to lie still.

"Tonight was awesome," she whispered. "Thank you."

"Let's do this every night."

"Okay," she said with a sigh. "Let's just live on the beach."

"Even better," I said as I ran my hands through her hair. It was a tangled mess from whipping in the wind in the cabin of my Jeep.

"What were you figuring out, Rafe?"

"My dad mostly. It's a long story."

"I know. I read about it online." I looked down at her. "He's an effing a-hole for doing that."

"He *is* an effing a-hole," I agreed as I pulled her tighter.

"So what was your dilemma?"

"To forgive or not to forgive." Before she asked, I answered, "I can't."

"I understand."

I looked down at her as she looked up at me. "Do you?"

"I really do. I mean, sometimes relationships with parents can be so toxic. You can't do anything but let go. I was so close to doing the same with my mom, but it worked out differently. We actually had a good time."

"That's so great, Alice."

"You have no idea," she said as she kissed my neck and my dick got instantly hard.

"It's a whole new world for her," she said as she sat up and begin to slowly unbutton my shirt, "and for me."

"Sex in the sand is not a good thing, Alice," I warned as my protest jerked in my pants.

"I just want to touch you a little," she said with sex heavy in her voice as her tiny hand slipped beneath my jeans and gripped my stiff cock. She gripped me firm as she released me fully from my pants, a sexy smile on her face.

I exhaled as her mouth trailed down my chest and lingered on my stomach. Her tongue did a wicked dance and then slipped out and covered the head of my throbbing dick. I groaned as she looked around us before she dove and swallowed me whole. I nearly jumped out of my skin as she sucked me ruthlessly and my eyes rolled back.

"Alice, Jesus. Alice, God...baby, wait...stop!"

"What?!" She sat back on her bare heels, stunned.

"Jesus, woman." I sat up slightly as I held her hands still. "You could suck the paint off a Chevy, but take it a little slower...Just at first, okay? Ease into it."

"Too much?" she said with wide eyes as she gripped me hard and my head fell back involuntarily. She swallowed me again in worship, and I nearly wept at the feel of it. The woman's mouth was magic. I came in minutes as she reveled in a job well done. I stared up at her, beautiful and on fire for me. I didn't deserve her, but I could see her love for me, and fuck if I didn't need it now. The woman was perfect for me. "Now take me home and bend me over," she said as she gripped the collar of my shirt. "And I want it *hard*, Rafe."

Yep, fucking perfect.

Andy flipped a one on the inside of his thigh and I shook it off. We hadn't been in sync in some time. Everyone on the team, even my manager, Jon, couldn't believe how bad we were sparring on pitch calls. With each month of the season that passed and every day that call didn't come, I'd felt my confidence start to slip, and I was doing a shit job of hiding it. Andy took off his mask when I nodded away another fastball and moved toward me.

"Rafe, that's twelve pitches in the last seven games," he hissed. "This shit can't keep happening."

"I'm not feeling it."

"Shake it off," he ordered as he looked down between us and dug his cleat in the dirt. "Trust my call and remember the game plan." Andy leaned in. "Horton can't wait on the change up."

Andy deadpanned at me as he looked up, and in his expressionless face, I still saw everything he wasn't saying.

"I'm good. Let's do it," I said as I kicked dirt at him.

Andy started to walk off and turned back suddenly. "You aren't alone out here." He walked back to the plate and got into position as Horton stepped back in.

I took a deep breath in attempt to clear my head and peeked over my shoulder to watch the slow creep of the first base runner. I fired a warning shot to buy more time. I flexed my shoulders one at a time and looked back at Andy as he held his pointer down again over his crotch.

Get ready to go skirt shopping, Horton. I'm about to make you my bitch.

I gave him nothing but menace in my stare. He would never be able to read me. I nodded sharp at Andy's signal and fired a ball into his glove.

Strike.

I smirked at the batter as he cursed and stepped out of the box.

When he stepped back in, he swung his bat in taunt. "How about some heels to go with that skirt?" I muttered as I wound up.

Strike.

I heard Alice holler for me first over the trailing noise of the crowd and smirked again.

I hear you, baby. This one is for you.

I fired low, watched his fruitless swing, and swiped my glove over my crotch with satisfaction.

You've just been fucked by Hembrey. Move along.

I let my head flop back in my recliner and turned my eyes heavenward as the incessant banging in my kitchen hit a whole new level.

"Sorry," Alice piped over my island as I remained planted in my easy chair, glove in hand as I watched the Sox dominate the Blue Jays. More chopping began and I turned up the volume to keep Alice and her workings slightly more muted. She'd come over after a day full of meetings with a brand new wok and bag full of shit I'd never seen and declared herself a sous chef. I'd hastily agreed to let her abuse my kitchen when I saw what she wanted to cook in.

Two hours in and I'd heard nothing but chopping and a repetitive "hmm" come out of her mouth and had yet to see her for more than a minute in the baseball covered apron and nothing else. I was pretty sure she had Googled "how to be a hot as fuck girlfriend" or something of that nature. That or she'd recently dined at a Japanese steakhouse and decided it was her next venture. Either way, the menu seemed seriously fucking complicated.

Another loud clack had me turning in my chair to look back at her. Over the counter between us, she pressed her lips together to keep from laughing.

"Seriously, woman," I grumbled until I saw the hint of a nipple peeking out of the side of her tiny apron. She followed my eyes and repositioned it.

"Dessert comes later."

"Dinner is loud."

"Fine, I'll wait for your game to end," she grumbled as her head disappeared and she began to rummage beneath my sink through the cabinet.

"What are you looking for?"

"Found it!" Seconds later, a pristine ass was on full display next to the TV as she began to dust my bookshelves with a rag in one hand and some Pledge in the other. I was sure then it was Google. I was sure she'd typed in "five ways to keep your man rock hard all day."

Objection popped into my head along the lines of "she didn't have to go there with cleaning," but nothing came out as I studied the curve of her tan legs up to the gradual, creamy white at the tops of her thighs. The back of the apron covered only a quarter inch of skin just above her ass. My eyes moved up to the small of her back and drifted to her delicate neck. Seconds was all it took for me to become fully hard as I dropped my glove in the newspaper basket next to my chair. She bent over slightly as she worked her way down the shelves.

"You never dust. Seriously, do you have any idea what this is?" She peeked over her shoulder as her eyes condemned me. "Its dead skin and a million other disgusting things. And where are your books, Rafe?" She continued as she picked up random memorabilia off my shelf and wiped it with the rag.

The game went to commercial and an ad came on with some cheesy pop song. Alice wiggled her ass a bit and my whole body tensed. Hell bent on being inside of her in seconds, I frowned as the commercial went off and her ass stilled. I reached over for my cell phone, completely stupefied with a million scenarios of how this would play out. I hit the shuffle button and The Weeknd chimed on with "Often". I muted the TV and turned up the volume. Alice froze, and I waited with a wolf grin.

Another look over her shoulder showed the evidence of her embarrassment. She looked so perfect in that fucking apron and it was all I could do to keep seated. Our eyes locked, and I pushed my chin out in challenge and encouragement. She blew out a breath and kept my gaze then began to slightly move her hips. I licked my lips and scraped the bottom with my teeth with another nudge in her direction as I scanned her. Ridding herself of the rag and polish, she giggled and turned to face the bookshelf, palms flat and began...to blow my fucking mind. I watched her pump her plump ass in perfect sync with the beat. It was the hottest thing I'd ever seen in my life. I released the button on my jeans and slid the zipper down as she pushed her ass away from the shelf and bent over completely, dangling it in front of me while still keeping time. I was about to reward her for her good rhythm with some of my own.

She slowly lifted, stood and turned to look at me. Her jaw dropped as she watched me stroke my cock. I fisted it hard and slow as she continued to move and slid her hands over her body in a sexy caress. I stroked harder as she worked herself into a full on sexual tease. "Don't stop," I gritted out as I pumped, hell bent on not losing my shit before I had a chance to get inside of her.

She worked her body into a sweat and stole every glance back at me she could. Determined to ruin me, she gripped the sides of the bookcase and bent her body backward in a roll. I saw her eyes widen as she screamed out in surprise as the bookcase began to fall. I was out of my seat in seconds, but I was too late. Alice was buried beneath it and my dick went instantly limp as my heart tried to break through my chest. I pulled the case away as I scanned her from head to toe. "Fuck, fuck," I cradled her head as she looked up at me with wide eyes. Seconds passed as I surveyed her body and asked her if she was in any pain. Her face twisted as I looked on and she began to laugh hysterically. I let out a harsh breath and cradled the back of her head in my hands.

After a solid minute of her laughter, she only slowed to scold me again. "If you would've had some books on it, bonehead athlete, it wouldn't have fallen…and I may have just peed a little." I chuckled as I scooted to lay next to her on the carpet.

"You sure you're okay?"

"I'm fine," she whispered over to me. "God, that would have been some good sex."

"Oh," I assured her as I studied her escaped nipple and ran the pad of my finger over it. "We're still having it."

"Meh, I'm not feeling it anymore," she said as she wrinkled her nose. I pulled her to me and looked down at her as we shared a smile. "What am I going to do with you?"

She looked back at me with hopeful eyes. "Everything?"

Alice drove with a smile on her face as she darted her eyes excitedly from me to the road. This morning, she woke me up early with her perfect mouth wrapped around me and breakfast in bed, which consisted of toast and Nutella. Well, what was left in the jar. I looked over at her now as she tapped her fingers to Peter

Cetera's "Glory of Love." I couldn't help but to chuckle at her and her blatant disregard for all things our generation. As if she read my mind, she quickly came to the defense of her movie playlist.

"It's better than that death metal you play in the Jeep."

"It's not death metal."

"It's loud and obnoxious."

I shook my head and frowned. "It's the Foo Fighters."

"What exactly is a *Foo* Fighter?"

Not able to come up with an educated explanation, I looked at her and deadpanned, "Isn't it obvious? They fight Foo." Her laughter was infectious, and I loved the sound of it.

"You're going to Google that later, aren't you?"

"Yep," she said as her chuckle slowed.

I looked over her and studied her beautiful profile in the morning sun. Her hair was pulled up in a messy bun. She had a t-shirt that said "I heart Jake Ryan" and some dark jeans that cradled her perfect figure, and high top Converse. I made a mental note to replace that t-shirt as she looked over at me and gave me a wide smile.

"Almost there!"

I'd seen the sign for the airport a few miles back and was pretty sure I knew what the surprise was, but I kept quiet. I studied the curve of her slender neck, the perfect shape of her chin and lips. Her features were severely feminine. Even her tiny ears were beautiful.

"Why are you staring at me?"

"Because I want to, and you stare at me all the time."

She quickly began muttering excuses, and I grabbed her hand and pulled it into my lap. "And I like it." She looked over at me with an embarrassed smile and gave me a sly nod.

I adjusted myself in the seat again, the top of my head grinding against the small amount of cushion on the roof.

"Such a big boy," she whispered suggestively. And that was all it took for my imagination to start wondering. I was on fire for her. The ache in my chest matched the throbbing of my cock. I'd just had her and I wanted her again. That well would never run dry, of that I was sure.

"Hold that thought," she said as she read my mind and exited the highway. Minutes later, my suspicions were confirmed as we pulled up and parked yards away from a pint-sized plane not much bigger than her Prius. "Today, you will be my co-captain, Mr. Hembrey. You up for it?" I remained quiet as I studied her body radiating the purest form of happiness. I nodded and swallowed the emotion in my throat for the second time that morning. She had a way of making me feel...everything, and not in small doses, but all at once. It was overpowering in a way. She still made me nervous, but not in a way that was unsettling. In a way that was purely addicting.

"Well, come on, hot shot." She winked as she walked toward the plane, where a man waited for us. Alice walked ahead of me and greeted the man with warm words. I caught up with her and scoured the small plane. There wasn't much to it, and I felt a small amount of unease as I studied it. She looked over to me as she nodded at the man who introduced himself as Byron.

"She's gassed up. You'll be speaking to tower four."

"Thanks, Byron."

Byron nodded and turned to me. "You're lit up this year. I'm a fan," he said as I offered my hand.

"Thank you, I appreciate it."

"I don't think you'll make it another month."

Alice looked offended as I winked at her in assurance. "Let's hope so."

Realization struck as she realized he was complimenting me, and then I saw the slight amount of fear cross over her features at the thought of me leaving. It vanished just as quickly as it came, but I caught it.

"So, what do you think about Columbia this year? That—"

"Sir," I said as I interrupted.

"Call me Byron."

"Byron, if it's okay with you, I'm going to spend the morning with my girl and not think about anything else."

He looked over to Alice, who snapped her attention to me with shock. A smile graced his face as he winked at me. "Understood."

"I'll have Alice send you some seats."

"That's not necessary."

"It's no problem," I said as I wrapped my hand around her waist. "Ready, baby?"

She nodded as she said a few parting words to Byron and then we made our way to the small plane.

"Rafe, you didn't have to do that," she scolded as we boarded and buckled our seatbelts. She handed me a headset. "I didn't mind you talking about ball, Rafe. It's your thing."

"I haven't thought about ball all morning, Alice."

Seeming satisfied, she looked over at me with pride and excitement. "Ready?"

"Hell yes."

She started the plane and adjusted various controls. I watched her completely relaxed and in her element. She spoke a few sentences over the headset as she taxied easily to a large runway. I sat back, slightly dazed and completely impressed as she looked over and said, "You look a little nervous."

"I'm good."

"Do you trust me?"

It all came down to that. And though I was sure it was in regards to her skill as a pilot, I gave no pause as I answered with a quick "yes." The question had me reeling.

Alice seemed satisfied as she pulled back on the throttle. We began the race between speed and the runway, and as I felt every single crack in the pavement, my thoughts raced along with the adrenaline rush. As soon as the plane hit air, I heard my exaggerated breath through the speaker.

"Rafe, you okay?" she asked tentatively with a quick glance in my direction.

"I'm fine, baby," I assured as we gained some height.

"You're a little green." She chuckled, her voice a mix of silk and humor.

I realized I was white knuckling the slack in my shorts and let go as I began to scan the ground beneath us. I looked over to the beautiful woman to my left as she spoke to me calmly. "I think it's time you saw Charleston the way I do." In complete control, she flew us over the barrier islands with ease as she pointed out the window and told me a few things even as a local I wasn't aware of. I looked down on my city with a bird's eye view and a new appreciation. It didn't take long at all for me to figure out what she meant. I grabbed my cell phone out of my pocket and snapped a few shots of the marshland and the harbor. I took a shot of the mid-morning sun nestled behind the two-mile-long Ravenel Bridge.

"This is fucking incredible," I noted as she kept the plane low, giving me a broad range of things to focus on. The peninsula seemed smaller and the land below felt more like a mystery than a place I knew I could travel by foot and never get lost.

"Alice...wow." I kept my eyes fixed on the city as she traveled a little further inland and pointed out Dutch's house, which looked like nothing more than a blip on the radar. I could hear the excitement in her voice as I remained glued to the window. Alice opened up about her fascination with planes, and that she loved the idea that something that seemed so impossible at one time actually became so incredibly useful and a part of everyday life. She loved the idea of being in one place and climate at the beginning of the day and landing somewhere completely different at the end of it. It was her fascination with the world and culture that fueled her as much as the plane itself as a tool to gain a taste of it. She felt that all things were possible in the air. That the world could be conquered and she was capable of doing it while she flew. I understood her love of it. I felt the same juice when I held the weight of the game in my hand.

And all too soon, I felt the tires touch the pavement as Alice expertly landed the plane and taxied us safely back to the hangar.

I looked over to her as the plane wound down and the engine stopped. When we both unbuckled, I pulled her into my lap, and she protested only slightly.

She looked up to me with a grin, her eyes relieved. "You liked it."

"I loved it," I said with certainty. I felt the same overbearing lump in my throat as my chest expanded again, full of her, full of Alice. With the same certainty, I looked down at her as I let my words fly. "I trust you, Alice. I don't trust the world, but I do trust you." I saw her perfect lips part as if she were going to speak as she looked at me with soft eyes and decided against it.

"What?"

"Nothing, I just...I know it was...hard for you to say that."

I shook my head in negation. "Not with you, not anymore."

"Why?"

"Because you're the most incredible, sincere, and beautiful woman I have ever met." She lowered her chin to my chest, and I lifted it up so we were face to face. I wrapped my arms around her as she gripped me tight. "You aren't alone anymore, Alice, and you never will be again, not you. You're too good for the world around you. And you *are* too good for me." Her mouth parted again as shock registered on her face and a silent tear fell down her cheek. "But the thing is, I love you, and I'll be damned if I give anyone else the chance to."

Frustration rolled off me with the knowledge that when she needed me down the road, I may not always be there. I may not always be present when she felt like a rolling stone and needed stability—needed *me*. Because as much as she craved adventure, I knew she craved a real home to belong to. And we were exactly the same in that respect.

It was selfish of me to ask her to take me the way I was, with only the time I could give, but I wanted her in a way I could never explain or try to. She had so much strength, so much ability. She was so fiercely independent at times; I couldn't believe she could need anyone at all. But she trusted me, she looked out for me, and when we were together, I could feel her need for me. She was everything I'd ever wanted and never thought I would find in a woman. And as she slipped her arms around my neck and returned my kiss with the same gentle fire, my heart solidified. It was Alice. It could only be Alice.

Alice: Do you believe in God?

Rafe: What? Why?

Alice: I just want to know.

Rafe: Isn't this a conversation for after sex.

Alice: You always fall asleep after sex.

Rafe: Exactly.

Alice: Rafe!

Rafe: Yes, I believe in God.

Alice: Thank you.

Rafe: What are you Googling?

Alice: Lifespans.

Rafe: Why?

Alice: I'm curious. The mayflies have the shortest life span. They live only a day. That's so sad.

Rafe: Terrible tragedy.

Alice: What would you do if you could only live for a day?

Rafe: I already do it every day. I play ball and then let you play with mine. :p

Alice: I can't believe you just texted that.

Rafe: Yes you can.

Alice: I'm forwarding it to my mom.

Rafe: Tell her we can send picture proof from home. Kind of like a new Hallmark card.

Alice: Ugh, never mind. You lack romance, Rafe.

Rafe: Alice, right now I have my arm soaking in a bucket of ice. My ass and thigh are killing me because I got nailed by a ball. My lips are chapped, and I have a fucking broken toe. Can we talk about God, lifespans, and my balls, and lack of romance when I get home?

Alice: Well...you didn't have to text back. Hurry home. I have questions and Vaseline. I'll make you look like you sucked off an elephant.

Rafe: I love you.

Alice: The longest living creature on planet earth is the bowhead whale...In case you were curious.

Rafe: I wasn't.

Alice: Now you know.

Rafe: Still needless information.

Alice: I'm educating you.

Rafe: On useless facts I'll never use.

Alice: Jeez, you're cranky.

Rafe: Again, arm in ice, dinger sting in the ass, broken toe, dry lips.

Alice: How is that brawn working out for you now?

Rafe: I'm on the bus, baby, headed home.

Alice: I want it hard.

Rafe: You've turned into a nerdy pervert.

Alice: Whatever, hard please.

Rafe: Gladly. I'll throw in some cuffs, rope, and anal play.

Alice: I'll have to do some research.

Rafe: You do that and get back to me. Just research with one of your pornos.

Alice: You looked at my browsing history!

Rafe: Every chance I get. You cover your tracks mostly, so I take it to the bathroom when you aren't looking. Did you really research the average size of the penis?

Rafe: What, no quick quip? No come back? At least you know you won the penis lottery. :)

Rafe: I miss your face. I need to look into those beautiful brown eyes.

Alice: I'm sorry about your game.

Rafe: Fuck the game. I want you here. I want to be inside you. Two more to play and the weather is shit.

Alice: Then I'll come to you.

Rafe: Really?

Alice: I'm on my way.

Rafe: Seriously, you're coming? It's a four hour drive and it's late.

Alice: Text me the address.

Rafe: Baby, it's raining too hard.

Alice: Do you want me to text Andy for it?

Alice: I just flew for three hours and almost cried when I touched down. I miss it. Can you talk? I feel like I'm about to crack.

Alice: I know you're busy with pre-meetings. Two more days and you'll be home. This really sucks sometimes.

Rafe: Baby, I'm sorry, are you there?

Alice: Rafe! I just played golf and it was sooo boring. Seriously, it was the beer that got me through it. I'm thinking men drink beer to get through boring rituals they create, thus making said ritual far more entertaining rather than to admit it was just a bad idea. I mean, couldn't they've just said, "Nah...it was good in theory but far too boring to execute." Golf...no.

Rafe: Alice, I'm pretty sure you need to Google the origin of the game of golf.

Alice: I still say they were drunk when they came up with it.

Rafe: Spoken like a new alcoholic. Take up knitting instead?

Alice: Har har.

Rafe: You're Googling knitting now, aren't you?

Alice: I just got finished with Dutch's yard.

Rafe: You are something else, Alice. That had to take you all day!

Alice: Two actually. I really stink at yardwork. I can hardly move.

Rafe: I've got two hands ready to take the sting out.

Alice: I was hoping you would say that.

Rafe: Are you alone?

Alice: Why?

Rafe: Because I want you to pull down your panties.

Alice: Thank you for the roses. I love them.

Rafe: You deserve them. I've got to go warm up.

Alice: Go get 'em, Bullet. XO

Rafe: Did you just hang up on me?

Alice: You are being paranoid. I'm not dealing with it.

Rafe: I'm four hundred fucking miles away and you send me a screenshot of you and some guy hanging out.

Alice: I was bored. He's married and he was just helping me with my painting. I was showing you my painting! You want me to sit at home two or three weeks out the month? Not happening.

Rafe: I can't fucking deal with this right now.

Alice: Then don't.

Alice: Fighting with you hurts so much, Rafe. Please don't ignore me. I miss you every day. I can't sit at home thinking about you. Nothing helps. My movies don't help. I think of you and only you. I wasn't doing anything wrong.

Rafe: I just don't think you know what that did to me. I know I handled that wrong, but I just can't see that shit, Alice.

Alice: You won't.

Rafe: I love you.

Alice: I love you, too.

Rafe: We okay?

Alice: Always.

Rafe: Hours ago, you were in my bed. You were telling me some usual random shit and all I could think about was sitting on this bus again and how badly I would want to be back in that bed hearing you go on about Michael Jackson's pet giraffe and all the other exotic animals owned by celebrities. To answer your question from earlier, no, I will not be buying a monkey or an albino snake. You make me laugh, Alice. You keep me going. You are the best thing that has happened to me in a very long time. If you keep waiting, baby, I'll keep coming home.

Alice: I've got you.

Rafe: I fucking love you.

I was in my office as I waited on Rafe to get back from a four-day stint in Myrtle. He'd pitched an amazing game, and I couldn't wait to celebrate with him. He'd called minutes after he got into town and insisted on picking me up. I was in no mood to argue, desperate to see him. It was an immeasurable high to belong to someone so talented, so insanely sexy, and so completely in tune with me. Our time together, though short in measure, filled me so completely. The sadness of my former life, which I'd now labeled the gray, had completely dissipated. It was a distant memory in my new life filled with color, adventure, and love. I daydreamed constantly about my new reality, which was actually better than the thoughts that swirled constantly in my head. I could replay them a thousand times and they would never be better than the real thing.

"You look hot, baby...God, you are so beautiful," Rafe said from the door as I looked up to him with a widening smile. The look on his face was almost one of pain, and I took it as a compliment. I'd worn a warm red, form fitting dress to work today, knowing it was his favorite color on me. I'd fixed my hair and lined my lips with the red lipstick he loved so much. I stood and quickly made my way over to him as he took a steady step toward me and pulled me into his arms before his mouth claimed mine with an urgent kiss. When I began to pull away, he gripped me tighter, his lips soft, and his warm tongue frantic and thorough. I moaned into his mouth and kissed him back with all of me. Rafe finally pulled away with soft whispers of 'I love you' and peppered kisses on my neck and chin. Both of our mouths were now scarlet red, and I giggled as I wiped the lipstick smear from his lips and the corner of his mouth. His eyes were gentle as he ducked in again and claimed my lips with a slow kiss. I sensed it then, in his grip, his desperation, and took a step back to look up at him.

I studied Rafe's face and the drop in my selfish gut was instantaneous. I pressed it back and found a sincere and proud smile. "You got the call."

He pushed out a breath, the worry in his features clear, and I shook my head.

"Don't, Rafe, this is fantastic! I'm so happy for you, really. Oh my God, this is really happening!" My facade was ice thin, and I already knew he could see the cracks.

"Happy?" He reached out with his hand and wiped the wetness away from my cheek with his finger.

"Happy tears," I lied as he pulled me to him and forced my chin up with a gentle hand.

"I love you," he whispered.

I said the only thing I could say. The only words the lump in my throat would allow. "I know."

Rafe wanted to stop at Andy's to give him the news before we went home. I was sure I was doing a pretty good job at hiding my devastation, but Rafe kept our hands locked and looked over at me every few seconds as he drove. I kept quiet, too afraid of the burn at the top of my throat. When I felt brave enough, I threw out questions.

"Where?"

"Denver."

"Are you happy about that?"

"Absolutely."

"When?"

He looked over at me with pause.

"I'm okay," I lied with a smile. "Rafe, when?"

"Tomorrow."

"Tomorrow," I repeated without emotion as my heart completely shattered. Tomorrow would be the worst day of my life. I made peace with it, swallowed, and gripped his hand as I turned to him. "You deserve this. It happened. It was always going to happen."

Rafe looked over at me and pulled my left hand to his lips. He kissed my empty ring finger twice and set it down. "No end, Alice."

We stood at the entrance of the bar I'd entered completely green only short months ago. Rafe gripped my hand tighter as I spotted Andy leaning over the well as he spoke to Mac, a regular I'd had a few conversations with. In fact, I knew the names of everyone on the stools. I'd found my tribe, my village, and with one phone call, I felt like I was about to lose it all. I prayed my smile was Oscar worthy as the second tear ripped through my chest. Andy looked up at us curiously as we remained where we were. A slow, incredulous smile covered his face as he looked at Rafe. "Listen up," Andy shouted over the chaos, his eyes still on Rafe as his smile remained. "That man standing at the door is Rafe "The Bullet" Hembrey and he's going to the show!" The whole bar erupted as Rafe began to walk forward and let go of my hand. Andy rounded the bar and met him halfway as they did the man-hug thing. Andy caught my eye over Rafe's shoulder, and I gave him a wink before I moved my gaze over to Kristina. She stood paralyzed as her solemn face searched mine for any sign of emotion. I kept my face firm as the entirety of the bar stepped up to congratulate Rafe one by one.

"Drinks on the fucking house!" Andy declared as the noise level increased. I let my face fail me briefly and saw Kristina move and shook my head in a firm no.

She nodded once and began to pour as orders were thrown at her in rapid succession. I moved to help her, but Andy caught my hand. I looked up to him as his gentle blue eyes peered down at me. "Kristina could use my help—" I laughed dryly "—and yours."

"Alice—"

"Please don't," I said as I ripped my hand away and walked behind the bar. Kristina and I knocked out the orders as Rafe and Andy chatted animatedly at one of the cocktail tables.

"Alice," Kristina said in a plea as she dried a highball glass with a towel, "God, are you okay?"

I blew out a breath. I was finally numb enough to answer. "I just wanted a little more time." I shrugged as another overwhelming round of pain shot through my chest. "It was too good to be true."

"You don't believe that."

"Men like that..." I said as I gripped Mac's empty mug and poured a horrible draft of foam. "Men like Rafe are too much to keep." I turned to look at Kristina and saw her eyes on Rafe. I took a step back as he glanced our way with a smile. I smiled back as Kristina averted her eyes. Realization dawned as I studied her face, the same devastation I felt etched all over it. Alarm struck me first as I watched her heart break. Slight anger surfaced as I realized how obvious it had been, and then an overwhelming sense of understanding replaced it. Of course she loved Rafe. God, I'd been so damned blind. She'd been nothing but good to me since we'd met, and not only that, she'd been forced to watch us fall in love.

My heart ached for her as I watched her eyes avert painfully, the same expression she'd worn a dozen or so times in his presence. I'd been completely oblivious, too happy in my newfound love and ignorant to her infatuation. I felt the guilt replace the anger as I stepped over to her and wrapped my arm around her waist in a half-hug. "The man we love is leaving."

Kristina looked over to me with tear-filled eyes. "Fuck, Alice, I'm so sorry."

"Don't, if you cry, I'll cry."

"Then I'll cry," Mac said in a drunken slur. Kristina ignored him as her eyes scanned my face for any sign of anger. I turned to her and pulled her to me with a whisper. "I love you, too, but back off my man, bitch."

She laughed as she pulled away from me and caught her tears before they escaped. "I've been so damned stupid. He never even saw me." She gulped back more tears as she began to wipe the water rings off the bar and looked over at me with clear guilt. "I would never *ever* do anything to—"

"I know." I picked up a bottle and poured two shots of something blue. She grabbed her glass and mine and threw the liquid in the sink. "That's not a shot, Alice."

"Make it strong," I urged as she began gathering bottles and I studied her. She was insanely beautiful. I would never understand it. "How could he not see you?"

"I guess he was waiting for you."

"You could have told me."

"Then *I* would have missed out on *you*."

Her lips pursed and her eyes closed with emotion as I questioned her. "Andy?"

"He knows," she said with the shake of her head. "He figured it out." She shook the tin filled with ice and liquor as she spoke. "I'm leaving for Atlanta in two weeks. Andy still doesn't want me to go, but I can't stay. I feel guilty, you know?"

"For not loving him?"

"I've reached the conclusion that I love them both," she said as she eyed their table and turned worried eyes back to me. "Please don't hate me."

"You could've hated *me*. You could've played it so differently. You never even threw your hat in the ring." I shook my head as I choked on the burn of the shot.

"I never had a chance," she said as she turned to me. "And I'm so happy for you both."

I shrugged. "It was a fairytale, and it's midnight. How am I going to do this without you?"

"Don't think like that," she insisted. "And I'm only going to be five hours away."

"I want this to be different for both of us," I said wistfully.

"Me too. But, hey," she assured with a shaky voice, "I'll find him. He's out there. Or you know what, fuck that. *He* will find me."

"Toast to that," I said as she filled our glasses again and I tossed back the sweet but potent concoction.

Kristina and I were a disaster an hour after that. We'd downed one too many shots and ended up spraying each other with the bar guns as angry patrons waited for beers.

Endless I love yous were exchanged between Kristina and I as Rafe looked on with a smirk, and Andy fought us for our guns and got soaked in the process. Dripping wet and still shattered, I looked over to Rafe as the worst of the buzz hit me, and I realized my mistake. My devastation must have reared its ugly head because minutes later, I was in his Jeep, staring at the sky above as I fought for breath.

Hours after I helped Rafe pack, I lay in his bed, wrapped in his arms, and stared at the ceiling fan in the dark. His room was half-lit by the moon coming through the window and the blue lights emitting from our charging iPhones. I couldn't bring myself to look anywhere else. I knew on the floor next to the bathroom was a set of bags that held his essentials for *months*, not weeks. I knew on my keyring on the table next to that luggage was a newly added spare key to his Jeep. He hadn't given me too many details, but I knew that soon the whole room would be empty and he would be living in Denver while I remained in Charleston.

He was leaving.

He was leaving to start his Major career, a career that would probably mean the end of us. I stared at the fan as it circled, and Rafe tightened his grip on me. It had been hours since he'd taken me and made me whole, only to rip me apart again with the look on his face. I braved a whisper in the dark, too afraid to look at him, and unsure if he was awake.

"Rafe?"

"Yeah, baby?" Tears threatened as I realized he was just as pensive as I was.

"I need you to teach me how to play it cool."

His lips brushed my temple as my chest finally exploded, and I stifled a sob. Soft lips brushed my shoulder before he moved to whisper softly in my ear. "I can't."

"Why not?" I heard my voice shake as he pulled me closer and whispered again.

"I fell for you the way you are."

"That's selfish."

"And I always will be when it comes to you."

"Promise?" I turned to look over at him, and despite the lack of light, I could clearly see the worry in his features. I hated myself for dampening a day that should be the greatest of his life.

"Alice—"

"You're right. You can't promise me anything. You never have."

"That's not true."

He moved to hover above me as he attempted to wipe the pain from my face with his fingers, and then with his words and kiss.

"Do you believe that I love you, Alice?"

I nodded, furious with myself. "Yes."

"That's my promise."

I nodded again as he kissed me deeply and sank between my legs.

"Alice, listen to me," he said as he eased my t-shirt up and over my head. "The world could disappear tomorrow and I'd only worry about a fucking tiny list of people. But the thing I would need in order to breathe again would be to see your face," he declared as he pushed his fingers inside me and my breath caught. I arched my back and spread wider as he sipped my nipples and then rubbed the thick head of him through my folds. I was deliciously sore but moaned my welcome.

"Rafe," I rasped out as he drove into me.

"We won't disappear," he promised as he pumped frantically. "We won't."

Heavy, that's the only way to describe the feeling throughout my body as I made my way past the game day flags and toward the entrance where I spotted Dutch. Her eyes scanned the crowd with hope until they landed on me. Her lips turned upward into a soft smile as I read her posture. She was sure I wouldn't show.

Andy was the reason I was there. Throughout the day, I couldn't imagine walking up the steps into the stadium without seeing the pitcher with the sharp eyes that I was madly in love with taking the field.

For Andy. This is for Andy.

The day after Rafe left, Andy had gone to the team manager, Jon, and asked for release from his contract. We were all surprised when he'd decided to end his last season early, and even more so when he'd mentioned they'd granted his request. We knew Andy was intent on quitting ball and dedicated to Rafe's promotion, but it wasn't until then that we knew just how much. Andy had surprised us all with his determination to end his career on his terms, in his time. What was even more surprising was that he could have easily been asked to the show with his record breaking stats this season. Rafe was still fuming over his decision and had told me as much in our last conversation.

The burn in my chest intensified as Dutch greeted me with a nod, and I lifted each foot with dread. Rafe was gone and would miss his best friend's last game. I let a tear trail down my face as I thought of everything that happened since I saw the flyer and trusted it to lead me where I needed to go.

My heartbreak cursed the damned insanity of needing to belong that day because I was searching for something...someone to belong to...and I'd found it with Rafe.

"He's going to hate not being here," Dutch remarked as we took our seats.

I nodded, unable to mask the pain that festered inside me, threatening to rear its ugly head at any moment. It had only been weeks and I felt like the only life I'd ever wanted had been taken away.

"Do you want a beer?" Dutch offered as I looked over at her.

I stood, looking for any excuse to keep from roaming the field and coming up empty. "I'll go."

"Stay where you are, missy," she ordered. "I can handle it."

"I'm sorry I'll be such poor company. Let me treat." I handed Dutch a twenty as I resumed my seat. She looked down at me with a sad twist of her lips and gentle eyes.

"I saw it, you know. I saw it the minute you two looked at each other. It was something to see. I don't think you're alone in feeling the way you are right now."

I wiped a lone tear from underneath my eye and nodded with a forced smile. "Thank you...f-for saying that. Go get that beer and let's toast to Andy."

"Coming up, missy," she said as she pinched the bridge of my ball cap and jiggled it a bit.

"Dutch?"

"Yeah," she replied quickly, her eyes covered in concern. I could feel her need to console me, and I hated that I was making a game that hadn't even begun so damned depressing.

"Thank you for this. Thank you for letting me sit in Herb's chair."

Dutch simply nodded before she moved to climb the few steps to reach the walkway that led to the concession stands.

"Ladddies and gentlemen, please rise for our national anthem!"

I stood with my hand over my disintegrated heart and glanced at my phone before I tucked it away in my pocket. I hadn't heard a word from him today. I knew he was busy getting acclimated with his surroundings and his new team, but I felt so disconnected from him already, so uncertain about our future. His words ran on repeat in my head.

"No end, Alice. No end."

I nodded as if he'd just whispered it to me. I was losing it, and I was doing it with an audience. Everyone around me glanced my way from time to time, no longer strangers but my true community. I looked to my right at the family man, who had attended nearly as many games as I had. He looked on at me with sympathy as his blond baby slept in his lap. He winked in reassurance, and I nodded with a disgraceful smile.

I heard the announcer start to tick off the lineup and took a deep breath.

"Ladies and gentlemen, tonight we salute number three, Andrew Pracht!"

I looked over to Andy as he took the field and waved to the roaring crowd. Minutes passed as the entire stadium stood and said goodbye to one of their favorites. Tears flowed freely down my cheeks as I clapped and whistled before I raised my hat in the air. Andy's eyes found mine and he lifted his hat up with a smile, a testament to our friendship. I laughed with pride as Dutch made her way back to us with frothy beers. We toasted to number three as we watched nine innings of Andy's best ball. He'd placed two runners at base and scored the point with a homerun in the eighth inning that won the Swampgators his final game. And in the time the first pitch was thrown to the minute I watched Andy stomp across home plate, I forgot about my aching heart.

Realization dawned as I turned to Dutch. "I'm in love with baseball."

"I know," she said without an ounce of surprise.

"I didn't," I said with a smile. "You wise old lady," I cracked as I gave her the elbow. "What else do you know?"

"Hush," she said as she nodded and the Gators took the field with Andy on their shoulders to give him one last walk around. Dutch and I raised hell as he looked over the crowd with appreciation and longing. When the field began to empty, I sat with Dutch as the crowd dispersed.

"It really is over," I said as I looked over at Dutch and cursed the fresh tears that brewed in my eyes.

"It's not over," she said as she looked on at the field. "The season isn't—"

The absence of light cut her off as the whole stadium went black. The announcer remained silent, which puzzled us all, and I heard a few people in the crowd voice their distaste.

"What the *hell?*"

"I can't see shit. They should at least give us a few minutes to get to the lot. Turn on your cell phone light—"

Then it hit. One guitar rift, one single rift had my mouth opening, and I looked over to Dutch. "Oh. My. God."

"What's going on?" Just as she said it, a solid line of fire lit up the sky and burst into purple fizz. Then another just as rapidly streaked the sky above the Jumbotron and burst into flowering, purple flames. The crowd paused as rapid cheers erupted around the stadium and my chest exploded with emotion.

"Rafe," I whispered as I clutched my hand over my chest to keep it from spilling out.

I looked over to Dutch as the levy broke, my voice raw. "One song can change everything. Did you know that?"

Dutch looked up as the sky burst with solid purple and Prince sang over the speakers. I felt every word hit me and began to cry openly as I finally let my love and heartache seep through.

"Rafe," I whispered again as I lost all sense of reality.

I looked up to the purple clouds above that lit the park with streaks of beautiful light designed specifically for me. I began to look around with desperate hope of any sign of Rafe and came up empty. Seconds later, my whole heart burst as I felt a hand clasp mine to the left of me and looked over to see Andy with an encouraging smile before he looked up at the colorful sky and shook his head with a smile. I could see the pride in his eyes for his best friend.

Rafe wasn't there...but he was.

For seven minutes of song, I was completely surrounded in Rafe's love for me, and that was enough.

I squeezed Andy's hand as he held mine back and let the river flow as the song hit its crescendo and sprays of purple rain glittered down into the stadium. The crowd roared back to life, completely blown away as I swallowed the last of my pain and whispered a thank you to the heavens for every single minute of the last months of my life. With renewed hope, I pulled Dutch into a reluctant hug.

"That was for you?" she asked as she finally squeezed me back with the hug of a momma bear. "Well, missy, I can say it twice. I told you so."

I nodded as Dutch looked on at me when I pulled away. "See you next game?"

"I'll be here," I said with enthusiasm as she made her way out of her second home, and I turned to Andy and collapsed into his hug.

"God, I love him," I whispered as the crowd again made their way out of the stands and the stadium lit up, illuminating the clouds of dissipating smoke.

"I believe the feeling is mutual, doll," he whispered back. I pulled away with a smile.

"Good game, Andy," I said with admiration as I looked up to him. "Are you okay?"

"Let's go nurse our broken hearts," he said with a quiver in his voice. I looked over at him as he shook his head in confirmation that Kristina left. I swallowed the slight agitation of her sudden departure without notice and decided it was for the best. We all needed time.

"Fuckin' A," I said with a nod as I followed him up the aisle.

"Hembrey, let's go," I heard my pitching coach call from just outside the bathroom door.

"I'm coming," I said as I finished the video of Alice. I saw it all. The minute she realized what was going on. My eyes stayed glued to Andy's cell video as her beautiful features contorted in shock and then the tears that followed. She'd never looked more beautiful as she smiled with her face lit up with firelight. I coughed at the pain that seared through me and the pang of jealousy of those around her.

When I'd left her at the airport, I had to push past every fucking emotion in my chest to leave her there. I didn't want to rush what had always come natural between us. I'd declared my love, I told her I wasn't leaving her, and she would never be alone, and I'd meant it. I would keep my promise but wouldn't ask for her future until

I was sure it was exactly what she wanted. Though she remained steadfast and strong as I kissed her with everything I had, I felt myself break apart as I reluctantly let her go and made my way into the airport without a look back. I fucking lost it shortly after and damned near made a fool of myself as I tried to catch her car as she drove away. I threw my glove at her Prius and just missed her by a foot when she pulled away. I had no idea what I would say, but as I watched her car pull away, I felt like it was pulling my whole goddamned chest with it, with her. I loved her completely, and the only way I could prove it and keep my word to her was over time and with dedication. I was completely torn apart, half of me intent on seeing my dream through, half of me hating the fucking fate that had me in knots, and in fear of losing the best thing in my life.

She'd given me everything when she'd decided to love me, and I would give her everything I could in this life. I had no idea how we were going to make it work, but I knew I wouldn't, for *any* reason, let her go. My phone buzzed right before I was about to throw it in my locker.

> **Alice:** You gave me my movie moment. I love you. I'll never stop loving you.
>
> **Rafe:** Sorry I wasn't there, baby.
>
> **Alice:** You were. You totally were. I felt you everywhere.
>
> **Rafe:** You can't talk like that right now. I'm about to warm up.
>
> **Alice:** Stay gold, Ponyboy. Stay gold.
>
> **Rafe:** Seriously?

18
Alice
2 months later

"Are you sure you don't want to stay, Ms. Boyd?"

"I am," I answered with certainty.

"What will you do?"

"I'm hoping for anything private or commercial. I want to get back in the air," I said as I gathered my purse and shook the hand of Garret, my supervisor. I'd managed to escape the rest of my contract, and they'd found a replacement without holding it against me. It was a small miracle, but one that left me just as unsure as I had been in the past month.

"You will be missed," he assured as he guided me out of his office. "The door is always open here."

"Thank you."

I packed up my Prius with a small box of crap I was sure I would throw away when I got home. I had a small amount of savings and wasn't sure what my next move was. I hadn't lied when

I told Garret that I wanted to be in the air again, but had no idea what was in store.

I thought of Rafe and sighed. He'd left Charleston only two months ago, and though we spoke every day and saw each other as often as possible, it was never enough. The first month I spent in complete denial. I relived our relationship by frequenting the places we'd gone, driving his Jeep, and sleeping in his bed. I'd also kept a stool warm at Andy's bar. Rafe's life had quickly turned into a circus, especially after he began to pitch, and pitch well, on the major level. His arm had started to earn him earnest fans, and his face and body...well, they had earned him a new popularity amongst the masses, namely women and the label of the next Derek Jeter.

The man I loved was the sports equivalent of Elvis.

And I was his faithful Priscilla.

I'd watched the miniseries "Elvis and Me" countless times when I was a girl. Priscilla, naïve and young, had been swept into a whirlwind affair with a larger than life megastar and had been abandoned for long periods with only rumors and mortifying articles to douse her hopes.

Rafe and I had FaceTime, daily texts and calls, and only a few stolen days a month to hold on to. We were sustaining, but my fingers where white knuckling the ledge. He'd never once made me doubt his love for me, but it was the distance that kept my heart in painful shackles.

As selfish as it was, and as happy as I tried to be for Rafe, I wanted our minor league life back. His publicist had all but sabotaged our free time together and seemed to hate me. She played heavily on his single, hotshot reputation that had made him sought after by the press. Everyone wanted a piece of Rafe, and I was the lucky woman who held his heart.

But for how long?

I'd grown close to Andy as we passed the time and attempted to grow used to loving Rafe from afar. Andy was actually doing better in the moving on department than I was and had gone on a few dates. He was open with me about his love for Kristina but came clean in that it was mostly infatuation. I *was* in love, dateless, and completely hell bent on waiting it out for Rafe. I played my part of the supportive girlfriend with endless patience and pretended often to be satisfied with whatever stolen moments we had. I was sure the more time that passed, I would grow used to it, but instead, it began chipping away at me and my resolve.

In the end, Elvis had come for Priscilla. And though I wanted no resemblance of their dysfunctional relationship, I couldn't help the question that was driving me insane.

Where the hell was my Elvis?!

I hadn't told Rafe about my decision concerning my job and was beyond thrilled that when the season ended we would have months together, but this season's end was still weeks away, and I was officially becoming a closeted stage-five clinger.

I couldn't understand why he was okay with the distance, with the amount of time we were away from each other. I could physically see his ache at times but never pressed for anything more than what he gave.

We spoke of the holidays and made plans to have a white Christmas in Denver. It was all that kept me hanging on at that point. When he wasn't in contact, he seemed light years away. Even while I'd visited him and attended the games, it was so much of a whirlwind being a part of his new world I'd felt slightly uncomfortable. We'd built our relationship in Charleston. It felt safe in Charleston. Our world seemed scattered now. I knew in my heart I had to be patient, to give him time to adjust to his lifelong dream turned reality, and if I had to, I knew I would wait forever. But it didn't stop me from being selfish in my longing.

What ate at me the most, and what I was sure Rafe didn't realize, was that I'd waited on him far longer than the months he'd been gone, and way before the moment we'd met.

I spent the afternoon in the mid-September sun staring at the waves as I tried to pour an ice bucket on my pity party. With my career move, I was stuck in an indecisive whirlpool where my options were limited. I would have to find a job that I loved. I would have to strengthen my relationship with Rafe when the season ended to the point where I would feel comfortable with the wait. I would find a way to have my Elvis.

I had no other choice.

He was at an away game. I could surprise him and make myself available, which I'd indirectly done by ending my contract at Boeing. But then what? With Rafe, nothing seemed permanent, and I would never press him for anything different, no matter how desperate I was to have him more present in my life.

"Rafe," I whispered as I watched a lonely wave roll in.

I reached for my cell and smiled at a text I'd gotten over an hour ago.

Rafe: I'm in pre-game and I can't stop thinking about my dusty apartment.

My fingers hovered over the keys as I thought of a sly retort, but my heavy, aching heart refused to cooperate. For once, I decided to break the promise to myself to remain strong. In a moment of weakness, I sent him a link to a song that let him know exactly how I felt, a plea from my heart to his.

Alice: Without You, Eddie Vedder

"Our boy is kicking ass!" Andy said animatedly as I opened my mailbox and pulled out a package.

"I saw," I said with less enthusiasm as I'd hoped.

"Doll, he'll be back in a few weeks."

"I know," I said distractedly as I studied the package with curiosity. I propped it on my hip as I took the stairs up to my condo. "But then what? More months together and then how many more alone?" Andy remained quiet as I once again cursed my dwindling resolve. "I'm tired, Andy. I just...this isn't how I thought it would be. I mean, I was hoping to see him a little more, you know. I didn't think I would feel like an army wife. He's just so wrapped up in the season. I feel like he's circling the world and I'm sitting here idle."

"He is and you are."

"Well, it SUCKS!"

Andy chuckled. "He loves you."

"He tells me every day. I just...miss him."

"Hang in there, doll."

"Andy," I whispered tearfully as I set the package on the counter, "please tell me this gets better."

"Come see me at the bar tonight," he said with obvious concern in his voice.

"I'm not up to it," I said as I opened the box and pulled out the t-shirt. I smiled as I studied it. It was a woman's cut, V-neck tee with Rafe's team logo. I turned it over and saw Rafe's number on the back, and above it in bold letters, "Rafe's Pussy".

I burst into laughter as I gripped the shirt to my chest.

"That sounded good," Andy said with a smile in his voice.

"Present from Rafe," I said as I sighed into the phone. "He's such a bonehead."

"A bonehead that loves you. Don't forget that. Talk soon, doll."

"Thanks, Andy."

I wasn't surprised by the knock on the door at 1 A.M. I assumed it was April. We'd been spending a lot of time together since we'd both ended up at the complex pool on a lazy Sunday. April was easygoing and had a knack for making me laugh with a brand of observant humor. I always thought of Andy when she was around and even tried to play cupid once by suggesting she come with me to the bar to meet him. She had insisted she was in no shape to date after her last disastrous love affair with a paramedic. I loved her company, and she made Kristina's absence more bearable. She was a 911 operator for the city of Charleston and worked odd hours, but knew today was my last day at Boeing. I figured she'd probably come over with a bottle of something strong and details of a juicy call from her day to distract me from my ever-present, uncertain future. I opened the door in my Rafe's Pussy t-shirt and boy shorts with a smile on my face. Standing in front of me was a disheveled and ridiculously sexy baseball player in full uniform. My chest quickly burst as I took a step forward, ready to tackle him, but he stopped me as he held up his hand.

"Turn around."

I froze as Rafe towered over me. I was in complete shock and couldn't believe he was standing in front of me. It was if I willed the moment into existence.

"Rafe," I said as my body vibrated with excitement.

"Alice Boyd, I just pitched a game, skipped a shower, and flew for five hours to see you in this t-shirt. Turn around."

He circled his pointer finger in the air as I smiled and slowly obliged.

"I could have sent you a picture," I teased as I came full circle with a smile on my lips.

Jesus, he looked good in that uniform. Hazel eyes studied me, and I saw the ache outlining his features. He let it show without apology or excuse. My eyes immediately filled with relief and the same need. My heart seized as he blew out a breath of frustration, his features filled with pain.

"I'm tired of pictures," he said in a raw and heated whisper as he threw his tote through the doorway. "I'm tired of fucking texts and voicemails," he gritted out as he picked me up underneath my arms. I wrapped my legs around his waist as he kicked the door closed behind him. He walked me to my counter and sat me there. "I'm tired of waking up and wishing you were there. Every. Single. Day," he whispered as he stood between my thighs and covered them with warm hands. "I'm tired of the space," he said as he leaned in closer, and I saw his eyes swell with emotion. "No more space. I can't take it anymore. I miss you too much. I love you, Alice."

I barely stifled a sob as I gripped him to me. "Thank God," I rasped out as I looked up to him, an utter mess. "I don't want to be without you anymore. I can't do it either, Rafe. It hurts too much."

"Oh, baby. I'm sorry," he said as he claimed my mouth possessively, and I let the pain radiate through me, uncaring if he saw, unable to hold back. I needed him to know. I'd never been anything but honest with him, and I'd only begun to lie when I thought he needed me to. "I miss you so much, too much. I'm totally lost here now. I can't go back to alone."

"I'm here," he said as he kissed my forehead, my eyelids, my cheeks, nose, and then placed a gentle kiss on my lips. "Being away is fucking tearing me apart. I can't pretend anymore that I'm not ruined when I can't see your face, can't touch you. I want you with me. This shit we're doing, it's not enough anymore."

"I wasn't truthful. I'm not happy. I can't handle it. I hate it." I let out another anguished cry as he pulled me tightly to him. His mouth crushed mine as our tongues thrashed in need. Nothing else mattered as we pulled each other close, our clothes a nuisance. Minutes of touches and kisses led to a more urgent need of skin on skin.

"You walked Wheaten today," I scorned as I pulled his shirt out of his pants and began to tug at his waistband. Nipping his neck, I pulled out his length and began to stroke it. His eyes closed briefly and opened with fire as he leaned in and kissed me until I was desperate.

"Shut up," he muttered with a smirk as he pulled away and I began to discard my shirt. "Fuck no. That stays," he ordered as he tugged my boy shorts down my thighs and threw them over his shoulders. "Spread for me." He pushed my knees apart as I leaned back and moaned. Slick and ready, I looked up to Rafe as he watched me twist beneath him. I stared up at him expectantly as he licked his thumb and began to massage me with it.

"Ah," I moaned as he stared down at me, blazed a trail over my face, and then moved his gaze down between my thighs. I followed his eyes as he stroked me reverently. "We both missed you," he said with a smug smirk as his thickness twitched in agreement. I huffed out a curt laugh, too entranced with the workings of his thumb. I gasped out his name repetitively along with several other words of love and devotion as he worshiped me with eyes and fingers. I chanted his name as he gripped my hips and pulled me onto him, inch by intoxicating inch, and then thrust in fully as he stole my breath. I arched my back in welcome and gripped the lips of the countertop behind me as Rafe lost himself and whispered my name. He was a fantasy above me, his hazel eyes lit with lust, his jaw tense as he licked his full lips. I studied his sculpted arms as they held me tightly to him. Dark, beautiful, sexy, and looking dangerous, Rafe rebranded me with every movement, every look, and every word he spoke.

"Rafe," I moaned as he thrust hard, slowly withdrew, swiveled his hips, and then pressed in deeper. I was seconds from an orgasm as he began to slow his pace.

"No," I protested in the depths of everything he was giving me. "I need this so much."

He pulled out and gently flipped me over, my feet barely touching the floor as he thrust in again and gripped the back of my t-shirt with his fist. I came with a shriek as he buried himself deep, and he followed close, groaning out his release. We collapsed bare-assed on the kitchen floor. He pulled me onto his lap and explored my mouth for endless minutes before he pulled back and declared, "No end."

Rafe and I spent hours in bed eating, sleeping, and laughing as we fell back into our old groove. I lied to myself every minute, pretending it would last. That it wasn't temporary. That he didn't have a flight to catch in mere hours.

Rafe lay next to me, screwing with his cell phone as I kissed the hard planes of his stomach and chest. Then threw the covers over both of our heads, making a tent with the blanket. Rafe's eyes drifted over me with amusement as I sat in the middle of our makeshift teepee.

"No cell phones allowed in the tent, sir."

"Give me two minutes."

I cupped his balls and squeezed. Rafe's stomach surged and he let out a grunt and dropped his phone on his chest.

"Baby, we need to talk."

I shook my head and cut him off. "They can have you back in a few hours, Rafe. I mean, you *are* leaving soon." I hadn't meant for my voice to sound so desperate, but he heard it.

Careful eyes watched me, and I turned away from him briefly and pulled the tent down. "Damn it. I'm sorry."

"Alice," he whispered as he tugged at my hand. "I want to take a picture."

"I'm not in the mood to smile, Rafe." Even hours after he swore to me our arrangement wasn't working, he was still returning to Denver, and our future remained unchanged. I didn't want to dwell on it, though I was furious with him.

He sat up and kicked his legs over the bed and crossed the room, gloriously naked, until he reached his tote. He pulled out a tiny glove and some boxers then walked back over to me.

I perked up a bit as I studied what was in his hand. "That's it?"

He smiled at me warmly as he pulled his boxers on and tossed it to me. He knelt by the bed as I studied it.

"So small," I noted as I attempted to shove my hand in. Rafe lifted his camera, and I heard the phone click just as I felt the warm, circular metal inside.

Stunned, I looked at him as he pulled me down to the edge of the bed and then stood me before him as I pulled the ring from the glove, my chin quivering.

"Alice," he whispered as he choked on my name. I looked down at him with tears streaming down my face and a loud yes on the tip of my tongue. His eyes watered as he strained to get the words out. In that moment, I felt justified for every minute I spent waiting, every second I mourned and missed him, and every second before when I dreamt of a someday with a version of him that he'd already surpassed. He pulled the ring from my hand and kissed my ring finger twice—the way he had just before he left. I didn't realize it then, but he'd made me a silent promise.

"I have a new future in my head and it has to be with you. I want you with me. I want this, us, for as many seasons as we have. I love you more," he whispered as he pulled the glove away from my hand and made sure I caught his meaning. "I love you so much more. Marry me?"

I nodded and whispered yes as I gripped him to me and kissed him like I no longer had to pretend, because I didn't and I would never have to as long as I had Rafe.

Later that day on a flight to Denver, Rafe and I clasped hands and spoke of our future. After a tongue lashing in the best way due to my omission about leaving my job, and an even sweeter exchange about the fact that I had no obligations left to keep me in Charleston, he insisted we start our life immediately and packed my bags for Denver with assurance we would figure out the rest later. Rafe had been just as miserable with the distance as I had and wanted no part of the wait it would take to get me to Denver. And I had no issue whatsoever with his argument.

My wait was over.

I helped him pack me, the only setback being to keep my clothes on while we did it. We'd barely made the flight.

Rafe fell asleep on the plane as I looked out of the window with the same hope and elation as I had when I landed in Charleston six months ago. Never in my wildest dreams did I imagine I would attend a baseball game that would change the course of my life so drastically. I admired my ring and then did the same as I looked over at my beautiful fiancée. I leaned in with a whisper, "I made you a seahorse." I chuckled as a slow, sleep-filled smile covered his face and he drifted off again.

It was the best day of my life.

19
Alice

Our wedding was a disaster, truly. It was an intimate, outdoor ceremony held at Dutch's place in Charleston. Though we'd move to Denver only a few weeks after Rafe's season ended, it seemed fitting we married in the place we fell so deeply in love. I actually felt a fondness for Denver, much like Charleston, though Rafe had strong objections to my new zest for an attempt at skiing and snowboarding, and any other activity that I wanted to try that he wasn't present for.

Charleston was ideal for both of us, and though we'd chosen early spring, two weeks before training began, a sudden heat wave had made an unwelcomed visit on our big day. So, while the groomsmen perspired in their tuxedos, my bridesmaids continued to cater to me by moving my dress out of the way while I peed... every two minutes.

Just as my nerves calmed and I floated down the aisle toward the most handsome groom ever, a massive thunderstorm hit. The wedding party and I, along with our drenched guests, made a mad dash for the picturesque barn we'd purchased specifically for the occasion. The doors on each side were open and helped to create a wind tunnel of epic proportions. Our four-tiered wedding cake and thousands in linens and décor toppled to the floor as the DJ, who assumed we were wed, scrambled to put on our song. "Free" played as Rafe grabbed my hand amongst the chaos while the others moved fruitlessly to close the doors and salvage what was left of months of planning. I could see the disappointment in Rafe's eyes as we danced, but it wasn't his own. It was for me. I looked up to my minutes-away husband in my designer wedding dress with a huge smile on my face.

"You don't have to hide it from me," he whispered as he dripped from head to toe in a mix of sweat and rain.

"Best day of my life, Mr. Hembrey. What do you say we find that preacher man and make it official?"

"You look so beautiful," he whispered with relief as his lips descended.

"Ah ah ah, you're going to have to wait for that kiss."

After our week long and amazing honeymoon in Ireland, we had a small party at Andy's bar to celebrate what had to be the worst wedding photos in history. Every single one, though perfectly lit and edited, showed the complete and utter disarray of the night. We'd all gotten gloriously drunk as it went on, so the pictures became legendary. Andy had blown them all up and placed them strategically around the bar as Rafe and I made our way around it. The laughter never stopped as we saw one horrid shot after the other. April soaked in her maid of honor dress, holding my destroyed bouquet with a cheeky grin. The well-tailored groomsmen with red stains on their white dress shirts from their corsages. Andy stood at the front of the line, a Cheshire smile in place as he twisted the nipple of Waters, who stood next to him, the agony clear on his features. The next picture showed my mother and her Uber driver turned live-in boyfriend and next minute fiancé taking cover under his jacket and laughing while doing so. Another candid picture displayed proudly the steady stream of guests and the horror on their faces as they ran in every direction to seek shelter from the lightning. Another shot was displayed of a pile of the muddied shoes of every guest at the wedding. Another showcased a perfectly captured ceramic bride and baseball clad groom on the floor of the barn, both buried in cake and debris. An eye brow raising shot of Andy and April was captured as they stood in front of the restroom, their posture intimate and hair mused up by more than the weather as they held hands—a story I still hadn't managed to pry from either of them.

Each photo represented the chaos and the resilient vibe of the day. The feeling inside that barn was the exact opposite of the weather. There wasn't a disappointed face in the group. It couldn't have been more perfect.

Rafe and I both paused at the last photo, hands clasped as we studied it. It was when we were announced man and wife and Rafe whispered "No end" to me. I smiled at him intimately just before the shutter was pressed and seconds before Rafe gave me the best kiss of my life. My wedding dress was caked in mud on the bottom and Rafe was clearly still dripping wet, but the looks on our faces could never be mistaken. It was the picture of a man and woman deeply in love and excited about their future. Rafe looked over to me, his hazel eyes filled with the same adoration reflected in the picture as the bar filled with another bout of laughter. And right before he gave me another kiss that could stop time, I couldn't help but to think: freeze frame, cue Thompson Twins "If You Were Here" and fade to black.

Rafe: What are you doing?

Alice: Looking for a four leaf clover.

Rafe: :) Any luck?

Alice: No, but I think I'm close.

Rafe: I'm sure you'll find it.

Alice: I better, I'm aging by the minute.

Rafe: I miss you.

Alice: Stop whining and get ready to pitch a perfect game.

Rafe: Someone misses me, too.

Alice: You got that from my text?

Rafe: Of course. Did you find it?

I opened the closet next to the front door of our expansive house and heard a loud squeal then quickly texted Rafe as our little girl waddled past me with a loud shriek as I lunged for her.

Alice: Found her!

"Clover," I protested with a grin as she ran through the house in nothing but her diaper. She was very much like her father in that she loved to be naked. I chased after her and she shrieked as I gained on her, a Denver t-shirt and a pair of jean shorts in hand.

"Come on, baby girl, we have to get dressed. We're going on the plane to see daddy!"

Clover stopped her feet, and though her looks and personality were more Rafe, I was sure it was the *plane* part that stopped her in her tracks. She looked up to me and raised her chubby arms so I could fit the shirt over her head. I looked into Rafe's hazel eyes as I brushed through her dark brown hair and secured it into tiny pigtails.

My phone buzzed again, and I sighed in defeat when Clover again took off with only the improvement of a shirt and fixed hair.

Rafe: I just don't understand why you didn't want to come this time. We could have taken her to the zoo!

Alice: Whining again?

Rafe: Fine. I love you both. See you Sunday.

I smiled knowing he was disappointed and probably hurt for the time being, but it was a price I was willing to pay. He was in the playoffs, and I was sure he was close to earning his first championship. Every season he amazed me, and I'd attended every game I could, rain or shine. I wouldn't miss this game for anything.

The perk of being a ballplayer's wife *and* a pilot was his eight figure salary. I did his laundry for a few years and he bought me a small plane. I was now flying private charters for Denver's wealthy while I attended Rafe's ballgames anywhere in the country. Sound like a dream? It was.

Pretty sweet deal for a bonehead athlete and a nerdy pilot.

Another text came through. It was a picture of Dillon at his third grade graduation. He looked adorable and was smiling big. The text underneath read:

> **Kristina: Clover's future husband?**
>
> **Alice: We have about twenty years to plan.**
>
> **Kristina: Miss you.**
>
> **Alice: I'll be there in two weeks.**
>
> **Kristina: Finally!**
>
> **Alice: I have to go chase your future daughter-in-law down, but are you going to tell me about the date?**
>
> **Kristina: I went home with my panties in my purse.**
>
> **Alice: That good?**
>
> **Kristina: I think he found me.**
>
> **Alice: You will tell me everything. Two weeks! :)**

Another text came through in a matter of seconds.

> **Andy: We just landed. See you in a few.**

"Clover," I begged as she ignored me. Clover pretty much

always ignored me because, well, she was two, extremely busy, and had no time for anything other than her own agenda.

"You can't finds me, Mommy!" I heard her taunt from the exact same closet I'd just found her in. For a brief moment, I was scared for her future. I laughed as she cracked the door slightly so that the light clicked on. She wasn't a fan of the dark, and I was surprised she'd lasted as long as she had. I looked down at my waiting baby girl as my chest squeezed.

The minute I discovered she was coming, I knew I'd have my clover. Rafe's and my relationship weren't exactly cut from the cloth of the norm, and our love was limitless. We fit, we complemented each other by being different, and that was a rarity, and our Clover was proof. Rafe had completely lost it when I told him he was going to be a father. He was reduced to tears in a *very* public display, and in that moment, I knew I could never love him more. He'd been a doting husband and gone above and beyond to make a very uncomfortable pregnancy easier on me.

Of all the long conversations Rafe and I'd had through our relationship, neither of us had really touched on children. I knew I wanted a baby eventually, and I was sure with Rafe and his love of kids he would, too. It was the weirdest part of our union in that it was just simply...a given. But neither of us knew how badly we craved a family until the day we found out.

It was the best day of our lives.

Clover came into the world, lungs full of protest and covered in jaundice. Rafe held our light yellow baby and started his campaign of favorite parent by declaring to her that I'd peed on her.

It was also the best day of our lives.

And the days kept coming.

Days like that day when I scoured our expansive one-story ranch home for our little girl and was hell bent on making it the best for my husband, who had trusted me with the rest of his days. I was more determined than ever to keep what he'd so generously given.

So on that day, I gathered our little girl, determined to follow my flight plan with a quick stop and then onto California to surprise him.

"Naw naw Duc!" Clover squealed as she saw Dutch standing at the door next to Andy. Dutch reached out and gripped her great-granddaughter tightly to her as a single, happy tear slid down her face. Andy smiled over at her as he winked and pulled me into a hug. "Good job, doll."

"It was all you, Andy," I said as we beamed back at Dutch and Clover.

We knew it was a big step for her. It was the first time she'd managed a trip to Denver and her first real trip anywhere since Rafe's grandfather died. Rafe had confessed to me shortly after our engagement that Dutch was his estranged father's mother, and that she, too, had sided with Rafe after her son had betrayed him. In a way, she'd lost her son and then shortly after lost her husband. She'd always been an introvert and uncomfortable with attention, so Rafe and Andy had protected her from the intrusive media by treating her as his biggest fan, which she remained to this day. But Dutch's love for her great-granddaughter was unmatched and seemed something like a new beginning for her. She'd managed to take leaps and bounds since her arrival. I never faulted Rafe for not coming clean about Dutch. He protected those he loved and trusted without fail, and I had to earn my way into that circle. It seemed Dutch's invitation for me to join her at each game had been a part of that push. She'd seen something in me for a reason she never explained, and I was forever grateful.

I knew months after our marriage and after several trips home that loyalty, the kind Rafe was capable of, was embedded in him and was one of the most amazing things about him. Though we had no abundance of free time aside from the winter months in the off season, we still managed to get to Charleston whenever our schedule allowed. For Rafe, Charleston would always be home, and it would always be where I'd found mine. And my husband never let any good amount of time pass without a visit.

We'd take Clover to the beach and fall asleep on the sand. We would stop by Peggy's Fish Camp and have dinner with Sue, or get our hands dirty in Dutch's yard. Our little girl would have roots and wings, and to us, that meant everything. We were completely focused on giving her the parents we so desperately wanted for ourselves. Though my mother and I had completely reshaped our relationship for the better, Rafe's relationship with his father remained non-existent, as did mine.

Though our new life together in Denver was different from where we began, Rafe remained the same man I fell in love with. He was grounded, faithful, loving, admirable, insatiable...and cocky.

When my husband was eighteen years old, though he hadn't known it then, he chose loyalty and love over fame and quick money. And as I think over our life now and his level of devotion, I'm convinced he saved those gifts for us, his family.

As we exited the truck and Andy, Dutch, Clover, and I gripped hands with each other to make our way toward the stadium, I felt nothing but elation that we were together for him on a day where I knew he wanted us with him the most.

It never ceased to amaze me just how different league games were from the minors to the majors. The stadium was filled to the brim with fans and the crowd was deafening as the players were announced. I spotted Rafe in the dugout as we took our seats to the left and gave us all the perfect view of him. I pulled Clover into my lap as my husband, clueless to our whereabouts, pulled his hat off, peeked inside the inseam, and gripped the small piece of paper. It was a note I'd written to him, a new ritual we'd started when we married. Sometimes I wrote random facts about movies, sometimes I got a little romantic, and others a little dirty. Today's note read:

Look to your left, Daddy

– Love, Clover

Clover had already spotted him as she frantically waved and called out "Daddy!" into the roaring crowd.

I saw Rafe's slow smile as he turned and saw the four of us. His twisted lips and face turned incredulous as he heard the announcement of his man crush throwing the first pitch. He zeroed in on the mound and then back to me with an awestruck expression. When his idol walked up to him minutes later, I watched the exchange with a happy sigh. I was sure Nolan was telling him just how persuasive his wife had been to get him there. I saw Rafe throw his head back with a hard laugh as he shot a glance in my direction and shook his head. After they exchanged a handshake, Rafe looked over our way until I was sure he met my eyes and mouthed "Best day of my life" and I returned it with an "Every day."

Andy, Clover, Dutch, and I sat in the stands as Rafe fired pitch after solid pitch, fulfilling his dream in the majors with a family behind him who adored him with a love that was anything but minor.

Listen to the
Anything but Minor
Playlist on Spotify

ALSO BY KATE STEWART

Room 212
Never Me
Loving The White Liar

...

The Reluctant Romantics Series
The Fall
The Mind
The Heart

...

KATE STEWART WRITING AS
EROTIC SUSPENSE AUTHOR ANGELICA CHASE

Sexual Awakenings Series
The Waltz
The Tango
The Last Dance
Curtains

...

Excess Series
Opulence
Reverence
Hindrance

...

Predator and Prey Series
Camouflage

ACKNOWLEDGEMENTS

Thank you to Beth aka Dutch and Jon Rustenhaven for your ball expertise and for answering my hours of questions. You two ROCK!

Thank you Benley Ramos for schooling me on all things MiLB at the game while you cheered for your brother and I cheered for his opponent.

Thank you Adrian West for being my kick ass cover model. I can't believe you won your second Emmy a week later!!

Thank you to LeRoy from Pixel Studios for your patience and guidance. The shoot was a blast and you made it even more so.

I have to thank my street team, Kate's Asphalt Asskickers:Stacy, Tabatha, Cindy, Akeisha, Sophie, Julie, Paula, Susan, Melissa, Theresa, Jessica, Jess B, Gia, Sarah, Vrsha, Jessica R, Jen, Kathy, Lina, SB, Donna, Karrie, Lisa D, Rachel, Kristan, Erica, Beth, Angela, Kelli C, Sharon, Beverly, Courtney, Jessica, Jen, Stephanie, Danielle, Jules, Yamara, Vrosha, Sopie, Christin, Karrie, Paula, Tristan, Sarah-Jane, Christy B, Cathy, Theresa, Malene, Kim B, Kathryn S, Cheryl, Jessica B, Suzanne B, Donna, Alison, Letitia, Stephanie, Katy, Kathy, Darlene, Marie, Heather, Cezanne, Keanna, Melissa, SB and Sanne, thank you for all you do and for having my back. I love you ladies and I love all the fun we have.

You ladies have been the driving force and reason for most of my sanity. It's been one hell of a year so far, and I just wanted to thank you for your love, friendship, and support. I cherish every single one of you and can't wait to see what happens next.

To my betas and partners in crime: Beth Rustenhaven, Anne Morrilo, Stacy Hahn, Sharon Dunn, Christy Baldwin, Beverly Tubb, Heather Oregon and Patty Tennyson, I can't thank you enough. This book scared the crap out of me in that it wasn't my usual genre, but your words of encouragement and awesome critique gave me the courage to keep going. I love you ladies dearly. Thank you!

Thank you to my amazing cover designer Amy Q. You little bad ass, you! Thank you for sharing your gift with me and reading my mind!

To my girls from Wrapped in Reading Patty, Mel and Dee. You are seriously the most amazing group of ladies. Thank you for being the women you are and for your unconditional friendship. I'm so lucky to have my three fairy godmothers in my life.

Thank you, Edee, my editor extraordinaire, for all that you do and the friend that you are. Fist bump soul sister. We finished another one. XO

Juliana Cabrerra, you make me a better human. I love you with all my wicked heart. I love that you know me as well as you do and still speak to me.

To my dear friend, Christine Stanley, I can't even believe what a golden person you are. I'm so blessed to have you in my life. I'm lucky as hell to call you friend. I love that you call me on my bullshit. I'm so thankful that you look out for me. I love you.

Thank you to all the bloggers for doing what you do. With so many books to choose from, I'm honored anytime you give my words a chance. I appreciate every single one of you. XO

Thank you to my Texas and South Carolina families for your love and support.

And a huge thank you to my husband, Nick, for being the safe, soft place to land. I can't believe your enduring love and that you haven't smothered me with a pillow yet. ;)

ABOUT THE AUTHOR

A native of Dallas, Kate Stewart now lives in beautiful Charleston, S.C. She lives with her husband of 9 years, Nick, and her naughty beagle, Sadie.

Kate moved to the city three weeks after her first visit, dropping her career of 8 years, and declaring the city her creative muse. Since the move in 2010, Kate has written and published 15 novels including Room 212, Never Me, Loving the White Liar and more.

Kate writes messy, sexy, angst filled romance books with 'hard to get' happy endings because it's what she loves as a reader. She has a scary addiction to chocolate milk and a deep love for rap music specifically the genius known as Marshall Mathers.

Email Kate - authorkatestewart@gmail.com
Follow on Facebook - https://www.facebook.com/authorkatestewart
Follow on Twitter - https://twitter.com/authorklstewart
Spotify - https://open.spotify.com/user/authorkatestewart

CHAPTER ONE
Taco Tuesday

"The cost of the rings alone is sickening to me. Let's say the happy, yet delusional couple, waits until they finish college. They are more than likely in debt up to their eyeballs with student loans already. Then they go buy a ring that they can't afford to start their 'new lives' together, forever.'

"BUT WAIT, that's not enough. Throw a last hoorah with all of their friends in Vegas with booze and strippers. I mean what says undying, everlasting love and faithfulness like lap dances and used up snatch picking $20 bills off someone's face?

"Then all of a sudden they wake up the next day and are never going to want it again? Yeah, right. Let me ask you, when is the last time you ate just one double stuff Oreo cookie?

"Don't kid yourself that eating just the cream inside isn't cheating, eating is cheating.

"The next time you see a stripper pole, or hell any pole for that matter, tell yourself you aren't going to remember the single most exciting night of your life.

"The same 'happy' couple gets ass raped for hosting an elaborate soiree to celebrate a marriage that will end up failing. Don't roll your eyes at me, it's fact. You know damn well they're fighting over the details of the damn wedding too. Can you feel the love? Me either.

"After the ass fucking, without lube, they spend a mint on a honeymoon where they spent ninety-percent of the time shit faced and fucking, seldom leaving their resort suite, yet it cost a grand a night.

"Now they have spent a minimum of ten grand themselves and that's if they didn't have to pay for the damn party celebrating their 'union'. Hell, I can celebrate a union with a fucking Happy Meal and a bottle of Jack. He brings his own condoms, now it's a fucking party."

"Kat?" Josie sighs.

"You asked how I felt about weddings. You know damn well I'm not going to hold back."

"What I was trying to ask is how you felt about mine. Blaine asked me to marry him last night. I want you and Cecilia to be in the wedding. I want you to be my maid of honor," she says as sweet as Josie is.

Fighting the urge to bash my head against the counter until I knock myself completely out, I answer the only way I can, "I would be honored."

She giggles. "Sure you would."

I bare my teeth trying my best not to growl. "You and Blaine are different."

She laughs. "How so?"

"His parents are loaded. I will assume you aren't paying for the wedding. I'm sure the ring isn't on plastic, you won't start out that way," I pause and try my best to dig myself out of the hole I've dug. This isn't easy for me; I normally don't give a shit if I offend. "Besides, you've been together four years now."

"Five, we graduated last year," she says.

"Right, well then, yours will be smooth sailing."

"We're moving about an hour from you," she says with a big smile, I don't even have to see her, I can hear it.

"That's so cool. I am off Sundays and Mondays every week. We'll get together."

"I'd love to, and maybe meet some of your friends?"

"Josie, I promise, I have real friends." I laugh knowing she worries about me, even though she knows I can take care of myself.

"No she doesn't," Ricco says walking out from the back of the shop.

"Jesus!" I jump covering my heart with my hand.

"Kat, why are you even trying to cover your heart, we all know you don't have one," he says and winks.

"Who was that?" Josie gasps.

"Who, Ricco? He's the jackass I hang out with here at the shop," I say as I flip him off.

"He has a very, very, nice voice," she whispers.

"He does not sound like the Taco Bell dog, Josie," I say to piss him off and embarrass her.

"I didn't say that," she gasps.

Ricco laughs and shakes his head. "I'm heading out."

"Jerry Springer call?"

He turns around. "I hope you get vaginal warts."

"Well, I hope you get three chicks knocked up and they all come after you at once," I pause, "Oh wait, you did already."

"Much love to you too, Kitty Kat." He flips me off and walks out the door.

I shake my head as I watch him swing his big old leg over *One and Only*, his Harley. Yes, that's its name.

"Sorry," I laugh.

"His voice, is..." she pauses and then whispers, "sexy."

I can't help but laugh. "There's a line that goes down the block to get inked by him. I can give you a 'jump-the-line' pass if you're interested in one last hoorah before your nuptials."

"Is there really?" she whispers.

"Apparently he's a hot commodity around here. Six-foot-three of inked, pierced, testosterone, who evidently has the stamina of twenty men, or so he says."

"So you haven't—"

"Oh hells no! Are you serious, the guy is an STI waiting to happen. He gets paternity suits delivered to him like a funeral home gets flowers."

She laughs. "How many kids does he have?"

"One for sure, two or three now just waiting to find out." I laugh. "It's almost comical. I have no idea what his aversion is to sane women, condoms, or just tossing his own meat. I mean really—"

Her laugh interrupts my rant. "Boy or girl?"

"Little girl, she's three," I answer.

"I can't wait to have babies," she says with a coo. "You need to get married so you and I can have kids—"

"Eww, no, not happening. They're little germ spreading, time suckers, who rip apart your vag. Not interested."

"Ever?" she asks.

"No. Not ever."

I know where this conversation will lead, hell I visit it at least once a month with my Mom-ster, I mean mother, so I decide to sway the conversation to my second least favorite subject, weddings.

"So, when is the big day?"

****

It's insanely busy for a Tuesday night at the shop. It's two others besides me; Marcus and Zack. Today's schedule was spot on, but we've had a few walk-ins, and the boys seem to think they're fucking supermen. Marcus knows his shit; Zack gets led by his dick. I haven't seen so many nipple and hood piercings since the owners left Ricco and myself in charge of FS.

Ricco puts up with it, he has no problem staying open past

closing. Me, I have little tolerance for the shit. We alternate weeks between opening and closing; this is my week to close. I am just coming off two days with no 'O's' in sight, due to mother nature's cruel joke to women, and I am a miserable bitch. Hey, at least I can admit it. *And,* it's Taco Tuesday at Mario's, so not cool.

"You pissed?" Marcus asks, setting the consent forms on the counter after checking out one of his regular customers.

"It's Taco Tuesday, what do you think?"

"I can lock up. You can go get your Taco Tuesday'ed," he winks.

"For your information, I wasn't going to hook up. *So* fuck you," I say grabbing his sheet and scanning it into the computer.

I look over and he is thumbing through Ricco's schedule book. He refuses to use the computer, says someday it will crash and we'll all be fucked, except him. We just barely convinced him to get a smartphone.

Marcus laughs and looks at me, then back at the book.

"What?" I ask stepping over to hand him the forms. He closes the book quickly and shoves it under the pile of supplier catalogs.

He reaches his long, thin, yet cut, arm, covered in some really cool ink, and pets the back of my head.

"Do I look like a damn dog to you?" I jerk away.

"No, Kat, no you don't. You look beautiful," he says basically cooing.

"One of us has to. Now get out of here and finish the bitch's ass you're inking."

Marcus is six-foot-tall, lean muscular build. You know the type of person you hate because they eat everything in sight yet still don't gain a pound? *Yeah,* he's that person. His face is chiseled, prominent cheek bones, square-ish jaw and a nose that I'm sure was perfect, until it was broken a few times due to fights. He's a tom cat. A ladies' man. The guy that will jump in the middle of an argument between two drunken lovers, stop it with his fist only to end up with the girl between his sheets. He's very high strung. I was sure he had too much energy to do this for a living but all that energy seems to turn into creativity.

Zack is a gym rat. Built like a house. He's not quite six foot, brown hair and the wildest colored eyes, almost violet. Against his tanned skin they pop. He's a pretty boy and the giggly girls love him. He loves them too.

Then there's Ricco. Six foot four, dark skin with green eyes. He's not pretty like Zack or stunning and sharp like Marcus. Ricco is big. A beast of a man really. He is broad, has a nice chest, nipples pierced, six pack abs, but not cut. Just...*big*.

His laid back attitude is what seems to appeal to the broads that walk in here seeking him. He doesn't smile a lot but he smirks. He has the devil in his eyes all the time.

When I first met him I wanted to gouge his eyes out. The way he would sit back so chill and stare at me made me uncomfortable. I went so far as to tell the owners I wouldn't work with him, that I would quit, but then Josephina told me to watch him when he wasn't looking, he was that way with everything. She was right. The man should be a cop. Doesn't miss a damn trick. Sees every *damn* thing.

Since that day four years ago, he has become one of my best friends, although I wouldn't tell him that. I enjoy giving him shit. He does the same to me.

The problem he has is his dick apparently has an aversion to sane women and condoms. I tell him all the time that he's gonna end up dead from a disease or from one of the bitches that drag him into court for a paternity test.

He tells me he's Catholic and doesn't believe in using protection. I tell him abstinence and no sex before marriage, those things are also in that Bible he picks and chooses from.

Religion, yuck!

ANYTHING BUT MINOR

Made in the USA
Columbia, SC
17 February 2019